Around the Way Girls 12

Around the Way Girls 12

Treasure Hernandez,

Marcus Weber

www.urbanbooks.net

Urban Books, LLC
300 Farmingdale Road, NY-Route 109
Farmingdale, NY 11735

Caught Between a Good Boy and a Bad Boy
Copyright © 2023 Urban Books, LLC

Lost and Found Copyright © 2023 Urban Books, LLC

ISBN 13: 978-1-64556-411-9
ISBN 10: 1-64556-411-8

First Trade Paperback Printing February 2023
Printed in the United States of America

10 9 8 7 6 5 4 3 2 1

*This is a work of fiction. Any references or similarities
to actual events, real people, living or dead, or to real
locales are intended to give the novel a sense of reality.
Any similarity in other names, characters, places, and
incidents is entirely coincidental.*

Distributed by Kensington Publishing Corp.
Submit Orders to:
Customer Service
400 Hahn Road
Westminster, MD 21157-4627
Phone: 1-800-733-3000
Fax: 1-800-659-2436

Around the Way Girls 12

Treasure Hernandez,

Marcus Weber

Caught Between a Good Boy and a Bad Boy

by

Treasure Hernandez

Chapter 1

Rinnnggg!

The sound of the bell should have told the students in Mr. Cline's senior English class that it was time to settle down. But it did no such thing. In fact, the talking and laughter got louder. It probably had something to do with the fact that it was the last day of senior year and they were all excited. Still, that didn't mean Mr. Cline didn't have a job to do. He adjusted the glasses on the tip of his nose and cleared his throat at the front of the classroom.

"Settle down, class. I understand that it's the last day of high school for most of you, but this is still a classroom, and you will respect it as such."

"'This is still a classroom, and you'll respect it as such,'" a boy in the back of the room mimicked.

Most of the students laughed, but one in particular looked over her shoulder at the boy with a disgusted look on her face. Kiesha Simmons was never too keen on class clowns, and that was exactly what Brandon was. He even dressed like a joke on purpose, wearing mismatched sneakers and a goofy hat on his head. Annoying didn't even cover the bases when describing him.

Ever since she was a little girl, Kiesha took her education seriously, all the way up to the last day of high school. She had beauty and brains, the best of both worlds. Brandon, on the other hand, looked at school as a distraction. Therefore, he tried to distract everyone else, and Kiesha wasn't having it.

"Shut up, Brandon. Damn. You're always doing the most."

"Ain't nobody say nothing to you, Kiesha! You always tryin'a save somebody," Brandon said.

"Thank you, Miss Simmons, but I can handle my own classroom," Mr. Cline said and rubbed his chocolate hands together. "As I was saying, before I was rudely interrupted by a student who won't be graduating on time—"

The class laughed, and Brandon slumped in his seat.

"I am so proud to have been your teacher this year, and I wish nothing but the best for you as you go forward in your journeys."

All year Mr. Cline had been Kiesha's favorite teacher. He was the kind of man who truly believed that a person could be whatever they wanted to be as long as they tried. In fact, he was the one who pushed her to follow her dream. Ever since Kiesha was a little girl, she was obsessed with commercials and how a few seconds could make someone want to get up and buy or experience something. There was a certain kind of power in it that she liked, and as she grew older, her infatuation for it only grew. And that was why in the fall she would be attending college at Howard University to pursue a career in marketing.

As Mr. Cline was talking, Kiesha felt someone tap her on the shoulder. She looked back and grinned when she saw her best friend, Stacy McAlister. Stacy glanced at Mr. Cline to make sure he was still preoccupied before she leaned forward to talk to Kiesha.

"You comin' out tonight, right?" she asked in a low voice.

"Coming out where?" Kiesha made a face like she didn't know what Stacy was talking about.

"Girl, stop playin' with me! To G Money's crib. You know his dad is throwin' him a pre-graduation party. I heard it's gonna be lit!"

"I don't know, Stace."

"You didn't ask your mom like I told you to, did you?" Stacy asked and rolled her eyes in an annoyed fashion.

"I guess I forgot." Kiesha shrugged.

"You ain't forget shit! You just didn't ask."

"Because you know how she is! Especially since there will probably be alcohol there."

Kiesha and Stacy had been best friends since sandbox days. They'd gone through everything growing girls could go through together and were thicker than thieves. In fact, just saying they were best friends didn't do them justice. Blood couldn't have made them any more the sisters they were. It was a beautiful feat because the two of them were as different as oil and water. Stacy was one of the most popular girls in school and the captain of the cheer team. Kiesha, on the other hand, kept a low profile and her head in the books. She was a beautiful girl with her light brown doe eyes and long, soft curls, but she cared more about school than she did partying or hanging out. However, somehow, she always ended up at some kind of party with Stacy.

Kiesha really did feel bad about not asking her mom about the party. Kiesha's mom wasn't super strict, but she did keep a close eye on her. She just didn't want her daughter to do anything foolish. She raised Kiesha to be bright, smart, and responsible. And because of that, Kiesha didn't want to hear the thousand questions that always came when she asked to go somewhere.

"Kiesh, I can't go without you. You know that's the rule! And you know my mom is gonna call your mom to double-check."

Kiesha groaned. Part of the reason she and Stacy were so close was because their parents were old college roommates. As single moms, they'd teamed up to help each other raise their daughters, and the teamwork still hadn't ended. Kiesha looked at Stacy's pleading face and groaned again.

"I'll ask when I get home. What time does it start?"

"Seven. And please do! Plus"—Stacy got a mischievous look in her eye and grinned—"I heard Malcom is gonna be there."

Kiesha tried to hide her smirk. Malcom Donald was the finest boy in school. He was a senior too, and she'd had a crush on him all year. He was cocoa brown, had the whitest and most perfect smile, and always wore his long hair in braids. Malcom had been the captain of the football team and brought them home a championship in the season. He was on the radar of any girl with eyes, but Kiesha had dreams of making him her boyfriend that summer.

"He doesn't even know I exist." It was Kiesha's turn to roll her eyes.

"Please, the last time I saw him he was asking about you. You might as well see what he's talking about later."

"Okay, I said I was going to ask. You don't have to throw a nigga's name in to get my attention," Kiesha said and turned around to hide her smile.

For the remainder of class, they went around the room and shared what they planned on doing once school was done for the year. Some students didn't have any plans but to work and hang out on the beach, and others had exciting summer plans. When Mr. Cline got to Stacy, Kiesha heard her giggle.

"I plan to enjoy my summer. You know, hang with my girls, shop. My mama already started me working at her clothing store, so I'll keep some dollars in my pocket. Then it's off to FAMU I go."

"Nice! What about you, Kiesha? Tell us what you have planned."

"I'll be interning most of the summer and spending as much time with my mom as possible."

"You're going to Howard, right?"

"Yep."

"I never thought I'd see the day you and Miss McAlister separated from the hip," he said with a good-hearted smile. "I'm interested—why not stay here and attend FAMU? What's so special about Howard?"

"I guess I'm just following in my mom's footsteps. Since I was little, she's talked about how great a school it is, and it's the only school I ever dreamed of attending. She claims it's where she awakened, and hopefully it does the same for me."

"So sentimental!" Stacy said behind her, and the class laughed.

Kiesha turned around to roll her eyes, and Stacy just shrugged. Sometimes it was hot and cold with her, but Kiesha always forgave her sometimey tendencies.

Mr. Cline wagged a playful finger at Stacy and turned back to Kiesha. "That's admirable, and I hope all your dreams come true up at Howard."

At that moment, the last bell of the day rang, and everyone jumped up to run out of the classroom. Kiesha tossed her bag over her shoulder and followed the crowd of students out into the hallway. She didn't know how to feel. Her high school journey was over. Well, almost. Graduation was in a few days.

She and Stacy walked to their lockers together to empty them. When they were done, Stacy pretended like she was smelling something delectable in the air.

"Ahhh, do you smell that? That's the smell of freedom!"

Kiesha laughed, but before she could respond, Malcom walked over to them. He was easily six feet tall looming over them. He smiled first at Stacy and then at Kiesha. She felt like her heart was going to pound out of her chest. He was standing so close to them she could smell the Armani cologne he wore. And he wasn't just fine, he was one of the best dressed students in school. He always had a pocketful of money, the kind that was able to keep Malcom laced in designer clothes and shoes every day.

"What's up, y'all?" he asked with his Florida-boy accent.

"About to run up out of here. I'm surprised you haven't left yet," Stacy said.

"I was, but then I saw the two most beautiful girls in school. I had to say somethin'."

"Nigga, you got all the game," Stacy laughed and pushed his arm.

Kiesha was still stuck on him calling her one of the most beautiful girls in school. They'd had a few classes together, but they barely spoke. Hell, she didn't even know if he'd actually looked at her long enough to see her features. But what he just said was all the confirmation she needed.

"Whatever. Y'all comin' to G Money's party tonight? I heard it's gon' be poppin' for real."

"We'll be there," Stacy told him and gave Kiesha a small nudge.

"Uh, umm, yeah. We'll be there," she concurred.

"Cool. I can't wait to see what y'all pull up wearin'. I know you're gon' be fine as hell," he said and winked at them.

She felt herself grow warm. If she weren't the color of peanut butter, she was sure her face would be bright red. When Malcom walked away to rejoin his group of friends, the butterflies in her stomach stayed.

"Girl, you see him checkin' for you? You really have to make sure Mama Bee says yes. Tonight might be the night you lose your—"

"Stace!"

"I'm serious. You don't want to enter college still a virgin, do you? You need some experience under your belt. And can you imagine a better-looking practice dummy?"

Kiesha laughed, but the truth was that her mind was going a hundred miles a minute. She'd daydreamed a thousand times about losing her virginity to Malcom. But not at a party, and not when he wasn't her boyfriend. But still, if it happened, she wouldn't be mad about it.

Chapter 2

"Ma!" Kiesha's voice rang through the foyer of the four-bedroom home she shared with her mother. "Ma!"

She went around the whole house in search of her mother, and when she didn't find her in any of the usual places, she went to the last possible option: the garage. Sure enough, when she opened the door from the kitchen, she saw her mom sitting at a long table in front of a canvas. She had her natural hair pulled up into a messy bun and wore an apron over her shirt and jeans. She'd been in the middle of painting a still life scene with beautiful pinks, reds, and greens. Kiesha almost didn't want to disturb her, but the party started at seven, and it was already three.

"That's beautiful," she said, and her mom stopped painting to turn around.

Upon seeing her daughter, Miss Simmons smiled big. She placed the paintbrush down and went to give Kiesha a hug. Her lips planted two soft kisses on Kiesha's forehead, and for those moments, Kiesha felt safe from everything in the world just like when she was a little girl.

"Hi, baby. I didn't even hear your car pull into the driveway."

"You never hear anything when you're in your zone. I didn't know you were painting again."

Miss Simmons had always been a woman of virtue. Kiesha had been blessed with a great role model for a mother. No matter how busy she was, Miss Simmons always made time for the things she enjoyed and loved. Kiesha remembered being a child and playing in the corner while her mother painted for hours. She was very good at it but never wanted to pursue a career in it. Painting was just a "release," she'd say, one she could speak all of her emotions to without receiving any judgment back.

Miss Simmons looked sadly from her masterpiece to her daughter. "I figured I'd better busy myself with something to prepare me for when the house is empty."

"Mama, I told you, if you want me to go to FAMU, I will. I got accepted there, too."

"No." Miss Simmons shook her head. "You've had your heart set on Howard since you were a little girl."

"This is true. They have one of the best marketing programs, but FAMU's is great too!"

"Girl, your mama will be just fine. I just need time to adjust. That's all. Anyway, how was your last day?"

"Fine," Kiesha said quickly and took her mother by the hand. "Come on, I'm sure you're thirsty. Let me fix you a glass of sweet tea."

"Mm-hmm," Miss Simmons hummed knowingly.

Still, she let Kiesha drag her to the kitchen table and make her a tall glass of sweet tea. Kiesha carefully placed the glass on a coaster in front of her mother and sat across from her. She watched like a hawk as Miss Simmons sipped the drink. She was trying to buy herself some time to figure out how to ask about the party. It was Friday, which they usually spent together doing a pizza-and-movie night. It was something Miss Simmons always looked forward to, and from the stack of DVDs on the counter, it seemed that this Friday was no different.

"All right, spit it out. I know you want something." Miss Simmons looked at her daughter over the rim of her glass.

"What? Me?" Kiesha feigned shock.

"Yes, you. I know you like the back of my hand, ma'am. Whenever you want something, you try to butter me up. So spill it before I spill this tea on you."

"Okay, okay." Kiesha took a big breath and spit the rest of it out quickly. "There's this party tonight, and I really want to go. Please, please, please, can I go?"

"And where is this party at?"

"It's at G Mon . . . Gregg's house. His dad is chaperoning it, so an adult will be there. All the seniors are going."

"Okay, you can go."

"Mom, please! I'm eighteen already. Technically I don't even have to ask permiss . . . wait, what?"

"I said you can go," Miss Simmons repeated. "It's the last day of senior year, you did amazing in your studies all year, and like you said, you're eighteen already. I think you should be able to have some fun."

"Really?"

"Yes," Miss Simmons said, smiling fondly at her. "A mother couldn't be prouder of her daughter than I am of you. Plus, your internship starts soon, I want you to have at least a little fun before then. Speaking of which, has Mr. Parks let you know an official start date?"

"June twelfth."

Antonio Parks wasn't just the top Realtor in Miami. He was the person Kiesha would be working with that summer. She felt beyond blessed to land an internship with someone so prestigious, and him being black was just the icing on the cake. She would be working hands-on with the marketing side of his real estate company, and she was excited. But first, like her mother had said, she wanted to have a little fun.

"What time does this party start?" Miss Simmons asked.

"At seven."

"Then you better start getting ready. I assume Stacy is going with you."

"Yeah," Kiesha said, pulling her phone out of her pocket and shooting her BFF a text message. "I just told her I'll be there to pick her up. She's so mad that her mom still hasn't been able to get her a car yet."

"Michelle is working her butt off just making sure they have a roof over their heads. The boutique is bringing in good money, but she has two other kids to care for. Stace will get a car in due time."

"I guess not everyone could be as lucky as me to get an accountant mom with only one kid."

"How fortunate you are." Miss Simmons winked. "I'm going back to my painting. Be safe tonight."

They both got up from the table and went their separate ways. Kiesha bounded up the stairs to her room. The first place she went was to her walk-in closet. She went to the back, where her more formal clothes were. Without even trying one on, Kiesha knew that she didn't want to wear a dress. She hated being confined in them and wanted something that would allow her a little more freedom. Her eyes fell on a brand-new light blue halter-top romper she recently bought. She loved it because it hugged all her curves and made her butt look huge. Not to mention, her peanut butter–colored skin really set the blue off. She snatched it off the hanger and went to take a shower.

The whole time the water was hitting her body, all she could think about was how she couldn't wait to see Malcom that evening. He was the kind of fun she was trying to have all summer, and she hoped that after the party he would feel the same. Kiesha had to be real with herself. She was definitely in her fairy-tale way of thinking. But at the same time she didn't care. She believed in fairy tales, and maybe hers was about to become a reality.

After she was finished washing her hair and body, she got out of the shower. After seeing in the mirror how pretty her hair looked, she opted to wear it just like that. She put some product in it to hold the curls and then wrapped a towel around herself to start her makeup.

She had just done her brows and foundation when she heard her phone ringing next to her makeup bag on the counter. It was Stacy. Kiesha answered it and put it on speaker.

"Hey, girl."

"What are you wearing tonight?" Stacy blurted out.

"Remember that cute blue romper I bought from your mom's boutique?"

"Ooh! Great choice. You're gonna be sexy as fuck in that."

"Thank you. What are you thinking about putting on?"

"That spicy red little number I've been saving for somethin' special. And I guess this is special enough. I just hope G Money doesn't think that just because I'm comin' to his party, I'm gonna jump his bones."

"Don't hold your breath. He's been trying to get you since the beginning of the school year."

"Yuck. I wish he'd give it a rest. I mean, he's not ugly. He's just not my type."

"Let you tell it, none of these niggas are your type."

"You got that right! Well, one is."

"Who?"

"Nobody you know. Anyway, do you think you're gonna get your cherry popped tonight?"

Kiesha heard the question as she contoured her face. Her virginity always seemed to come up in their conversations recently. She felt like Stacy was more concerned about it than she was. Kiesha just felt like it was because they had always done everything together or around the same time. Stacy had lost her virginity the summer before their junior year. It was something she said she didn't regret and enjoyed doing. Kiesha, on the other hand, just hadn't met the right person to give it to. Nor had the setting been right. She wasn't waiting for marriage or anything, but she didn't want to give away something so sacred to just anybody, despite her lustful thought of Malcom earlier at school.

"I guess I'm just not looking to let someone fuck me at a party. That isn't how I see myself losing my virginity," she said absently, finishing her face. It wasn't until Stacy grew quiet that Kiesha remembered that was exactly how she had lost her virginity. "My bad, Stace. I just meant—"

"I know what you meant. Don't worry about it. What time do you think you'll be by to pick me up?"

"I'll probably be there at seven exactly."

"Good. We don't want to show up super on time like some lame bitches. Okay, I'll let you finish getting ready. I'm going to call my girls, so just let me know when you're outside."

"Okay!" Kiesha said, and the phone disconnected.

She hoped that she hadn't hurt Stacy's feelings. She truly just hadn't been thinking. If she had, she would have never said anything at all. But Stacy knew her heart.

After putting on her lashes, Kiesha grabbed her romper and got dressed. To accent the blue, she selected a small cream-colored purse and slid on a matching pair of sandals. Once her look was all the way together, she stared at the finished product in the full-length mirror in her bedroom. She was almost blown away by her own reflection. The romper fit better that day than when she tried it on. She glanced at the digital clock on her dresser and saw that it was time to go.

"Ma!" she called when she ran down the stairs, stuffing her phone and car keys in her purse. "Ma, I'm about to go!"

"Okay, baby. Have fun and be safe. Please be home at a respectable hour!" Miss Simmons called from the garage.

Kiesha sent Stacy a text that she was on her way and ran out the front door.

Chapter 3

"I told you this bitch was gonna be jumpin'!"

Kiesha barely heard Stacy's voice because she was too busy looking incredulously around the inside of G Money's lavish beach home. She'd been to a lot of nice homes for gatherings, but this by far was the most luxurious. They were right on Darwin Beach and had a beautiful view of the water. Not to mention that G Money's dad had really gone above and beyond for the party. There was a live DJ, and waiters were walking around with food and drinks.

Kiesha maneuvered around the crowd inside with Stacy until they were outside on the luxurious terrace. There were a lot of people there too, but there was more room to move around. It was beautiful, and Kiesha was tempted to wander down to the beach, especially after Stacy's cheerleader friends came over to them.

Piper, Kennedy, and Myra were also super popular. They reminded Kiesha of the movie *Mean Girls* because they acted like they were better than everyone. They didn't bother Kiesha too much, not after she beat Piper up freshman year. Piper thought she was going to get away with making a slick comment about the small painting Kiesha had in her locker. Her mother had made it special for her since she was starting a new school journey, and she wasn't going to let big-nose Piper get away with calling it trash. Her nose was leaking blood and had swollen to a size bigger by the time Kiesha was done with her.

"Hey, babes!" Myra said in a fake, valley-girl voice. She was from the hood, but when her mom remarried, to a wealthy contractor, he moved them into a big house on the good side of Miami right before their freshman year. She practically reinvented herself to match her new lifestyle. She wore an expensive Fendi romper with the matching hat. She embraced Stacy before taking a step back and holding up her cup.

"What's this?" Stacy asked, her nose hovering over it. She sniffed.

"Bitch, don't smell my drink! Just taste it!" Myra exclaimed.

"Fine." Stacy took a sip and made an impressed face. "Bitch, is that tequila I taste?"

"Casamigos, to be exact."

"G Money's dad let him have alcohol at his party?" Stacy seemed even more impressed.

"Better." Myra grinned devilishly. "He snuck it in. Come on. It's upstairs in his room."

"You comin'?" Stacy asked, turning to me.

I shook my head. "I think I'm going to stay out here and enjoy the view. You go ahead."

"Lames weren't invited anyway," Kennedy said with a smirk.

"The only lame thing is that you only got accepted into community college with your dumb ass," Kiesha shot back. She watched Kennedy's light-skinned face turn red.

"You're such a bitch," Myra said, turning her nose up.

"She came for me. I sent back. Who's the real bitch?"

"Come on, you guys, not here," Stacy said, rolling her eyes. "I'll see you a little later, Kiesh."

Most people would feel a way about their best friend's other friends not liking them or that Stacy left her standing alone to go off with them. But it wasn't the first time Stacy had ditched Kiesha at a party, and it wouldn't be the last. She checked the time on her phone and wondered if Myra would give Stacy a ride home if she left early.

Kiesha looked around and spotted London, a close friend of hers. She was standing by the twins, Cleo and Clifford. There was a time when they all had been almost as close as she and Stacy were, but then senior year picked up, and Kiesha wasn't able to hang out as often. London didn't live far from her, so the two of them had kind of grown up together. It would be cool to just hang out with them that evening.

Before she could make her way over to them, she felt a tap on her shoulder. When she saw who had touched her, she felt instant butterflies.

"M . . . Malcom. Hey."

"Hey," he said, looking at her and smiling. "Wow. You look amazin'. I've never seen you wear your hair like that before."

"I do, just not at school." She shrugged.

"You should more often. It really brings out your eyes," he said seriously, but she laughed. "What?"

"I've just never heard anybody say that in real life. Just in movies."

"Well, this ain't no movie. This is real life, baby. Punch?"

It was then that Kiesha noticed that he had two cups in his hand. She'd been raised to never take a drink from a man if she didn't see it get made. She hesitated for a second, but eventually she took it—not the one he was holding out to her, but the other one.

"Your mama raised you right, I see." He grinned. "But I promise you I didn't spike these drinks with drugs."

Kiesha smiled back and took a gulp of hers. It was good, but it burned going down, and she gagged a bit. "Damn. What's in here?"

"I said there weren't drugs in there. I never said there wasn't any alcohol."

"I can't believe you."

"It's good though, right?" Malcom asked.

"It's okay," Kiesha said, making a face that caused him to laugh again.

It wasn't the first time she had tasted alcohol. It just wasn't her favorite thing. Plus, she'd watched enough movies to know that getting drunk at a high school party wasn't necessarily the smartest thing to do. However, any uneasy feeling she had washed away the moment Malcom grabbed her hand and led her to a sitting area. They sat side by side but faced each other. She couldn't help staring into his face. That might have been the closest she'd ever been to him. Her eyes lingered on his slightly wet, full lips, and she wondered what they tasted like.

"I really like this blue on you," he told her, touching her thigh. "And damn, I never knew you were this thick."

"That's because you were too busy dating the cheerleaders to notice," she said, feeling goose bumps rise.

"You might be right there, but I'm tryin' to see what's up with you now. Tell me, do you have a man?"

"Maybe."

"Lies."

"And how would you know?"

"Because you wouldn't be sittin' here with me, lookin' at me how you're lookin' at me."

"And how am I looking at you?"

"Like you want a piece."

And he was right. He was looking delectable in the floral button-up shirt that he wore open, revealing his muscular chest. It was taking all of Kiesha's mental power not to rub her hand across it. Knowing she might not be able to control her urge, Kiesha took another gulp of her drink.

"I do think you're very handsome. And maybe it's the liquor that's giving me the courage to say this, but I've been feeling you all year."

"Word? Why didn't you ever say anything?"

"I don't know."

But really she did know. The girls she always saw him talking to were known for giving it up. At the time, she didn't even want to swim in those waters, even if it meant getting her crush to notice her. But now things were different. Her body was yearning for something it had never had before. Kiesha had never even let a boy go down on her because she was scared he wouldn't want to stop there. However, she had masturbated before and knew what it meant when her clit got to thumping like it was right at that moment. She could feel the secretions flowing between her thighs, and the alcohol wasn't making it any better. That mixed with the way he was eyeing her down.

"Do you want to go inside to somewhere less crowded? G Money's crib is crazy. There are about five empty rooms upstairs."

His question caught her off guard. Because it was happening. Malcom wanted to get her alone. And she knew what that meant. He was so fine, and she wanted to go. It was like he had her in a trance. He held his hand out to her, and she was about to take it and follow him wherever he led her, when she felt someone sit on her other side.

"Girl, I've been looking all over for you!"

The voice belonged to London. London, an earthy girl, was rocking a pair of bell-bottoms and a top that barely covered her breasts. The goddess braids in her hair went past her butt, and her makeup was beat to the gods. She was like Kiesha: beautiful and low-key.

"Hey, London. I'm fine, as you can see," Kiesha said and tried to give her a hint with her eyes that she was interrupting.

London didn't pay her any mind. "Good. The twins and I are going over to the water. Join us?" London smiled big at her and kept ignoring Malcom.

"We were about to head inside for a second. I can meet you down there," Kiesha told her.

"Yeah, don't worry. She'll be in good hands," Malcom said innocently, but Kiesha caught the glare London gave him.

"Kiesh, you know Cleo and Cliff leave right after graduation for their summer trip. We might not see them again before we head off to college. They would love to see you."

There was something about the way she was urging her to come to the beach that caught Kiesha's attention. She looked back to Malcom's eager face. He stood up and held out a hand to her, but at the last minute, she shook her head.

"I'll come find you after I talk to my friends," she said to him.

"That's cool." Malcom shrugged and walked off without another word to her.

She was glad he didn't take it too badly. She turned back to London and cut her eyes at her. "Now why'd you come and do that?"

"Do what? Cockblock?"

"Yes!"

"I was coming over here to get you anyway, but then I heard him say he wanted to take you into the house. Girl, you knew what he wanted to do, and it wasn't to go to second base!" London gave her a knowing look.

"I know, bitch!"

"And you were ready for all that? Ain't nothing wrong with wanting to rock the boat. But you really would want your first time to be with somebody as run through as Malcom? He's damn near fucked all the girls in school!"

"That has nothing to do with me. I like him. That's all that should matter."

"You shouldn't like his type at all." London rolled her eyes. "Trust me on this one. He's a sleazeball, and if you knew what I knew, you'd let that go."

"Whatever. Come on so we can meet the twins."

Chapter 4

By the time midnight hit, Kiesha was tipsy and all smiles. One thing about her girl London was that she knew how to have a good time. They had danced on the beach until they couldn't anymore, and then they just collapsed in the sand. It was almost hard to believe that they weren't kids anymore, that in just a couple of months the carefree pieces of their lives would be swept away. She would miss those days, which was why she cherished those moments on the beach, swapping stories with London and the twins, laughing until her stomach hurt, and looking up at the stars.

"Hey." London nudged her and pointed at the house. "It looks like everybody is clearing out."

Kiesha looked back up to the terrace and saw that she was right. There was hardly anybody standing there besides a few kids. The cleaners G Money's dad must have hired were already outside picking up after the careless teens. Kiesha sat up and dusted the sand off her romper and legs. When she stood up, Cleo gave her the biggest hug.

"Girl! If I don't see you before you leave, just know I'm going to miss you!" she said.

"Hell, pray we even make it back, period," Clifford said, wiping sand off his chest. "Since our dad died, our mom wants us to get closer and closer to our black roots. She might drop us off at an old plantation and never come back to get us! Like, girl, I might be light skinned, but I'm black as fuck. I don't need any lessons, especially from a white lady!"

Kiesha laughed and gave him a hug too. She was for sure going to miss his flamboyant self. One thing about him was he would never hesitate to speak his mind. Kiesha had known all of them for almost as long as she'd known Stacy. Although Stacy was her best friend, they were her tribe. They were the ones who got her and didn't care about social status. Her heart tugged knowing they were about to go off into the world and shape themselves into whatever they wanted to be. And that meant they might grow apart. Her eyes began to water, but she blinked her tears away, not wanting to sully the moment with waterworks. She hugged Cleo and Clifford one more time before she and London headed up to the house.

"Do you need a ride home?" London asked when they were inside.

"No, it's okay. I drove. I have to find Stacy though. I'm her ride."

There were still people there, but for the most part everyone had filed out. Kiesha surveyed the crowd but didn't see Stacy. However, she did see Myra and her puppets.

"Hey, do you know where Stace is? I'm about to leave," she asked when she approached them.

"Stace?" Myra asked and turned around. When she saw who was asking, a sly smile came to her face. "Oh, Stace. I think she's still upstairs in one of the rooms."

"Okay." Kiesha rolled her eyes.

"I'll come with you," London offered before shooting daggers with her eyes at Myra.

"No, you get home. I'll be fine."

"It's not an issue, girl. My dad's out of town anyway for business. No curfew."

The two of them found their way to a winding staircase. Kiesha kicked cups and plates out of the way as she made her way upstairs. There were still a few people up there, but none of them were Stacy. She peeked inside each room but found nothing. It wasn't until she passed a room with a closed door that she heard the familiar sound of Stacy's voice. She was giggling at something.

"Here, I'll get her. You go bring the car around," London said and tried to step in front of her.

"She's my best friend. I'll get her," Kiesha said and gave London a look. She pushed her out of the way and opened the door. "Stace, I've been looking for you everywh—"

She stopped talking midsentence. Kiesha had indeed found her best friend. Stacy was in the middle of planting a wet kiss on someone while pulling her dress down over her exposed bottom. The room was hot, and both Stacy's hair and the bed behind her were disheveled. Kiesha didn't need three guesses of what had taken place in the room. Upon seeing Kiesha standing there, Stacy jumped back, and the someone she had been kissing spun around. It was Malcom.

"Kiesha, what . . . what are you doing in here?" Stacy asked nervously.

Kiesha was still stuck in her shock. Her eyes kept going from the bed and back to them, and each time, she saw something new. Like the condom wrapper on the floor and Stacy's thong resting on one of the bed pillows. It was like someone had punched her in the chest.

"How long?" she was able to get out.

"What?"

"How long have you been fucking him?" Kiesha asked louder.

She couldn't tell if her heartbeat had slowed down or sped up. Stunned wasn't even the word to describe what she felt inside. Malcom looked like a deer caught in headlights as he looked back and forth between the girls. Slowly but surely, the shocked look on Stacy's face subsided only to be replaced with a smug one.

"I guess since the cat is out of the bag, I might as well tell you I've been fuckin' him since December."

"But—"

"I knew you liked him? So?" Stacy rolled her eyes dismissively. "It made doin' it more exciting. Especially since you always felt like you were better than me."

"What are you talking about?"

"You know exactly what I'm talking about. You think just because you live in a nice house and your mom can afford to give you whatever you want, you're better than me. Well, I got something you wanted and couldn't have. And the dick is good as fuck. But you wouldn't have been able to handle it with your virgin ass."

"Kiesh, she's drunk. Let's go." London tugged at Kiesha's arm, but she snatched away.

"You're supposed to be my best friend, Stacy. Best friends don't do this kind of shit to each other."

"You're so fucking sentimental! Malcom, isn't she so sentimental?" She laughed loudly, but Malcom just looked uncomfortable.

"And you," Kiesha addressed him. "Why would you try to get me to come to a room with you if you were fucking her?"

"You did what?" That was news to Stacy. She looked incredulously at him.

"You said she had a big crush on me, and when you told me she was a virgin, I couldn't resist," Malcom told her sheepishly. "And what guy doesn't want to smash two best friends?"

"Asshole!" Stacy said and hit him on the arm.

"Ay look, I'ma let y'all sort this out. I'm about to go holler at my man G Money."

He left the two of them to glare at each other. Kiesha felt like she was looking into the face of a stranger. She didn't recognize the person standing in front of her one bit.

"I can't believe you, Stacy. I don't even know what to say."

"I don't care. You know why? Because pretending to be your friend has been the hardest thing for me to do for a while now. I faked it. I mean, we're cool and everything. But the only reason I've kept you around for so long is because my mom wouldn't let me leave the house unless I was going somewhere with you. You became like a pet to me. A pet with a car and money."

"Why would you hype up me and Malcom though? That's a stupid game to play with someone."

"Don't people throw their dogs bones all the time?"

Her words stung, and the fact that she meant them hurt even more. Kiesha sucked in her breath to keep from letting the tears fall. Maybe Stacy was right. Maybe she was too sentimental. Or maybe she just really thought Stacy had her back. She felt a soft touch on her shoulder and whipped around to glare at London.

"You knew, didn't you?" she asked.

"I . . . I saw them at a party a few weeks ago," London admitted. "That's why when I heard him say he wanted you to go to a room with him, I butted in. Losing your virginity to him would have been a total mistake."

It was all too much. Kiesha had to get out of there. She pushed past London and ignored her calls. All she wanted to do was rush home and curl up under her covers. What a great way to end her senior year.

Chapter 5

It was no secret that Kiesha had been quieter than usual. Her spirits had been killed after the party, and she shut everybody out. No matter how much she tried to block it out, she just kept replaying what had happened over and over. It was the darkest truth she'd ever encountered, and she couldn't run away from it. Ever since she was little, people had told Kiesha that she was mature for her age, but her teenage heart felt every bit of it breaking.

London tried calling several times, but Kiesha wouldn't answer. The twins tried calling too. Kiesha was sure London had told them what had happened. She didn't answer for them either. She just wanted to be left alone. So many thoughts were racing through her mind when it came to Stacy. Like, had she really ever truly come to Kiesha's aid when the other girls would tease her, or did she just laugh right along with them when Kiesha was gone? She searched her brain for signs, but there were none. Stacy had played her role well, and now that school was over and she wouldn't need her mother's permission to do anything, her use for Kiesha was over.

Kiesha sulked in the house for days all the way up until the day of her graduation. It felt like she was mourning a loved one because she was. The Stacy she knew and loved had died a long time ago and had been replaced with a shell of her. Kiesha's mother noticed the sulking and let her daughter be, but she drew the line when she wasn't even excited to put her cap and gown on.

"All right now, what the hell is going on?" Miss Simmons asked, putting her hands on her hips. "You sleep all day, you won't eat, and now this! What's wrong, Kiesha?"

The two of them were standing in the middle of Miss Simmons's bedroom as she put the finishing touches on her daughter's hair and makeup. Kiesha was as stunning as any mother hoped their daughter would be on an important day like that one. However, instead of a happy expression, Kiesha wore a sad one. All the makeup in the world couldn't cover her frown. No mother liked seeing her child gloomy, especially not on a day as important as their high school graduation. Miss Simmons tried to put a hand to Kiesha's cheek, but Kiesha moved it aside.

"I'm fine, Mama," she said and sat on Miss Simmons's king-sized bed.

"Did you forget I popped you out of my coochie? This one right here." Miss Simmons pointed toward her crotch. "I know when something is wrong with my baby girl. Did something happen at that party?"

Kiesha shrugged and let her eyes fall to the ground. Miss Simmons's eyebrow shot up in a concerned manner. Kiesha knew that her mother's mind had probably gone to some boy doing something to her. But Kiesha didn't have the energy to clear it up. She didn't even want to think about it. She'd already replayed the sight of Stacy kissing Malcom in her head more times than she would have liked to. It made her sick to her stomach, especially when she thought he had finally seen her. The whole time he was plotting.

"Kiesha, I'm not going to drop it. So just tell me, please."

"Fine. Fine!" Kiesha finally gave in, knowing that her mom would keep her word to not drop it. She looked up from the ground and into her mother's eyes. "Stacy and I got into a fight."

"Oh, is that all? You two will be back again in no time, just like when you were little."

"This isn't like when we were little. I can't stand that bitch!"

"Oh, but you don't mean that, ba—"

"Yes, I do! She was just using me for my car and so her mom would say yes whenever she wanted to go somewhere. And she . . . she's been having sex with the boy I liked this whole time! This whole time!"

Kiesha burst into tears, and Miss Simmons rushed to comfort her. She wrapped her arms around her and rocked her back and forth, letting her get it all out. Kiesha sobbed into her mother's neck and inhaled the coconut oil on her skin. When she was calm, she sniffled and sat up straight. Miss Simmons wiped the excess tears away and looked caringly at her.

"I'm so sorry that happened to you, baby. I'm so sorry. Was it that Malcom boy?" Miss Simmons asked, and Kiesha nodded. "But how do you know she slept with him? You know kids spread nasty rumors all the time."

"This isn't a nasty rumor. I walked in on them at the party."

"She slept with him at a party you were at? Wow. I'm going to have to talk to her mother."

"No! I just want it to be over. The things she said to me a person can never come back from. Let's just drop it."

"The only way I'm going to drop it is if you cheer up. If you've already made your decision to cut Stacy out of your life for now, then walk in that decision. Don't let the pain she caused rule you. You're better than that."

It took a moment for the words to set in, but when they did, Kiesha felt loads better. There was something about a mother's love that was healing. Maybe it was the hug. Or maybe it was that Miss Simmons's words were exactly what Kiesha needed to hear. Because she was right.

Kiesha was positive Stacy wasn't sulking about losing her as a friend, so why was she?

"Thanks, Mama." She kissed Miss Simmons on the cheek and got up to fix her makeup. As she did, the doorbell rang. "Who's that?"

"Probably London," Miss Simmons said and placed a hand on her hip. "I thought the two of you could ride together since she lives in the neighborhood. Is that okay?"

"Yeah, it's cool."

"Good. And I'm glad you told me what happened, because I planned on prying it out of London. I was going to figure out what was wrong with my baby one way or another."

"A mess!"

"No, a mama. When you're done, come on out here so I can get pictures of the two of you."

Her mother went and let London in while Kiesha finished getting ready. When she was done, she went out to the front room. London offered her a kind smile, a gesture that Kiesha didn't return. They both were wearing their gold and black gowns over dresses. Kiesha slid into her mule heels, and they all went outside to take pictures in front of the house.

When they were done, Miss Simmons promised that she would be right behind them. She just needed to finish getting dressed. Kiesha and London got into London's car and drove toward the convention center where the ceremony was being held. The two girls had seen each other earlier that day at the graduation rehearsal but hadn't spoken a word to one another. Kiesha couldn't lie. She was still upset with her friend. How could she not tell her about Stacy and Malcom? The whole ordeal made her look like a joke.

"I take it you're still mad at me," London said as she drove her Buick LaCrosse. Kiesha didn't say anything. "Come on, Kiesh, you can't ignore me forever."

"Why can't I?"

"Because you just can't."

"Just like you just couldn't tell me what was going on behind my back?"

"I didn't want to hurt your feelings. I also never thought that Malcom would try you."

"Gee, thanks."

"I'm just saying, like, you weren't his type. He likes the easy girls. He's not the type to want to work for anything, so I thought your crush on him would blow over eventually. But I guess Stacy telling him you're a virgin still sparked his attention. I'm sorry, Kiesh."

Kiesha didn't say anything. But after a few moments of staring out the window, she knew she couldn't be mad at London. She didn't know what she would have done if the shoe were on the other foot. Kiesha let out a long breath.

"It's okay. I'm still just processing it all, you know? Forget Malcom's trifling ass. I can't believe Stacy said all those things to me."

"You can't? I could have told you a long time ago that girl wasn't your friend. Any chance she could get, she ditched you. Popularity definitely got to her head. But fuck her too. You have me, and I'll never fuck the nigga you like."

"Thanks."

It was all Kiesha could get out without getting choked up. She got herself together quickly. She wouldn't let something like a disloyal bitch ruin one of the most important days of her life. And it wasn't just about her. Her mother had worked too hard to get her there.

When they got to the convention center, they went to where they'd been directed to meet the other graduates and helping staff. They were among the last to arrive and stood in the back. The principal was in the middle of giving a speech and telling them how proud of them she was. Kiesha could barely hear anything she was saying, however. From where she stood, she could see Stacy standing with Malcom. Not only that, but they were also holding hands.

"You okay?" London whispered.

"I'm good," she answered and focused back on the principal.

Shortly after, they were told to line up in alphabetical order according to last name because the ceremony was about to start. Kiesha and London hugged, promising to find each other when it was all over, and went their separate ways. Kiesha stood in her designated spot and almost rolled her eyes when she saw Myra come and stand directly behind her. Instead, she opted to ignore her. Myra, however, wouldn't have any such thing.

"You look like you picked yourself up out of the shitter finally," she said in a low tone as the long line of students walked out to a hallway. Kiesha still didn't say anything. "Did you run home and cry to Mommy that night?"

"You must take pleasure in other people's pain," Kiesha finally responded.

"No, not people. Just you."

"I would ask why, but if you're as sick and twisted as Stacy, I don't want to know."

"You really thought she was your friend, didn't you? She was just using yo—"

Kiesha stopped walking and whipped around to face her. She mustered the vilest look she could and glared into Myra's eyes. The gloating expression faded quickly from her face, and she stepped back.

"Good idea, because if you say one more thing to me, I'm going to do you worse than I did Kennedy."

Kiesha turned back around and continued walking. Shortly after, she heard feet moving behind her, letting her know that the line had resumed moving. Myra heeded the warning and didn't say anything else to her.

"Bitch," Kiesha mouthed.

The only sound Kiesha heard next was the deafening sound of cheering when the graduates entered the stage area. She saw her mother in one of the ground seats waving at her like a maniac. Kiesha had to admit, that sight made her smile.

Ahead in the line of graduates, Stacy looked back, probably hoping that Myra was tormenting Kiesha. What her eyes were met with was a middle finger. Shocked, she turned back around.

"Ladies and gentlemen, our Rose Hill graduates!" a voice said, flooding the space through the speakers.

More cheers followed, and it hit Kiesha that it was her moment, one of the most important ones in her life. Stacy had made her choice, and now Kiesha was making hers by focusing on what really mattered. Her future.

Chapter 6

A Week Later

The sound of sucking and slurping filled the air. Bright sunrays shone through the floor-to-ceiling windows inside the master bedroom of a high-rise condo. The rays fell on two naked bodies as they were entangled in lust.

"Damn, girl, you're sucking the fuck outta that dick," Adrian Parks moaned.

He gripped the back of the Latina woman's head and forced her to gag on his thick penis. The feeling of the back of her throat on his tip made his eyes roll. She didn't seem to miss a beat. Her lips wrapped around his shaft, and her tongue licked as she sucked up and down. The warmth and wetness of her mouth were too much for him. His breathing was labored as he felt his climax building up. She knew that he had reached the point of no return and mixed her suck with a two-hand twist combo. That was what did it.

"Ahhhh!" Adrian jerked as he shot his cum down her throat.

She kept swallowing until he was completely drained. She tried to snatch his soul by continuing to suck, but he pulled his dick out of her mouth and leaned back onto one of the big pillows on his king-sized bed. The woman looked very pleased with herself, and he had to admit he was impressed by her skills.

"Was that good for you, daddy?" she asked.

"Very," he responded and reached into his nightstand. From it, he pulled a small wad of hundred-dollar bills and handed it to her. "Your tip is included in that payment. Go and get dressed. I have to leave soon."

She smiled big and took the money from him. When she got out of bed and got dressed, Adrian stared at her voluptuous body. It was then that he realized that he didn't remember her real name. She was just a chick he'd met on Instagram. Bad as hell, pretty face, nice body. He could see her surgery scars and assumed she had a BBL. That didn't matter to him though. He wasn't trying to fuck her. He just wanted some good head. Women on the internet always acted so above certain things, but dangle some hundreds in their face, and they were down to do anything.

"Maybe we can do this again?" she said hopefully when Adrian walked her to the front door of the condo.

"Hsssss," he hissed, making a face. "About that. I have a policy that I never see the same woman twice."

"What?" she asked, clearly confused.

"Look, Selena—"

"Sonia," she corrected him tersely.

"Whatever. You're nice and all, but I just wanted to get my dick sucked. You got some money out of the deal, so we both won."

"You're an asshole."

"I'm not actually. I just have certain boundaries that I don't cross. And one of them is not dating women who suck dick on the first meetup. Have a good day."

He opened the door for her, and she stomped through it. He watched, amused, as she made her way to the elevator at the end of the hall. Adrian had another rule: while women were on his floor, they were his responsibility. It was his duty to make sure they made it to that elevator safely. After that, his job was done. When she got into the elevator and turned to see him still watching, she flicked him off. He waved goodbye and shut his door.

Adrian was a very good-looking man who could have any woman he wanted. He knew that. However, a relationship or anything close to it just wasn't on his mind at the moment. That was why he'd stopped dating entirely. Even when he tried to casually see people, they would grow too attached to him. He knew he wouldn't be able to give a woman the time she deserved or needed, so it wasn't fair to either one of them. That was the reason it was just easier for him to buy pussy when he needed it. The unspoken "no strings attached" clause that came along with that fit his lifestyle perfectly. Not only did he get to experience different beautiful women, but he also didn't have to worry about them blowing up his phone afterward or anything else.

At age 22, Adrian was a very successful man. One of the reasons was because his father was Antonio Parks, owner of Parks Realty. As soon as Adrian graduated, he got his own Realtor license and began working in the company. He had since worked his way up and was now the leading marketing exec for the business. Two things he could sell were the dream of owning a property and the property itself. It was a gift.

He spent the rest of his morning eating breakfast and getting dressed. Sonia had definitely put him in the zone. He was ready to go to the office. Only, he didn't know that the office was coming to him. The knock at his door while he was putting on his diamond cuff links caught him off guard. At first, he thought it was Sonia coming back to cuss him out, which was why he checked the peephole before opening the door. It wasn't Sonia in the hallway. It was his father.

"Dad, what are you doing here?" he asked, opening the door.

"I didn't know I needed a reason to come visit my own son," Antonio said, taking the fedora off his head before stepping inside.

"You don't, but it's early. Most people call before they just show up at someone's home."

"Hm," Antonio chuckled slightly and sat down on one of Adrian's couches. "This unsavory welcome must have something to do with that pissed-off Hispanic chick I saw leaving the building."

"I don't know what you're talking about."

"You don't, huh? Maybe she was muttering about another Adrian in this building being an asshole then." Antonio playfully tapped his chin, and it made Adrian drop his poker face.

He grinned big and sat across from his old man. Since Adrian was a boy, his father had always been able to get the truth out of him. Antonio used to joke and say that it was his superpower. But really it came from just being a good father.

"Okay, okay, you got me."

"Son, how many times do I have to tell you to be careful dealing with all these women?" Antonio shook his head. "Women are delicate creatures. What can happen if you shatter glass?"

"You can get cut."

"Exactly!"

"But, Pop, this isn't like that. These women know what they're walking into when they deal with me."

"Tell that to the angry Latina outside."

"Hey, I don't sugarcoat a thing. She wanted to see me again, and I had to let her know I wasn't with that. Sticking to my boundaries makes me wrong?"

"All I'm saying is that one day you're going to meet that one special girl and your womanizing past is going to come back and bite you in the dick."

"Well, until then, I'ma keep doing me." Adrian grinned again and leaned forward in his seat. "Anyway, I know you didn't come all this way just to lecture me on women. What's up?"

"There's a convention in Atlanta that I've been invited to, so I'll be gone for a week." Antonio leaned back on the big gray couch and smoothed his tie down.

"Okay. You need me to hold down the fort. That's not anything I haven't done before. I got you."

"I know you've done it before, but this time will be different."

"How so?"

"My intern starts on Monday, and I want to make sure she'll be in good hands while I'm gone. She's a very bright young lady, and I want her to have the best experience with Parks Realty."

"You want me to babysit a nerd? Got it. Easy peasy."

"This is serious, Adrian. She's going to Howard in the fall for marketing, and I figured it would be good for her to shadow you while I'm gone. You are the best at what you do, after all."

"What's in it for me?"

"The love of your father." Antonio winked.

"Too bad I already have that. What about this?" Adrian asked and rubbed the fingers on his right hand together. "I do better work when dinero is involved."

"How about a summer vacation completely paid for by me?"

"As long as I get to pick the location, that's fine with me, old man."

"Also, make sure she doesn't find out about the other side of our business."

"You already know that's going to be on lock." Adrian grinned.

Happily, Antonio slapped his hands together. He got up from the couch and went back toward where he'd come in. On his way there, he patted Adrian on the shoulder. Being Antonio's only boy, Adrian had always felt a pressure to make him proud. Even though Antonio constantly reminded him that he was the best son a person could have, Adrian still thrived to make his father's life easier. That was why he worked so hard for the company. And that was why he was going to stand in for his father with the nerd. He just hoped the girl wasn't too weird.

Before his father left, he turned to his son at the door and made a face.

"You need to get a cleaning lady up here expeditiously. It smells very strongly of ass and titties."

Chapter 7

Two Weeks Later

"Kiesha!"

Kiesha heard her mother shouting her name. However, she thought it was in her dream. Along with Miss Simmons's voice, there was an annoying bell that kept sounding over and over. She just wanted them both to stop, but they didn't. Not until she felt a strong arm jerk her. She opened her eyes and realized that she was nestled comfortably in her bed. Standing over her and staring wide-eyed at her was her mom. Kiesha knew that whatever the cause of her expression was had to be serious because she had both hands on her hips.

"Whaaat?" Kiesha moaned into her pillow.

"Do you know what today is?"

"It's Monday, right?"

"Yes, but it's a very important Monday. It's the day you start your internship!"

"What?" Kiesha exclaimed and sat up so fast she got lightheaded.

She snatched her phone up from beside her and checked her calendar. Miss Simmons was right. It was the start date for her internship with Antonio Parks. The annoying alarm sound was coming from her clock, and she hurried to turn it off. Slowly her memory was coming back to her. She'd set her alarm so that she would wake up on time for her important day. But she'd also stayed up late binge-watching movies, which explained how she'd slept through her alarm for almost thirty minutes.

Kiesha still had a little over an hour to spare, but it would take a good thirty minutes just to drive to the realty office. She jumped up and rushed to the foot of her bed. The one smart thing she'd done was pick her outfit out the night before like it was the first day of school.

"Yeah, you better put some fire under that ass! I can't believe you."

"Mama, you're not helping!" Kiesha groaned as she put her hair up into a bun.

"Mm, well, how about I help by making you something to eat in the car since you aren't going to have time to sit at the table?"

"That would be great. Thank you!"

"Mm," Miss Simmons said again and left the room.

Kiesha rushed to shower and throw her cute pastel pink skirt suit on. Before she left the room, she made sure to give her baby hairs some love and threw a scarf on for them to dry on the drive. She left her room, and when she passed the kitchen, her mom handed her a plate with a bagel that had her favorite strawberry cream cheese spread on it. She kissed her on the cheek and made her way out the door.

"I love you. Drive safe! Tell me all about it later!" Miss Simmons called from the porch.

"I will!" she called back from her car.

She drove off in the direction of Parks Realty. She just knew that traffic was going to be bad since it was a Monday and almost 9:00 a.m., but surprisingly it wasn't. It might have had something to do with the fact that school was out. Whatever the reason, she was grateful. She demolished her bagel and took the scarf off her head right before she pulled into the parking lot. She saw a Rolls-Royce Cullinan parked in the spot that read ANTONIO PARKS, and she felt herself growing antsy. It was really settling in that she was doing a paid internship with the most successful black Realtor in Florida. It was more than a blessing, especially since she was getting the opportunity to do work in what would be her actual career field.

Before she got out of the car, she fixed her blouse and her jacket. After one last glance in the mirror, she opened the door and made her way inside. She coached herself as she walked. Confidence was key, and she didn't want anyone to think she was nervous even though she was. Deadly nervous.

The cool air inside the building hit her and soothed her skin. A short distance away was the front desk and the pretty, young receptionist sitting behind it. She wore a bright smile and looked to be in her early thirties. Kiesha couldn't help but notice that her wig was laid to the gods and her lash extensions were flawless.

"Hi, I'm—" Kiesha tried to say when she reached the desk, but the receptionist interrupted.

"Kiesha Simmons?"

"That's me."

"Perfect. I was expecting you. I'm Talia, the receptionist. But you can call me Li Li. Here's your badge." Li Li handed Kiesha a white badge that had on it the picture she'd sent in. "That will get you through any door in this big building except Mr. Parks's office."

"Thank you," Kiesha said and then looked around. "Do I wait here then?"

"No, I'm sorry. Go straight down that wide hall there. We call it the Executive Hall. At the end of it you'll see the main office. Mr. Parks is waiting for you."

"Thank you."

Kiesha did as she was told and went down the Executive Hall. On the way to her destination, she found herself wondering if she would get an office. She doubted it. She was just an intern. She'd be lucky enough if she got a desk by a window.

When she reached the office at the end of the hall, she noticed that the door was open. She stepped through it, and it felt like the energy around her had shifted. There was a faint scent of expensive cologne, and everything inside the office was lined in gold, literally, including the big mahogany desk. The chair was facing the other way, but she could hear papers being sifted through, and that let her know someone was sitting in it. She cleared her throat to announce her presence. Instantly the chair swiveled around, and she smiled big to greet Mr. Parks. Only the person in the chair wasn't Mr. Parks. It was someone she had never seen before.

"Who are you?" she blurted out.

The man sitting in the chair resembled Mr. Parks, but he was way too young to be him. He didn't look much older than Kiesha. If she weren't so busy being shocked, she might have noticed how good-looking he was in his navy suit and clean line up. He chuckled at her outburst.

"I guess having manners was on the bottom of the internship requirements," he said.

"I . . . I'm sorry. I didn't mean to be rude or anything. It's just that you aren't who I was expecting. Li Li told me that Mr. Parks was in this office."

"I am Mr. Parks, just not the old one." He smiled charmingly. "My name is Adrian. And you must be Kiesha."

"That's right." She nodded. "You're Mr. Parks's son then? Or maybe his nephew."

"You were right the first time. Antonio Parks is my father. I'm just filling in while he's away on business."

"Away on business? Didn't he know I was coming today?"

"He did. And that's why he put me in charge of making sure you're on the right track while here."

"He put you in charge? But you don't look much older than me."

"That's because I'm not. Perks of being the son of a boss man. Age doesn't matter. Skill and work ethic do, which is why he trusts me to run this place while he's gone."

"Oh." Kiesha wasn't able to hide the disappointment in her voice, and Adrian chuckled again.

"I didn't realize until this very moment how tough it is to fill my father's shoes," he said astutely and stared into her face. "But I promise you that you're only stuck with me for a week. Let me show you to your office."

"Office?"

"You didn't think we would have you working from a corner desk by the window, did you?" Adrian winked at her.

She smiled sheepishly, not wanting to admit that that was exactly what she thought. She followed him out of the office and halfway down the Executive Hall. When he opened the door, she couldn't help the smile on her face. The office wasn't huge like Mr. Parks's, but it was the perfect size for her. There was an L-shaped desk for her to sit at, a minifridge, and a couch against the wall. The room wasn't decorated, but she would soon change that. She sat down at the desk and noticed the desk nameplate with her name on it.

"Wow, this is so nice," she said, admiring her new space.

"I'm glad you like it. My actual office is right across the hall, so either way we won't be too far from each other."

"So what is it that you do here, Mr. Parks?"

"You can just call me Adrian," he said and smiled at her.

That time she did notice how fine he was. His skin was like smooth chocolate, and the gaze from his piercing eyes made her want to blush. Her eyes travel down to his broad shoulders and muscular build. She wondered how many hours he put in at the gym a week to get so sexy. He complemented the tailored suit he wore, not the other way around. Before she started to drool, she snapped out of her short-lived trance.

"Okay, Adrian, what exactly do you do, um, around here?"

"I'm head of marketing. That's what you're going to school for, right?"

"Yes. Did you get your degree in marketing as well?"

"Uh, no," Adrian laughed. "Another perk of having Antonio Parks as a dad. I hated school, and he knew it. Luckily for me, I had a dad who focused on the other things I was good at."

"And that was?"

"Selling things. I could talk a cat into buying claws if I wanted to. So when I graduated, my dad gave me a choice: live on the streets or join the family business. It's obvious which one I chose. Now I'm responsible for bringing in clients, and the rest of the team is responsible for sending them out as happy campers."

"That's amazing. I can't begin to tell you how excited I am to be interning here this summer. What are we doing today?"

"I'm glad you asked. Today we're going to make a campaign for a few new listings we just got this morning. Our TikTok and Instagram have over two million followers, combined. Also you're going to help me with an idea for a commercial we're shooting next week."

Kiesha was happy they were jumping right into work. She followed Adrian out of her new office and to another part of the building that required key card access. It was a large room with a few cubicles and desks with computers on them. There were half a dozen people back there working and on the phones. Adrian led Kiesha over to one woman in particular. She was very fair skinned and pretty. When she saw them approaching, she smoothed out her blouse and stared curiously at Kiesha.

"Megan, this is Kiesha, our new intern. Kiesha, this is our leasing consultant," Adrian introduced them.

"That's the official title they give me, but really I do a little bit of everything," Megan said, smiling at Kiesha. "I didn't know we were getting an intern."

"You know my dad likes to make plans in silence. We're about to get started on the campaign for the beach homes."

"I'm glad you're going to start on those, because you know once Sheraton Realtors gets a hold of them, they're going to try to close before we do."

"And that's why it's great that we got a week's head start on the properties. Is anybody using the conference room?"

"Not until one o'clock. It's all yours."

"Thanks."

Megan smiled at them before they walked away, but there was something about the way she looked at Kiesha that made her feel that it wasn't genuine. It was like the woman was sizing her up. She looked to be about the same age as Li Li, but she definitely didn't have the same welcoming energy.

The conference room was the same as every conference room Kiesha had ever seen: long rectangular desk with about ten chairs, a few laptops, a projector, and a white board. She sat down and waited patiently. From a file cabinet, Adrian pulled out a folder full of the campaign ideas and set it in front of her. As she looked them over, she couldn't help but be impressed. Adrian was definitely an out-of-the-box thinker when it came to getting people's attention.

"What do you think?" he asked.

"I like it. A lot. You're dope," she said with her eyes still on the pages. "I'm trying to figure out what you need me for. This is great."

"It's missing something. The razzle-dazzle. Everything is about timing, and the goal is to already have buyers before the other realty companies find out about the gold."

"I get it." Kiesha's voice was low. That happened when her mind was going full throttle. In just a few seconds she had an idea. "If timing is of the essence, why don't you just knock out two birds with one stone?"

"What do you mean?" Adrian said, coming to stand closely behind her as she pointed at the papers in front of her.

"Once you release the campaign, the other Realtors are going to find out about the properties anyway. So instead of releasing it and waiting for people to contact you for a viewing, why not just host a viewing for the public? Call it 'Sandy Dreams.' And what's a more beautiful place to shoot a commercial than the beach? You won't even have to pay extras to be in it because a crowd will already be there."

When she was done speaking, the room was quiet. Maybe she should have kept her mouth shut. She was certain Adrian hated her idea. However, when she glanced up, she saw his lips slowly forming a smile.

"I like that. I like it a lot. So much that I think we're gonna go with that instead."

"For real?"

"Hell yeah! One thing you'll learn about me, Miss Simmons, is that I have no ego. While you're here, we're a team. Wow, beauty and brains. Did God save any for the rest of them?"

She knew that he was truly giving her an innocent compliment, but still she felt her face grow warm. He grabbed the papers from in front of her and crumpled them up. She was glad when he turned his back to throw them away. He had been standing so close to her—too close to her.

"Kiesha. You can call me Kiesha," she heard herself say.

He turned back and paused. There was still a small smile on his face as he looked at her. She wished he would stop. It was her first day, and he was the boss's son. She didn't want to have any extra thoughts about him. She was there to work and that was it. But there was just something about the swagger in his walk and the confidence in his voice that she liked. He was just a . . . man.

"Okay. Kiesha it is," he finally said. He was about to say something else, but then his phone's ringer went off. He glanced at it and held up a finger to her. "I need to step out for a moment. You start working on that campaign."

He left in a bit of a hurry, but Kiesha still waited to make sure he wasn't going to pop back in. Once the coast was clear, she pulled her phone out to send Stacy a text about how fine her boss's son was. But then she remembered that Stacy wasn't her best friend anymore when she couldn't find their text thread. Kiesha wanting to text her had been such an automatic feeling she almost got sad. But then she stopped herself, remembering that she still had a real friend. She opened her text thread with London and grinned big as her thumbs moved.

Bitch! This nigga is fine as fuck!

Chapter 8

Adrian kept a smile on as he walked all the way to the back of the building. It quickly faded when he exited through the back door that led to the alley. Parked there was a red convertible with a man in the front seat. The man wore his hair in a low fade with waves so deep they could make you seasick. He was no stranger to Adrian, although he wasn't happy to see him, not there anyway. His name was Cameron Bailey, and he flashed his pearly whites at Adrian, who didn't return the favor. The two men were by no means friends, not anymore. They could be considered business associates.

"Cam, what the fuck are you doing here?" Adrian asked.

"I thought you said you wanted to meet today."

"Did I ever give you a time and a place, nigga?"

"Nah. That's why I pulled up. Time is of the essence, and that pack is waiting to be moved. So what's the word?"

Adrian ran his hands over his face and sighed. The truth was that he had completely forgotten that he was supposed to be meeting with Cameron that day, hence the reason he'd never given him a meetup time. He'd been so focused on filling in for his dad in the office that he forgot he needed to fill in for him in the streets, too. There was another reason Antonio Parks was one of the most successful men in Florida.

His beginnings were very humble. He started off as a dope boy, and working his way up in the ranks, he eventually became the biggest drug kingpin in Florida. However, when he got older and started a family, he knew that being the face of such a dangerous operation was risky. That was why he decided to go legit in eyesight and run the streets from the shadows. When Adrian came of age, he showed him the ropes of all his business dealings, even the illegal ones. He was grooming him to one day take over everything, and he was proving himself with flying colors. However, there always seemed to be one person who had trouble following Adrian's instructions. That person was Cameron.

Cameron was the son of Antonio's right-hand man, Carrington. When Antonio fell back into the shadows, he still called all the shots, but it was Carrington who carried out his orders. He was the new face of the operation, which was why it was assumed Cameron would be next in line for the throne. Antonio wasn't going to force his own son to take his place unless he wanted to. It was his choice, and he chose to one day be the head of both businesses. That meant that Cameron worked under him.

The two men were the same age and had been raised like brothers. However, they didn't get along. They were loyal to each other, but they were more like frenemies.

"You know not to pull up here like this. You should have texted me," Adrian finally said.

"I did. Three times."

Adrian checked his phone and saw that Cameron was being honest. There, in fact, were three missed texts from him. Adrian was almost lost on how he didn't see them, but he remembered. He'd been distracted by the new intern's pretty face. He hadn't even thought to look at his phone. He had been too busy sizing her up. And then she went on and impressed him with her brain. Nothing else had crossed his mind.

"My bad. It's been a busy day."

"I bet. But I'm not here to listen to you vent about it. People are waiting to hear about this weight."

"No doubt. You know what to do. Make the rounds but hold Drako's order. That nigga owes me twenty-five K. Until he pays up, his camp is gonna starve."

"Say less," Cameron said and rubbed his hands together.

"When did you get this bright red shit anyway?" Adrian asked, looking at the car.

"It's nice, huh?"

"It's straight, I guess."

"It's nice. I know, nigga! You hating!" Cameron laughed. "But you know that nigga Jerry from Opa-Locka?"

"Drako's old connect." Adrian nodded.

"Yep. Well, since nigga went down for a RICO charge, they auctioned off all his shit, including this car."

"Nigga, you for sure gotta get up from around here now in this hot-ass shit!"

"Chill out. It was white and on chromes when I got it. I got it painted and went regular on the shoes. You can't even tell it's the same whip."

"Whatever, fool. I still say you're tripping."

"Yeah, yeah. I'm about to go handle that though and let you get back to doing the suit-and-tie thing. Hit me if you need me."

Adrian shook his head and slapped hands with Cameron. He watched him drive away before going back inside. He went back to the conference room to find Kiesha where he'd left her. She barely even noticed when he walked back in, but that was fine with him. He put his hands deep in his pockets and leaned against the far wall, just watching her work.

When she first stepped foot in the office, he'd wanted to compliment her choice of attire. The skirt suit hugged her body beautifully, and the pink accented her skin. When his father told him they were going to have an intern for the summer, he didn't know why he'd imagined a geeky, scrawny girl who would probably get on his nerves. He hadn't for a second expected a thick, beautiful black queen.

The sound of someone clearing their throat interrupted his concentration.

"Mr. Parks, I need you to help me with some work if you don't mind." Megan had stepped into the conference room.

He glanced at Kiesha one last time before nodding and exiting with Megan. She had some papers in her hands, and he assumed she needed him to look at them. He followed her into a room down the hall. However, it wasn't until they were inside that he realized he hadn't been paying attention at all to where she had taken him. She flicked on the light and revealed that they were inside of the company's spacious supply closet. She dropped the papers to the floor, revealing that they weren't anything but blank computer sheets. Before he could try to leave, she blocked the door and locked it.

"You know that's my favorite suit of yours, right?" she said seductively.

Her eyes stared at him hungrily. It was then that Adrian regretted sleeping with her the week prior, but he couldn't help himself. Megan was a sexy woman, and he wanted to see what cougar pussy was about. She had exceeded his expectations, but he had his rule: one and done. He never planned to go to bed with her again. It was already messy enough that they worked together. When she reached to massage his crotch area, he moved her hands away and stepped back.

"Megan, what are you doing?"

"What does it look like? I want some dick. Right now."

Her assertiveness was turning him on. That, mixed with the low-cut blouse she wore. He could picture her light brown nipples and remembered the feel of them on his tongue. She bit her bottom lip at him the same way she had when he was ramming her from the back. One more second and he was going to hike her skirt up and do it again, but he snapped out of it.

"We can't do this here, Megan."

"Are you telling me that my pussy was weak or something?"

"Not at all, but I was under the impression that you knew it was a one-time thing. I'm not looking for anything ongoing with anyone right now. Especially anyone I work with."

He'd cut straight to the point, and he could see that she wasn't too happy with his choice of words. But he didn't care. She could deal with it or leave. That was the biggest problem with having good dick—some women didn't know how to let go. However, the disappointed look on Megan's face subsided.

"I understand. This was very inappropriate of me. I just thought this would excite you. I guess you're too young to appreciate a woman like me."

Without another word to him, she scooped her papers back up and opened the supply door. When she did, however, they both were shocked to see Kiesha standing on the other side. Her eyes opened wide when she saw the two of them in there together, but she didn't say anything. Megan cleared her throat and stepped past her, leaving Adrian alone with her.

He blurted out the first thing that came to his mind. "Kiesha, that wasn't what it looked like."

"I . . . I just came to get some computer paper. There was none in the conference room. What you have going on with her is none of my business."

"There's nothing going on!" he exclaimed and then quickly lowered his voice. "There's nothing going on. She just needed some help with . . . something."

"With the door closed?" she asked, and he swore he saw an amused glint in her eyes.

He had to admit it sounded ridiculous, and he soon found himself smiling sheepishly. He shook his head, grabbed a pack of printing paper for her, and exited the supply closet.

"All right, how about we start whatever business relationship we'll have on an honest note?" he asked when they got back to the conference room.

"Deal. So what was that all about?"

"That was about a one-night stand that I shouldn't have had."

"I knew she was looking at me funny when I walked in with you!" Kiesha laughed and sat back down in front of the laptop. Adrian sat across from her at the table. "So what, is she hooked on the D now?"

"I wouldn't say all that, but what you saw was her trying to get it again. I'm sorry you had to see that. It isn't how I want this company to be depicted. We are professional people here."

"But you're young and handsome." She shrugged. "It comes with the territory."

"You think I'm handsome?"

"I, uh . . . Look at what I came up with!"

She slid the laptop in front of him, and he dropped the topic, not to spare her from being put on the spot, but because what she had come up with in that short time frame was brilliant. He looked at her and then back at the computer.

"Aw yeah, we might have to hire you for real!"

Chapter 9

Say you my nigga, I'ma be your killer
Nobody gon' play with you when I'm with you

Cam found himself rapping loudly along with Kodak Black as he breezed through the Miami streets. It had been a few hours since he left the real estate office, and he was getting to the business he and Adrian had discussed. He'd made his rounds and dropped off product to people who needed their pack. However, there was one more left. It was supposed to be Drako's, but if he didn't pay what he owed, Cam was sure he could find someone to pick it up. Drako operated out of Little Haiti and had a reputation of doing what he wanted to, which was why Cam tried to advise Adrian not to let him in on their operation when Jerry went down. But he wasn't trying to hear it. To him, the more hands pushing the work, the faster the money would come in. He was right, but Cam always had a bad feeling about Drako.

He stopped his car in the lot of an autobody shop and hopped out. Before he could even take two steps, six men came out of the garage to greet him. One of them was a tall, dark-skinned man with a beer belly poking through his wife beater and wick locs on his head. The bright gold teeth were almost blinding, and he stared strangely at Cam.

"What's good, Drako?" Cam asked, nodding.

"Shit, just wondering why you showed up here so light," Drako responded in a gruff voice.

Cam knew he was referring to the fact that he had stepped out of his car empty-handed. However, they had business to square away first. He surveyed his surroundings and took note of Drako's men also glowering at him. These weren't men he knew and had been doing business with. They were all just now starting to build a rapport, and Drako seemed like he didn't know how they liked business to be done.

"I can't drop off more work if you haven't paid the five for the last drop. You owe us twenty-five big ones, Drako. Before I can give you the pack, you gotta come up off that."

Drako scoffed at him, then gave a flat-out laugh. The men around him joined in, but Cam kept a hard face. He didn't find anything funny. Drake rubbed his hands together and stepped toward Cam, wearing an evil smile on his face. Cam stood his ground and didn't even move when he and Drako were toe-to-toe.

"You come to my territory and tell me what you aren't going to give me, nigga? Are you stupid?"

"The real question is, are you stupid? You seem to have forgotten whose money you're playing with." Cam turned his nose up.

"I play with my money," Drako said and laughed again. "When Jerry was here—"

"Well, he ain't here, motherfucka! So you have two choices: pay up or lie the fuck down."

Cam's voice was calm, but even a deaf person could hear the menacing undertone. He didn't care a single bit how Jerry did business with Drako. And if he ever let anyone slide off with that much money, he was a plumb fool.

"And what if I don't?" Drako tested his temperature. "What if I go to that car of yours, take the drugs, and leave you leaking where you stand?"

"I'd say you really are dumber than you look," Cam snickered. "You can kill me right now, but that won't change the fact that you owe Antonio money. And if you take the drugs, you'll owe him that, too. One thing he doesn't play about is his business. So go ahead and make your move today. I bet you'll be dead first thing in the morning."

"He can't touch me!"

"Nigga, anybody can touch you right now. Jerry's whole operation went down, and y'all are the last ones standing. And that means you have no protection. You shouldn't be trying to make any enemies in such a fragile state. Now I'm not going to say this again. Pay up."

Cam could see Drako's thoughts turn as he leered at him. The two men had a stare down for a few moments before Drako stepped back and motioned to one of his people. The man didn't say a word. He just went back into the garage. Soon he returned with a black duffle bag and threw it at Cam's feet. Cam unzipped it and was happy to see all of the hundred-dollar bills staring up at him.

"It better all be in here, too," he said as he tossed it into his trunk. In exchange, he grabbed a different duffle bag from the trunk and threw it at Drako. "Same time next week. Word of advice: keep the bullshit on ice and everything will go smoothly. I won't be so nice next time."

Drako snorted but didn't say another word as Cam got into his car and drove away. The thing about Cam was that he mastered the ability to show his gangster without ever untucking his pistol. His father, Carrington, had told him that a real man didn't need weapons to make those around him fall in line. His presence should be enough. They were words that Cam carried with him. He was glad that he was able to handle the situation without calling in reinforcements. The last thing he wanted was for his dad to come back from the business trip he was on with Antonio and see that he had fumbled the bag. He would keep what happened with Drako to himself. It was under control.

Chapter 10

Kiesha successfully made it through her first three days as an intern for Parks Realty, and she could honestly say that she was still on a cloud. She didn't know what she expected before, but the actual experience was way better than what she could have imagined. She'd hoped to work closely with Antonio, but he would be back by the end of the week, so she could wait a little longer. Also, working closely with Adrian proved to be pretty cool. Not only did she get to work with a fine and young black man, but he was also truly gifted at what he did. And that made it even more of a treat to know that he was impressed by her.

"Girl, I know you aren't over there thinking about that man again."

London's voice interrupted Kiesha's thoughts. When she snapped back to reality, she realized that there was a small smile on her lips. She tried to stop, but that made her smile even harder. London was looking at her like she was crazy, and she had to laugh.

"I'm just in a good mood, that's all!" Kiesha said and fell back into the pillows on London's bed.

She had done that day what she had done every day since she started her internship, and that was go straight to London's house when she was off. Kiesha was in her normal spot on the bed, and London swiveled back and forth in her computer chair, eating a bowl of peaches. Of course, Kiesha told her all about Adrian. There was no way she would be able to hold that water, not when the man gave her insane butterflies whenever he was around.

"I'm just glad you're in a better mood, because for a second there I was a little bit concerned."

"It just took me a little bit of time to remember what matters, that's all."

"Has Stace tried to reach out to you at all?"

"She knows better." Kiesha made a face at the thought. "After all the shit she said to me, there ain't no coming back from that."

"I hear you, but aren't your moms like really good friends?" London asked, slurping a peach in her mouth.

"And they can stay really good friends. That has nothing to do with me," Kiesha said and felt her vibration lower. "You know what really bothers me? It's the fact that Stacy was in my life for years. Like, how did I not see that she didn't like me?"

"Because I'm sure she loved you. It's hard to explain, or to understand for that matter, but it's possible for someone to love you and not like you. Especially if they're envious of you. Envy is one of those feelings that just will fester until a person can't control it anymore."

"Look at you being wise," Kiesha teased.

"Shut up. I'm serious. Have you ever looked at yourself? I mean, really looked at yourself?"

"In the mirror every day."

"Okay, have you ever really seen who you are? And I'm not talking about the shit that's just on the surface."

"I don't know. Maybe."

"I'm telling you that Stacy saw you. It's hard for people to touch greatness and realize that they're only a fragment of that. I don't think it hit a lot of our peers that high school was just a part of our journey and who you grow into after is what really matters. Fucking idiots. Most of those hoes are going to crash and burn. Crash and burn, I say!"

London was the only one who could make Kiesha belly laugh in a moment of seriousness. And while she was in the middle of cracking up, she felt her stomach growl. Her eyes went instantly to the bowl of peaches in London's hand, but she was in the middle of eating the last one.

"Are there any more of those?"

"Last can. But we can go to the store real quick. Grocery shopping for the house is my summer chore."

They left London's room, and Kiesha waited for her to grab the money her mom left her from the kitchen before they left. They took London's white Dodge Charger and rolled the windows all the way down, enjoying the Miami air. They sang their hearts out to Summer Walker's latest album until they reached their destination.

"Damn, I forgot to make a list," London groaned when they got inside and grabbed a basket.

"Bitch, we don't need a list. We just need food!"

The girls laughed and proceeded to throw things into the cart. It wasn't until they reached the meat section that Kiesha felt the undeniable urge to use the restroom. Public restrooms were disgusting, but she couldn't wait. She told London she would be right back and made her way to the back of the store where the restrooms were. As soon as she stepped inside, she remembered why she usually waited. It wasn't dirty in there, but it smelled strongly of vagina and poop. All she could do was hurry up and squat over a toilet and relieve herself, which she did in a hurry. One more minute in there and she was going to throw up all the nothingness in her stomach. She all but ran out of there after she washed her hands, and apparently she wasn't paying attention, because she crashed into somebody.

"I'm so sorry!" she exclaimed, looking up into the man's face.

"You're good," he said and then looked quizzically behind her. "I mean, are you good? You ran up out of there like Michael Myers was behind you."

"Have you ever smelled a girl's restroom? That shit is worse than Michael Myers!" she stated seriously, but he laughed.

He was handsome. Beyond it. He had brown skin and a cocaine white smile. Fresh, too. Kiesha took notice of the Amiri jeans and T-shirt he rocked with a pair of Jordans. He didn't look much older than her, and she liked that he didn't have a ton of facial hair. She liked the baby-face look.

"You're funny and beautiful. Maybe you bumping into me was a sign."

"Not hitting me with the game!" she teased, and he cheesed harder.

"I'm just talking how I talk, shawty."

"Yeah, yeah."

"For real. I'm just saying it's not every day a beautiful woman falls into your arms like this. I don't think I'm supposed to let this moment pass without at least getting your name."

"It's Kiesha."

"Well, Kiesha, it's nice to meet you. I'm Cameron. Call me Cam. Are you from around here?"

"Yeah, I am. I just stopped by to grab a few things."

"Same. Would it be too forward to ask for your number?" he asked with a hopeful look in his eyes.

"Um . . ."

"What, you got a man or something?"

"I gotta have a man to not give you my number?" she asked, putting her hand on her hip.

"Either that or crazy."

"Confident. I like that." She bit her lip and thought about it. She didn't know about them meeting by fate, but she did know that later on, when she thought about the sexy man in the grocery store, she would regret it if she didn't at least take his number. "Put your number in my phone."

Kiesha handed him the device. Her intention was to take his number and hit him up when she was ready, but Cam had other plans. After he put his number in, he called himself from her phone so that he would have her number too. She smiled because she had to admit he was smooth with it. He winked at her when he handed her phone back.

"You thought I was going to wait two weeks to hear from your fine ass? Nah. You're crazy."

"It wouldn't have been two weeks. Maybe two days though." She grinned.

"That's still too long when I'm trying to take you out tomorrow."

"Oh, really?"

"Yeah, really. But we can talk about that later. I need to get out of here and make some moves. Have a good day, Kiesha."

Cam smiled at her one more time and walked away. Even his walk was smooth. She couldn't lie. He had definitely sparked her interest, and she found herself wondering what kinds of moves he had to make. She could tell by the diamonds on his neck that he made some big money, but she didn't want to make any assumption of what his job could be. She guessed she would find all of that out on their date. If he really followed through.

Unexpected things just kept happening in her life. It wasn't a bad thing. In fact, she welcomed them, because when she moved away for school, she knew her life was going to change drastically. That was why she didn't see any harm in having a ball until then.

As she walked to the meat section, she felt her phone vibrate in her hand. It was Cam sending her a message with a location and a time for them to meet up the next day. She guessed he was serious. She felt a small flutter in her stomach. The summer vacation had just started, and it was looking up already.

Chapter 11

The next day came faster than expected, and Kiesha tried to keep her head out of the clouds in the office. She and Adrian were working on putting the showing together and wanted it to be like a celebration, complete with food and drinks. There would even be a DJ. If everything went as planned, Adrian had high hopes that someone would make an offer on at least one of the houses at the showing. "Rich people and alcohol are always a good mix," he'd told her.

She couldn't believe she hadn't even been there a week and was already working on her first big campaign. And because of that, she and Adrian had to spend almost every minute together. She ignored Megan's mean mugs because she knew the woman was just mad. But she would be too if someone like Adrian were treating her like nothing but a fly on the wall. She tried not to rub it too much in Megan's face. She knew what it was like to want someone who was only interested in one thing.

At lunchtime, Kiesha sat alone in her newly decorated office eating a salad and watching a show on her phone. She understood why, in the movies, people spent so much time in their offices. It was peaceful and quiet there. She had filled it with all the things she loved and stocked her fridge with all her favorite snacks. The sun was peeking in through the window, and she had a beautiful view of the company's garden. It was the most perfect place for her. There was a knock at the door, and when she looked up, she saw Adrian standing there. She stopped eating and took her earbud out, smiling at him.

"Hey," she greeted him.

"Hey." He smiled back and pointed at her salad. "Please don't tell me that's all you're having for lunch."

"Um, it's all I brought today," she said, glancing down at the half-eaten chicken Caesar.

"There's this amazing taco joint I was about to head to. I was coming to see if you wanted to join me."

"Oh." She checked the clock and saw that she only had fifteen minutes left on her break. "My lunch is almost over."

"Girl, ain't nobody tripping over your lunch breaks. Come on."

He waved for her to follow him, and she had to admit, tacos would taste so much better than the Caesar salad. She didn't make him ask her twice. She threw the salad away and followed him outside to his car.

"This is your car?" she asked, impressed with the Rolls-Royce Cullinan.

"Yeah. It was a gift from my old man. You wanna drive?" He held up the keys to her, and she shook her head feverishly.

"Nope! I cannot afford this car, and my mama would kill me if I hit something in it. The passenger seat is fine with me."

"I hear you," he said, and they got in.

The seats in the vehicle were powder white, and it was so clean inside that Kiesha almost didn't want to even put her feet on the floor. The car freshener smelled like the cologne Adrian wore, and she inhaled a big breath of it. She had never sat in anything so expensive, and there he was, driving it casually. It was lunchtime, and traffic was congested even on the regular streets, so the two of them just spent time trading off songs in the car. They had similar tastes in music. However, when Adrian told her that he wasn't too big a fan of Summer Walker, she almost set it off in that Rolls-Royce.

"You what?"

"I don't rock with her like that. I mean she can sing, but damn, all she does is cry over niggas. Like damn, let that hurt go, shawty."

She almost didn't even care that he was slowly but surely letting his professional guard down with her. Kiesha just couldn't believe he didn't like her girl. Summer was the one who helped her get over the Malcom situation, and she wasn't about to let anybody up and slander her.

"She makes music for people going through real things. A lot of women can relate to the words in her music."

"Well, I'm a man who wants to vibe out, not have the vibe killed. I like listening to old-school R&B. You know, from the '90s and early 2000s. They talked about the same kind of stuff, but the delivery wasn't all sad."

"I can agree with you on that. My mama put me on to all the old-school jams. She said she thinks the world went dark after men stopped crying and singing in the rain. Now all the music is doing is telling men to have multiple women and treat them like shit. They've even made money and gifts regular because it doesn't mean anything."

"You might be on to something there."

"You must relate," she said, and he shrugged.

"I mean, a little bit. I would feel like I'm disrespecting shawty if I hit and didn't at least get her some flowers or something. Women are beautiful and delicate creatures. Just because you as a man aren't ready to settle down doesn't mean you have to treat them like shit."

Kiesha was almost stuck. She knew Adrian was 23, but at times she felt like he was much older. He had a surety and wisdom about him, so much so that when he spoke, even when his opinion was different from hers, she couldn't do anything but respect it. He lived his truth unapologetically and reminded her that although life between the two sexes wasn't always a fairy tale, there was still magic.

"You're not ready to settle down? I mean, you're young and successful. That's the only thing that's missing, right?"

"Wrong. There's a lot missing still, and that's why I can wait on love. My life doesn't really have room for all of that right now."

"I see. Is that why Megan is mad?"

"Maybe." He shrugged again. "But I'm upfront with every woman I connect with."

"They probably think they can change your mind," she teased.

"Ha. Yeah, right. You see how strenuous the work is that we do. That's the only thing that's on my mind. What about you?"

"Are you asking if I have a boyfriend?" she asked, and he nodded with his eyes on the road. "No. I'm just chilling."

"That was a nigga answer!" He laughed and she laughed too.

"Definitely a nigga answer," she agreed. "But for real, I'm trying to enjoy my summer. Be beautiful, let my hair down a little bit. I just want to become the person I need to be right now. So if love comes, it comes. If it doesn't, I know it will eventually."

They grew quiet, and she wondered if it was because there was nothing left to say or because they had finally gotten to the taco spot. Either way she was glad. The last thing she wanted to do was vent to her boss's son about her life. Her phone vibrated in her pocket as he ordered their food at the window. She pulled it out of her purse and smiled when she saw Cam's number pop up. Her head instantly went back up into the clouds as she thought about their date that evening.

Chapter 12

After shooting Kiesha a reminder text about their date that evening, Cam tucked his phone back in his pocket. There was something about her that he liked, but he couldn't put his finger on it, and that was why he wanted to find out more about her. He could tell that she was a little younger than him, but he liked the way she carried herself as a lady. He hoped it wasn't just a façade like the hood rats he was used to dealing with. They weren't good for much but some head and a quick nut.

He leaned back in the seat of his car and surveyed the area. He wasn't in his convertible. That day, he'd opted for his black Tahoe. It was a common car, not the flashy kind that made a person stare. And he was definitely trying to be inconspicuous as he scoped out one of Drako's trap houses. There was something about him that Cam just didn't trust. Men like him didn't just conform to a new order. They pretended until they could find a weak spot. And that was why Cam had to find one first.

"What you think is going on in there?" a voice in the passenger's seat asked him.

It belonged to his blood cousin and best friend, Hoody. Hoody was the only one who Cam told about the run-in with Drako because he was the only one he knew would see things for what they were. Something was just off. And the last time Cam had that feeling it was about a man named Steelo. He was the same age as Carrington and Antonio. He had come up with them since they were boys, but Cam never trusted him or regarded him as an uncle. Adrian didn't either. It was one of the only times the two agreed on anything. And they were right to not trust Steelo. Not only did he single-handedly try to take down their entire operation from the inside, but he was also working with a dirty cop. If it weren't for Antonio's moles in the Feds, they all would have gone down. But that situation was handled clean, and Steelo was exiled from the state of Florida. If anybody in their camp were to see him, they would gun him down on sight.

"I don't know. That's what I'm trying to find out. Something ain't right about these niggas here, man," Cam said with a sigh as they watched people leave and enter the house.

"I coulda told you that. Them niggas ain't nothing to take lightly. I heard they're the reason Jerry went down in the first place."

That was news to Cam. He hadn't heard anything like that before. Hoody's serious expression sparked his curiosity. Jerry had gone down on federal charges, and in order for that to have happened, there had to be some kind of airtight evidence against him. Jerry had always been the type to cross his t's and dot his i's. In fact, when he went down, it made Cam tighten up everywhere. "You think somebody in his camp was snitching?"

"I don't know. I think somebody in his camp was plotting. Big time. You don't think it's strange that out of all the crews down with Jerry's shit, Drako's is the only one left standing? And y'all gon' let this nigga in on our shit."

"That wasn't me. That was your boy," Cam said, speaking of Adrian.

"Nah, that's your boy."

"Fuck out of here." Cam waved him off. "Our dads are thicker than thieves, and that makes us family. But it doesn't make us friends."

"Nigga, we family. We ain't friends?"

"Shut up, Hoody."

"Man, whatever. One day, you niggas are gon' kiss and make up. That shit that happened is in the past. Y'all used to be tight like how we're tight."

"That shit changed once his pops upped his rank, didn't it? I'm the one out here putting in all the work while that motherfucka sits in an office barking orders at me. We were supposed to be partners. That power got to his head."

"Maybe it did, but there ain't nothing wrong with reminding him that he ain't shit without you. In a healthy way," Hoody added.

"Man . . ." Cam started to respond, but then he saw something that made his blood run cold. "Hoody, look at that."

He pointed toward the trap house. A silver Mercedes-Benz had just pulled into the driveway, and a man stepped out. A truck pulled behind it, and people spilled out of it. It wasn't unusual to see that kind of thing at a spot like that. However, it was unusual to see the person who'd gotten out of the Mercedes.

"I can't be seeing this right. Is that who I think it is?" Hoody asked.

"Nah, you're seein' it right. What the fuck is Steelo doin' back in Miami? And even better, why is he comin' to visit Drako? I knew somethin' wasn't right about that nigga!"

"You gon' let your pops know?"

Cam thought about it. It would be the best thing to do, but Carrington and Antonio were in the middle of an expansion deal in Atlanta. He didn't want to interrupt such a huge money move with something he'd just be told to handle. He wanted to call his shooters right then to run up in the spot, guns blazing. However, then he would never know what was going on. He needed to do more digging.

"Nah," he said, snapping a quick photo before Steelo disappeared into the house.

"Okay, let's call the niggas in from the block to handle this fool."

"I'm not with that move either. Steelo is known to work with the Feds, and for all we know, they're watching this shit right now. Let's play this shit smart. First let's figure out what the fuck this nigga is doing back in Miami. I need all feelers out. If we know he's here, someone else does too. And that means they know why."

"I'm on it," Hoody said and pulled his phone out as Cam drove away.

Chapter 13

"How do you even know this boy?"

Kiesha almost laughed when she looked up from her vanity and saw her mother standing there with her hands on her hips. She had a satin bonnet on her hair and a robe wrapped tightly around her. When Miss Simmons spoke, it sounded like she had something in her mouth, but the carton of Ben & Jerry's in her hand explained that.

"Ooh, can I have a bite?" Kiesha asked. Her mom knew chocolate chip was her favorite.

"No," Miss Simmons said and held the carton closer to her. "Plus, one bite of this and you might pop out of that dress."

She pointed at the satin black dress Kiesha had opted to wear that night for her date. The back of it was completely open, and it might have looked like a tight fit, but it was actually very comfortable. She decided on black heels and gold jewelry to accent it. She'd been wearing her curls more often recently and had put a side part in her hair, tucking the left side behind her ear.

"That's not very nice," she said to her mom and went back to putting on her lipstick.

"What's not nice is not telling your mother, the woman who gave you life, who you're going out with tonight."

"I'm just meeting a friend. That's all."

"Kiesha Shanelle Simmons, who do you think you're fooling? You are not meeting a friend dressed like a movie star. No, spill it."

"Fine. He's this guy I met. He's super cute and nice. He asked me out. I said yes. There, are you happy?"

"No, I'm not. What's this guy's name?"

"Cameron."

"How old is he?"

"Twenty-two," Kiesha guessed, realizing she hadn't asked.

"Uh-huh. Make sure you take your Mace with you. And your switchblade."

"Mama!"

"I'm serious. And send me your location. I'm not playing with you. And one more thing."

"What?" Kiesha groaned.

"Wear your Versace perfume tonight. It would go well with this dress." Miss Simmons walked into the room and kissed Kiesha on the forehead. "All mom talk aside, I hope you have a great time, baby."

"Thanks, Mama," Kiesha said and turned to hug her mom and bury her head in her stomach.

When she let go, Miss Simmons kissed her forehead again and left the bedroom. She finished the final touches on her face and took her mom's advice by spraying herself with the Versace perfume. Miss Simmons had been right. It brought everything together. She looked at her watch and saw that she was running late. Cam said their reservations were for eight, and it was already almost seven thirty. Kiesha put her shoes on, grabbed her purse, and hurried out of the house.

Cam chose a fancy steakhouse called Strucks for them to dine at. Kiesha arrived with a few minutes to spare, and he told her he was already inside. The hostess took her to the table in the back, and suddenly Kiesha felt herself growing nervous when she saw him. She didn't know if it was because it had been a long time since she'd gone on a date, or if it was because he looked so delicious in his mustard yellow button-down. When she got to the table, he stood up to pull her chair out.

"Wow, you look amazing," he told her, and she felt his eyes gazing at her.

"Thank you," she told him and felt her cheeks grow warm.

When he sat back down across from her, she wanted badly to let her eyes lower to the table, but she forced them to stay on him. She was already there. There wasn't a point in her acting shy now. Still, his presence was doing something to her. And by the way he was looking at her, maybe hers was doing the same thing to him. He licked his full lips and flashed his pearly whites. She pursed her lips to stop the wide grin from coming to her face.

"Don't do that," he said. "If you want to smile at me, smile, shawty. Ain't nothing wrong with showing a nigga you're happy to see him."

"Why do you think I'm happy to see you?" Kiesha asked and rolled her neck slightly.

"Girl, you didn't get all dolled up for anybody else in here. And if you did, point him out so I can bleed him."

"You wouldn't do all that for little old me," she said, but her Cheshire cat smile said what she really wanted to say.

"You're a princess. I'd move a kingdom."

"Game!" She laughed as the waiter set their menus in front of them.

Kiesha looked at the menu even though she already knew she was getting salmon, loaded mashed potatoes, and asparagus. She still looked at the menu in case something else caught her eye.

"Can I get you anything to drink?" the waiter asked them.

"A lemonade," she answered.

"No wine? We have a very nice Chardonnay."

"Oh, no. I'm only eighteen," she said, and the waiter raised a brow at Cam.

"I'm only twenty-two, partna. We're legal over here!"

Kiesha didn't know why that made her laugh so hard, but it did, mainly because Cam was so serious. She didn't know if he was saying "legal" as in he could drink or that he wasn't that much older than her. Either way it was hilarious, especially watching the waiter gather himself.

"I'm sorry. You both just look so mature for your ages. I apologize. Can I get you anything to drink, sir?"

"I'll keep it PG tonight. Just bring me a Coke."

The server left to get their beverages. Kiesha fought her shyness, but it was hard. Why did he keep looking at her like that? His eyes never left her face. They brushed across her eyes and nose and lingered on her lips—the same lips that bent upward, that time with ease.

"Are you examining me?" she asked in an amused fashion.

"I just like to pay attention to detail, that's all. I hope you know what you're ordering, because here comes Alfred."

Kiesha had to hold back her laugh as she ordered. She was certain that wasn't their server's name, but it was very fitting. He was an older gentleman with a comb-over and a thin mustache. It also didn't help that he stood with his back so straight it looked uncomfortable. After they were done ordering, Kiesha swatted Cam's hand playfully.

"You abusing me already, woman?" Cam asked and pretended to be shocked.

"You're just goofy as hell! About to make me laugh in that poor man's face like that."

"That's just me. In my line of work, it's good to laugh sometimes."

"And what line of work is that? I see you shining over there, so it must be something that pays well."

"Just the family business," Cam answered casually. "My dad and his business partner own a lot of businesses around Florida. I just get in where I fit in, really. What about you?"

"I'm interning right now before I leave for Howard in the fall."

"Howard? Impressive. You must be smart as hell."

"I do my thing in the books, I guess," Kiesha said shyly.

"So if this becomes a thing, you okay with long distance?" he asked with a smile.

"That depends if it becomes a thing."

Cam was smooth, and Kiesha had to admit she liked it, mainly because he didn't pull away when she told him she would be leaving in the fall. The two of them continued to flirt back and forth until their food came. Even while they were eating, their conversation seemed to flow. She found herself growing comfortable with him and was happy that she had come out to dinner. By the time they left the restaurant, her cheeks were sore from laughing so much. Cam walked her to her vehicle and held her door open for her.

"Next time you'll have to let me be a real prince and come pick you up," he said.

"I guess you can do that now that I know you aren't a crazy-ass nigga."

"Could never be that!" He laughed and kissed her on the cheek. "Get home safe, shawty. I'ma be on that line, too. Thirsty with it, so make sure you hit me back!"

"I will, I promise."

Kiesha got in her car and drove away, feeling the butterflies in her stomach fluttering like crazy. She didn't know what was happening. But even if it was just game, there was nothing wrong with a little summer fairy tale.

Chapter 14

"What the fuck do you mean you saw Steelo?" Adrian's angry voice sounded.

The tie he was tying was black, but all he saw was red. He stood in front of his living room's full-body mirror, staring at Cam, who sat comfortably on his couch. When he showed up at his door that morning, he'd told Adrian that he had some urgent news that couldn't wait. The news was the last thing Adrian expected to hear.

"Just like I said. I saw him."

"Where?"

"When I was scopin' out that nigga Drako's spot."

"Wait." Adrian made a face. "What were you doing there? I thought you already made the drop."

"I did. But somethin' told me that some shit wasn't right with that nigga, man. He's not solid, and I went to scope his shit out. If I were wrong, I would man up to it, but turns out I wasn't. When me and Hoody were watching the trap, Steelo pulls up in broad daylight."

"Steelo and Drako?" Adrian asked, rubbing his chin. He tried to make sense of it but couldn't. "That shit doesn't even add up."

"Here, just so you don't think the words comin' out of my mouth are cap."

Cam tossed Adrian his phone. Adrian caught it and looked down at the photo on the screen. There Steelo was, plain as day, walking into a house. Whatever he and Drako were cooking up couldn't be good, especially since Steelo was known for working with the Feds. It put Antonio's whole operation in the line of fire, and it was Adrian's fault. He didn't want to admit it out loud, but Cam had been right about Drako all along. He now knew things about their operation and could be feeding the information to Steelo right that very second. They both had to be dealt with expeditiously.

"You call your dad?" he asked Cam.

"Nah. Every time some shit happens, we gon' call our daddies? I came to you first to see how you wanted to handle it."

Adrian nodded. Cam was right. They needed to handle it, and before their parents got home.

"My pop called me this morning before you got here to tell me they'll be gone at least another week," he said. "We need to dead this shit before then."

"What you got in mind?"

"First I want to know exactly what ties the two of them have. I heard Drako has a thing for whores."

"On it. I'll be in touch." Cam got to his feet and walked to the door, shaking his head. "I told you not to do business with that nigga."

The entire ride to the office, Adrian's thoughts raced. He didn't like the feeling of not knowing what was going on around him. He felt himself cautiously looking in his rearview mirror for police cruisers. Walking on thin ice wasn't his thing, and he wasn't a fan of it. However, his unease subsided slightly when he arrived at his destination and was met with Kiesha's smile.

"You're late, but let me guess—perks of being the son of the boss, right?"

She grinned at him and handed him a coffee before he took his seat. Whatever fragrance she was wearing was almost as divine as the yellow bodycon dress hugging her curves. Something about her radiant presence calmed his mind, and he was able to leave the streets in the streets. He pulled her laptop in front of him to take a look at how far she'd gotten with the campaign and saw that she was almost finished.

"How long have you been here?" he asked.

"I came in a little early. I hope you don't mind. When ideas come to me, I like to get them out as soon as possible. Otherwise, ya girl goes crazy!"

"I don't mind at all," he told her in an impressed manner. "I need to clean it up a little bit, but other than that, good job. Now all I need to do is hire caterers and the DJ."

"I already did that," she blurted out, and he looked taken aback. "I'm sorry. I saw their contact numbers and thought I'd take a load off your shoulders."

"Don't apologize. I already told you, when you're ready, you'll have a job here waiting for you."

Adrian pushed the laptop back in front of her and leaned back in his chair. He watched her tuck her hair behind her ear so that she could see the screen better. The side profile of her face was just as beautiful as the front. Her eyelashes were so long that they looked like extensions, and her chin was perfectly chiseled. Adrian found himself taking in every small detail of her face. He counted two beauty marks on her smooth skin, and he noticed that when she was deep in concentration, she did a thing where she bit her bottom lip. When she finally noticed him staring at her, a bashful expression came over her.

"Is there something wrong, Adrian?" she asked in her soft voice.

"Nothing. Just watching you work, that's all," Adrian said, even though he wanted to tell her how attracted he was to her.

Something stopped him from speaking his mind, but he was sure his eyes said it all as they lingered on hers. Usually with women the only thing he thought about was how good they would look underneath him, but with Kiesha he just wanted to get to know her more. It was a strange feeling for him, and it made his nerves jump with her. He cleared his throat suddenly, and they shifted their gazes at the same time. He pulled his phone out to casually scroll the screen. He wasn't looking at anything in particular. He just needed to focus on something else. She went back to working on the laptop.

"I'm thinking of hosting the event on Wednesday. Do you, um, do you think you'll be able to make that?" he asked.

"I'm sure my schedule is open."

"Good. Take my card and find something nice to wear," he told her and removed a credit card from his wallet.

"What?" Kiesha asked, staring wide-eyed at the card. "Oh, Adrian, I couldn't."

"Oh, but you can. You deserve it after all the work you've put in. And you'll have a plus-one as well since I probably won't be much company. I'm usually too busy trying to sell."

"Wow, this is so nice of you. Thank you!"

The happy look on her face brought a piece of joy to Adrian's heart. He wasn't sure what she was used to. Maybe this was a first. He wouldn't mind introducing her to more than just spending a couple of dollars on her. He opened his mouth to say something else, but his phone rang from inside his pocket. When he saw that it was Cam, he knew he needed to answer it. He held a finger up to Kiesha and excused himself from the conference room.

"What's the word?" he answered as he made his way to his office.

"Nigga, you aren't going to believe this shit."

"Hold on," Adrian said and forced a fake smile to his face as he passed his colleagues. He picked up his pace to Executive Hall, and when he was there, he hurried into his office and shut the door. "My bad. What's going on, Cam? You put a bitch on Drako yet?"

"Didn't need to. Get this, I just got word that Drako is hostin' a party Friday night. A welcome home party. One guess for who."

"Steelo."

"Ding, ding, ding. This shit is all over social media."

"That motherfucka is exiled. What the hell are they having a welcome home party for? He's not safe here if I have a say-so."

"Well, nigga, you might need to say so. Because this is a bold move, and it's gon' speak loudly if we don't do somethin'."

"Say less."

Chapter 15

Curiosity nipped at Adrian like the cold in a winter in Nebraska. There was no way he was going to be able to wait until Friday to confront his opposition. He didn't know what he would be walking into and needed to do some deep-sea diving. That was why he decided to leave work early the next day. He and Kiesha had wrapped up all the finishing details of the showing, but his head wasn't there, especially when he started to connect the dots.

He kept asking himself what Drako and Steelo had in common for them to do business together. What would put them on the same team? And that was when something clicked with him. If anybody would know anything, it was Milk. He was an old friend from high school. The two of them were on opposite sides of the fence, being that Milk had worked for Jerry, but they had remained cool over the years. Adrian made a call to him and set up a meeting in the hope that he could shed a little light on the situation. That meeting was why he needed to leave work earlier than usual. He packed his things into a briefcase and made to leave the office, but he almost crashed into Kiesha on the way out.

"Oop! My bad. I didn't know you were in such a rush to leave me," she said playfully, putting her hand to her chest.

"If I didn't have to leave, I would stay here staring at you all day," he said absentmindedly, looking at his watch. "I just have somewhere to be at three."

"Oh, well, um . . ." Kiesha seemed to fumble over her words, and it was then that he realized exactly what he'd said.

"I didn't mean to make you—"

"I just came to bring you back your credit card," she interrupted him and handed him the black card. "Thank you again. I found the perfect dress. And I hope you don't mind, but I snuck some shoes into the transaction, too."

"Jesus, woman, wait until we're married to take the mile," he joked with a wink that made her look away. It seemed almost natural when he cupped her chin and gently forced her gaze back on him. His smile brought one to her glossy lips. "Much better."

"Will you be back today?" she asked almost hopefully when he let her chin go.

"No, I'll see you at the showing tomorrow. We can go for a walk on the beach after."

"Oh, I—" she tried to say, but he breezed right by her.

"I'll see you tomorrow!" he called over his shoulder as he headed for the door with his briefcase in tow.

The moment he started his Rolls-Royce, he pulled off in the direction of the place he and Milk agreed to meet. As he drove, he loosened his tie and played with the idea of giving his father a call to let him know what was going on. However, he thought better of it. He couldn't run crying to his dad whenever something happened. Not when he would one day wear the crown. Still, he knew his father would be a little upset that Adrian didn't tell him that Steelo had slithered his way back into the garden. When and if Adrian did decide to make that call, it would be when Steelo was gone again or in the dirt.

Finally, Adrian arrived at the Turner boat dock Milk had given him the address to. He'd been instructed to park by the boat named *The Milky Way*. Before he got out of the vehicle, he grabbed his pistol from the glove compartment. He cocked the loaded weapon and tucked it in his pants. Adrian stepped out of the Cullinan and instantly felt the sun beating on his forehead. He took a few steps toward the boat, but before he reached it all the way, Milk stepped out of it and onto the dock. He was a stocky man with average height and had skin so light that if it weren't for the kinks in his sandy brown hair, a person would mistake him for a white man. It was how he'd gotten the nickname Milk. He slapped hands with Adrian and glanced over his shoulder as if to make sure he wasn't followed.

"It's just me," Adrian assured him.

"Yeah, well, you can never be too sure these days," Milk said, shaking his head. "After all that shit with Jerry, man, things ain't been the same. Muthafuckas don't even trust their own mamas right now."

"And why is that?"

"Listen, you know how your pops runs his shit? That was the same way Jerry ran his. He was smart, way too smart to go down the way he did. The whole bust was too calculated."

"Hell yeah. I know Jerry kept his shit tight. He and my pops had a lot of respect for each other. They never stepped on each other's toes."

"Jerry had a lot of respect, but he must have had just as many haters. Because somebody set that shit up, and that's a fact."

"How do you know that?" Adrian asked, raising his forehead.

"Jerry rotated pickup and drop-off spots every week, and it was never the same rotation. Never. But somehow the Feds knew exactly what houses to hit, and they got every last one. That ain't no coincidence."

"Hell nah it ain't," Adrian agreed, rubbing the hair on his chin. "Damn. I hate that that happened to Jerry."

"Me too. They auctioned off all his assets. My guy ain't never seeing the outside again."

"Who all knew the rotations?"

"Jerry, me, my nigga Amir, and Drako."

"And everybody from that camp is locked up besides you and Drako," Adrian noted, and Milk puffed his chest out.

"Nigga, what you tryin'a say? I ain't no fucking rat."

"That's not what I'm trying to say. I'm just making an observation. I know you're loyal. Ain't got an ounce of snake in you. Back in school you always had my back."

"And you had mine," Milk said and sighed. "I have some simple shit going for myself now, though. The money back then was good, but the risk was too great for me, you know? So I got out of the game when my girl had the twins a few years back. Bought a boat. Shit, I've just been living life. Jerry wasn't a 'one way in, one way out' type of nigga. He was more than a boss to a lot of us. More like a big brother. He respected me and proved his loyalty tenfold when he didn't drop my name to the Feds. Everybody else got caught up only because they were in the houses during the raids."

"So that leaves Drako. Damn." Adrian shook his head as he looked out at the water.

"I heard he was working for you now."

"A decision I might soon regret."

His heart had gone out to Drako when he found out Jerry's whole operation had gone underwater. People had families to feed, and he could use the extra hands. That was why he extended Drako's camp an opportunity to make some money with him. On the outside, Drako seemed thorough, but Adrian should have known better than to go based only on appearances.

"Wait, you tryin'a say that Drako had something to do with Jerry going down?"

"That's what I'm trying to figure out, but it's looking that way, yeah. I need to get some more information."

"Let me know what's good with it all when you do."

Adrian looked from Milk to his boat. His friend had truly gone on to live a simple and peaceful life. A part of Adrian felt guilty for even bringing all of that to his attention. Milk was a soldier, one of the best shooters Adrian had ever seen with his own two eyes. Not only that, but he was also loyal. He would want to get whoever had turned on Jerry back in blood, and because of that, Adrian made the silent decision to leave it right there with Milk. He was out of the game, so he would stay out of the game.

"No doubt," Adrian lied through his teeth and shook his hand.

When he got back inside his vehicle, he knew the only way he would get all his answers was to show up to the party on Friday. But first, he had to put on his professional hat.

Chapter 16

Kiesha was truly in awe of herself as she swayed in her bedroom mirror. The gold fabric of her dress fit perfectly over her shape. It wasn't too tight, nor was it too loose. It was perfect. Her hair was pinned up in a bun, and her edges were laid to the gods. She couldn't wait to arrive at the showing. She truly felt like Cinderella right before she went off to the ball to meet her prince.

Light hums escaped her lips as she closed her eyes and danced around her bedroom. She pictured strong arms wrapped around her, holding her in a warm embrace as she nestled her head in his chest. She felt safe as a rush of happiness overcame her. She was right where she was supposed to be. Except when she looked up into her prince's handsome face, it wasn't Cam who was holding her. It was Adrian. His smile was like a ray of light, and when he leaned down to kiss her, Kiesha jerked her eyes open from her daydream.

A hand went to her chest, and she sat down on her bed. She didn't know if she was out of breath from the dancing or from her thoughts. She tried to make sense of Adrian sneaking into her daydream. Especially when Cam was the one who'd be there to pick her up any minute. She'd invited him as her plus-one since Adrian had told her she could have one. She thought it would be a cool way to show Cam what she was busy with that summer. But the butterflies she felt at the thought of Adrian were making her wonder if she had made a mistake.

She liked Cam a lot and enjoyed talking to him, but she couldn't deny that Adrian was starting to grow on her. She'd only known both men a short amount of time, but she had spent a good amount of it with both of them, Adrian at work and Cam outside of it. She shook the thoughts from her head. She was dating Cam, and that was who she would focus on. Adrian couldn't like her like that anyway. Plus, he'd already told her that he wasn't looking for anything special with any woman. Yes, he flirted with her sometimes, but he was just teasing. Probably.

Kiesha slid into the matching golden shoes that she got to go with the dress and was glad she'd gone with the shorter, more comfortable heel. She had never been to that kind of showing before and had no idea how long she would be on her feet. After that, she put some finishing touches on her makeup and went into the living room to wait for Cam to pick her up.

"Oh, my God!"

The exclamation almost made her jump out of her heels when she got to the living room. There, waiting for her, were both her mother and London. Both of their jaws dropped when they saw her step out of the hallway. Kiesha was surprised to see London there. She hadn't told her that she was coming over. Plus, she was sure that she'd told her that she had plans that evening.

"London, I thought I told you about the showing."

"You did, and I decided to come over and see you off and be here when you get back so you can tell me all about your date!"

"You're dragging it!"

"No, I'm not. A good friend is happy for their friend's happiness. So I'm going to run to the store and grab us some snacks for when you get back." London squealed and took her by the hands. "You look so gorgeous. I don't even think you were this fine on prom night!"

"Gee, thanks," Kiesha teased.

"She doesn't mean it like that, baby. You just look really good!" Miss Simmons gushed. "This guy must really have you in a daze. You've been glowing since you've been dating him!"

"Or it could be my job. I really like it. I want to make a good impression with the clients. Is this too much?" Kiesha asked and smoothed down the sides of the dress.

"Not at all. Now go stand by the mantle so I can get a picture before you leave."

"Ma!"

"Aht, do it now," Miss Simmons said and pointed to where she wanted Kiesha to stand.

Kiesha rolled her eyes. However, she did what her mother said. She posed away for the camera until the doorbell rang. She tried to get to the door first, but Miss Simmons beat her to it. She swung the door open and revealed a very dapper Cam standing on the front porch. He had a fresh haircut and wore a tailored black suit with diamond cuff links.

"You must be Kiesha's mother. I see where she gets her beauty from," he said, offering a kind smile.

"Flattery will get you nowhere," Miss Simmons said dryly but then broke into a grin. "Except inside of this house. Come in."

She moved out of the way so that Cam could step inside. The smile on his face faded when he laid eyes on Kiesha. An expression of wonder replaced it as he looked her up and down. His speechlessness made her nervous. Maybe she had done a little too much with the gold dress. It wasn't like she was walking the red carpet or anything.

"Wow," he finally breathed. "That dress is . . . wow. You took my breath away."

"Um, Mama, London, this is Cam. Cam, this is my mom and my close friend," she said, not knowing how to respond.

"It's nice to meet you both," he said and held out a hand to Kiesha. "You ready? I don't want you to be late to your event."

"Oh, you're right," Kiesha said. She grabbed her purse from the living room couch and took his hand. "I'm ready."

"Have fun and be safe!" Miss Simmons called after them.

Kiesha blew her a kiss before shutting the door behind her. Cam walked her to his SUV and held her door open for her. He didn't let go of her hand until she was safely seated, and when he got into the car, they pulled off from the house. She kept seeing him sneak glances of her as he drove, and she wanted to laugh so bad. They'd seen each other almost every day since their first date, but every time he saw her, he made her feel like it was the first time.

"Don't crash trying to look at me," she said, poking fun at him.

"You're in good hands, shawty. Believe that."

"I believe it," she told him.

When they got to a stoplight, Cam turned so that he could look at her without the road as an interruption. Kiesha's eyes had a mind of their own as they traveled down to his lips. He'd just licked them, so they were glistening. She wondered how they tasted. Every time he had kissed her, it had been on the forehead or cheek. She wanted more. When she looked back into his eyes, she could tell that he did too. Slowly, they leaned in toward each other until their soft lips met. Their kiss was slow to start, but it grew deep and passionate. Their tongues danced to a tune that hadn't been made yet, and when they parted, they had to catch their breath. By then the light had turned green, and he had to drive, but his free hand found its way to hers. She gladly held it.

"Everything about you is amazing," he finally said. "I'm really feeling you."

"I feel the same about you."

"Maybe after this you can come to my spot?" he suggested.

When he said those words, she realized that she'd been dreading them without even knowing it. She still hadn't told him that she was a virgin, mainly because she didn't know how. Being a virgin used to be normal. However, in this day and age, people looked at you as if you were an alien. She didn't want him to reject her after finding out, and until she knew if they were going to get serious, she didn't want him to look for affection elsewhere. She took a deep breath and looked at him.

"Cam, I need to tell you something."

"What?" His eyes got wide at the seriousness in her tone.

"I don't want to go back to your place."

"Oh. That's cool." His voice was even, but there was a look of disappointment, almost sadness, on his face.

"It's not because I don't actually want to. I just don't want to give you the wrong idea."

"Kiesha, I don't have a problem with takin' things slow."

"It's not just that, Cam. I'm . . . I'm a virgin."

A silence fell inside the car, and Kiesha could tell that he was shocked by her words. She'd known he would be. They drove in silence for a while before he broke it.

"Like, a *virgin* virgin?" he asked.

"Yes."

"Ohhhhh. So you've never gotten head or anything?" he asked.

"Nope."

To her surprise, he started laughing. In fact, he laughed so hard that it annoyed her. She snatched her hand away from him and faced the window.

"Wait, shawty. My bad. I'm not tryin'a make you mad. I just don't know what to say. I guess I'm just intrigued, that's all. I've never dealt with a virgin before. But ain't nothin' changin' between us."

"You sure?"

"Yeah, girl. I fuck with you. You ain't gotta worry about me pressurin' you or none of that. I done had a lot of pussy. I'm actually enjoyin' just getting to know your mind right now. If that's cool with you."

"That's cool with me."

A weight felt like it had been lifted off her shoulders. She didn't know how truthful he was being about being okay with it, but when he took her hand in his again and kissed it, she eased up a little bit more. Only time would tell.

Chapter 17

Adrian was blown away at how amazing the event had turned out. The view of the ocean set the tone for the whole evening. The music, food, and drinks were just the icing on the cake. All the homes had been staged with beautiful furniture, and he'd hired a contractor to build temporary walkways from one house to another. When the sun started to go down, small lanterns lit the way. The aesthetic of the whole showing was magnificent. And the turnout? More people came out than what even he'd expected. He couldn't wait for Kiesha to get there to bask in the moment with him. It was, after all, as much her vision as it was his.

"Excuse me, Mr. Parks?" a voice sounded as he was making his rounds through one of the properties.

He turned around and saw a Caucasian couple standing there with their arms linked together. The man looked to be in his forties, and the woman was way younger than him, with a deep tan. They were dressed elegantly and stared eagerly at him. He'd been in the business long enough to know what that look meant, and a smile came to his face.

"Is there anything I can help you lovely couple with?"

"Yes. We're Rebecca and Rob Stephenson. This house is absolutely lovely!" the woman said, brushing her hair out of her hazel eyes.

"I think so myself. Did you have time to look at the double pantries in the kitchen?"

"That's my favorite part! We have three kids who eat us out of house and home, so it would come in handy. I also love that the master bedroom overlooks the ocean."

"Overall, we want the house," Rob butted in. "Has anyone made an offer on it yet?"

The night had just started, and the truth was that nobody had put an offer on any of the houses. However, a good businessman knew not to say that. If you wanted the most bang for your buck, you had to set the demand for the product. And at that moment, the demand would be the illusion of a bidding war.

"I actually have gotten three offers so far, and the night has only begun, so I expect to get more," Adrian said, waving Megan over to him. "However, my colleague will be more than happy to help you out from here."

Megan already knew what to do. She winked at Adrian as she passed and led the Stephensons over to a table where they could fill out some paperwork. Adrian did a little fist pump in the air knowing that he would probably sell all the homes before the other real estate companies even got a whiff of them. He was definitely smelling himself and had a natural high. He looked around and saw many Parks employees helping out the guests, and he figured it was time to move to another house. He walked out of the house with a little swagger in his step and a smile on his face. It grew wider when he saw Kiesha wearing a beautiful gold dress and making her way over to him.

"Oh, my God, this all looks great!" she exclaimed. "It's so fancy. I've never seen a showing like this before."

"No one has." He grinned at her. "Thanks to you, we got our first offer."

"Already?" she asked, shocked.

"Yup. They're doing the paperwork now," he said and took her image in. He had the sudden urge to wrap his arms around her slim waist and pull her in for a big hug. "You look gorgeous tonight."

"Thanks to you. Do you like the dress?" she asked.

"I do. I really do," he told her, but instead of looking at the dress, he held her gaze.

There were a lot of unspoken words that happened between them in that moment. And it was then that he realized he liked her. As in *liked her* liked her. Adrian didn't think he ever felt like that about anyone, but Kiesha made him want . . . more. From her and from himself. He opened his mouth to ask her if they were still on for their walk on the beach after the showing, but then someone appeared at her side.

"Cam?" Adrian asked, confused.

"Adrian?" Cam looked as shocked as he did.

"Wait." Kiesha put her hands up. "You two know each other?"

"Yeah, we grew up together. And I guess you can say we're business partners," Cam answered. "Hold on, your internship is with Parks Realty?"

"Yeah. Adrian is, I guess you can say, my boss."

"Wow, small world." Cam grinned and held his hand out for Adrian to shake it.

With low energy, Adrian shook it. Kiesha was standing there looking uncomfortable and avoiding Adrian's eye contact.

"How did you two meet?" Adrian couldn't help himself from asking.

"I saw shawty in the grocery store, and we've been rockin' ever since."

"Nice," Adrian said. "Well, I'll let you two enjoy the event. There's food and drinks, virgin for you, Kiesha. I'm about to go try to sell the rest of these houses."

"Shouldn't I be with you?" she asked.

"You've done more than enough," Adrian responded a little harsher than what he intended. He saw the hurt in her eyes, and he instantly felt bad, but not bad enough to continue standing right there. "Cam, call me later."

Cam nodded and Adrian walked away. The high he had felt minutes before was long gone and probably wasn't coming back. He didn't know why he was so upset, but he felt it sitting in his chest. He wasn't happy at all to see Kiesha and Cam together. And if that was who she was dealing with, why did she look at him like that? He avoided the two of them the rest of the night, but that didn't stop him from catching a few displays of affection between them. He even saw Cam kiss her.

After that, things became a blur for Adrian, and he began downing back-to-back drinks. He was thankful that there were other Realtors from Parks Realty working the showing. By the end of the night, they'd gotten quite a few offers on each house. When the event was over and almost everyone had left, Adrian found himself inside the master bedroom of the home the Stephensons loved so much. They were right. The view was amazing from there.

"Hey! This was a great turnout!"

The voice belonged to Megan. He would ask how she knew where to find him, but she'd been watching him like a hawk the entire night. The buzz he felt sent his eyes straight to the cleavage in her dress.

"Why haven't you left yet?" he asked.

"I can ask you the same thing," she said, walking up to him. "Kiesha is outside looking for you. She wanted to say goodbye before she and her date headed out."

He didn't like how she said the word "date," as if she were letting on that she knew something she wasn't supposed to know. She was being a bad girl, and bad girls got punished. Megan got so close to him that he was sure she could smell the alcohol on his breath. She smirked up at him.

"Why are you smiling at me like that?"

"Oh, nothing. What should I tell her?" she asked seductively.

"Nothing. Because your mouth is going to be too preoccupied with other things."

Adrian backed into the master bathroom and unzipped his pants. He pulled his already-hard manhood through the slit in his boxers, and Megan grinned wide. She followed him inside the bathroom, shutting and locking the door behind her. He didn't have to tell her what to do next. She dropped to her knees and gobbled his dick up like it was her favorite meal. As she sucked and slurped, he suddenly had flashes of Kiesha on her knees for Cam, pleasing him like Megan was doing. Adrian's hands found the back of Megan's head, and he started to fuck her face, feeling the tip of his manhood jabbing the back of her throat. She was a champ and didn't gag once.

Suddenly, Adrian withdrew from her mouth and forced Megan to her feet. She submitted to him as he bent her over the double sink and hiked her dress up. She wasn't wearing any panties, and he was staring right at her beautiful, voluptuous bottom. He knew she was a freak, so when he spread her cheeks and slid his sopping wet dick into her ass, she moaned loudly.

"Oh, Adrian. You're sooo nasty, baby. Fuck my ass. Yeah, fuck me!"

And that he did. Her tight asshole felt so good around his shaft as he plunged in and out of it, making her cheeks shake like an earthquake. She threw it back at him, and he caught it like a pitcher. Flashes of Cam fucking Kiesha that way kept sneaking into his mind, and they only made him stroke harder.

"Adrian! Adrian! Oh, daddy! Yessss!"

"Shut up and take this dick!" he breathed.

"Okay! Yes, daddy!"

Thick juices slid down Megan's thighs every time she came from the anal pleasure Adrian was giving to her. When he finally felt his own climax building up, he thrust into her a few more times before exploding deep into her anus. He threw his head back and held back his moan, fearing it would come out as a name. He caught his breath and pulled his limp penis out of Megan's ass. Adrian cleaned himself up with the decorative towels in the bathroom and zipped his pants back up.

"I'll see you at work in the morning," he said and left Megan quivering on the counter.

Chapter 18

The showing had turned out better than Kiesha could have ever imagined. It was the most amazing thing, seeing something she'd worked so hard on come to fruition. If that was what she had to look forward to when she got her degree, she was all for it. Cam had been the perfect gentleman, and the thing she liked most about him was that he wasn't afraid to give her affection in the public eye. He made her feel like a princess and even got her home by midnight.

Kiesha still couldn't believe that Cam and Adrian knew each other. Not only that, but they were business partners. She was trying not to think about it because it was making her head hurt. She also didn't know why the thought made her stomach turn so much. Why did she care if they knew each other? Still, she couldn't wait to tell London about this new revelation.

When she walked through the door, all the lights in the house were off except the plug-ins in the hallway that led to the bedrooms. Miss Simmons's door was slightly ajar, but when Kiesha passed the room, she heard light snores letting her know that her mom was knocked out. She'd fill her in about the night in the morning. Kiesha hoped that London was still awake, because she had to tell someone about the things that transpired. She was happy when she saw a light was on in her room and hurried to open the door.

"London, girl! Tonight was so amazing! You won't believe what happ—London?" Kiesha abruptly stopped speaking. London was indeed awake and sitting at Kiesha's vanity, but her face was buried in her hands. "London?"

London's shoulders quivered, and Kiesha heard her sniffle. Kiesha looked around the room for any signs of what was wrong. She didn't see anything but a bag of snacks on the bed and the TV frozen on the Netflix home screen. She moved closer to London and put a hand on her shoulder, but her friend jerked away.

"No, don't!" London said tearfully.

"London, girl. What's wrong? Why are you crying?" Kiesha asked and pried her hands from her face. When she did, Kiesha gasped in horror. "London! What happened to your eye?"

London's left eye was completely swollen and had started to bruise. She also had a busted lip and a few cuts on her face. That wasn't at all how she looked when Kiesha had left, and alarm set in. Tears streamed freely down London's face as she looked into Kiesha's. There was both sadness and anger in her one good eye.

"They jumped me," she finally said.

"Who? Who jumped you?" Kiesha asked, feeling anger form in her chest.

"When I was at the store, I ran into Stacy and her crew. Malcom was there, too, with a few of his people. I was in line, and they stood behind me on purpose to talk dirt about you so I could hear, I guess. And you're my friend, so I stuck up for you. I wasn't going to just let a bunch of whores talk about you. Afterward, they followed me to the parking lot."

"And they jumped you there?" Kiesha asked, and she nodded. "Ooh, I can't stand those bitches! I can't believe they did this to your face."

"They didn't. Malcom and his friends did."

"What?"

"Stacy's friends can't fight like that. But Stacy and I were getting down, and I guess I must have hit her too hard, because that's when Malcom jumped in and punched me in the face. I . . . I fell to the ground, and all I remember is feeling his friends kicking me."

"London!" Kiesha cried.

She plopped onto the vanity seat and wrapped her arms tightly around her friend. While she was having the night of her life, London was going through hell. All to grab some snacks for them. Tears fell down Kiesha's face onto London's shoulder, and the two girls cried together for what felt like a long time.

"That bitch and that nigga are going to pay," Kiesha said when they finally pulled away from each other.

"No, Kiesh. It will blow over."

"I can't keep letting this kind of shit slide. She only did this to get to me. And I never pegged Malcom as the type to hit women."

"I've been hearing a lot about him over the last few days. He was never who we thought he was. His family is heavy in the streets. So, Kiesh, for real. Just let it go. You have so much going for yourself, and Stacy is just jealous."

London got up from the vanity and crawled into Kiesha's bed. Kiesha watched as she wrapped herself in the covers and turn to face the wall. Kiesha wished she could just let it go. She really did. But she couldn't. If she didn't do something about it now, Stacy would feel like she could bully her. And not just Kiesha, but her friend too. She didn't know yet what she was going to do, but one thing she knew for sure was that this was the last time Stacy was going to cause turmoil in her life.

Chapter 19

The events from the night before seemed like a blur to Adrian when he got into the office the next day. Regret seeped from his pores as he remembered his sexual encounter with Megan. He'd broken his own rule, and he didn't know what to expect with her. It was obvious that she wanted more from him than he was willing to give, and now he had fed into that fantasy. That was why he planned to avoid her for as long as he could. He knew he was probably in the clear that day since she would be busy closing deals. But that could only last so long.

Kiesha had called in late that morning, and Adrian tried not to imagine the reason why. He kept telling himself that what she did in her free time was her business and none of his concern. However, truly feeling like that was the hard part.

Knock! Knock!

Adrian had been in the middle of sorting out some paperwork when the knock on his door came. He looked up to see Cam entering his office. Cam made himself comfortable by sitting on the opposite side of his desk, leaning back in the chair, and clasping his hands together over his stomach.

"You rang?" he said.

"I got some new information about Drako," Adrian said.

"From who?"

"You know Milk, right?"

"Yeah. Light-skinned motherfucka who used to be down with Jerry."

"That's him. I paid him a visit the other day, and he had some pretty interesting things to tell me about Drako. You already know how all that shit went down with Jerry, right?"

"Yup."

"His operation was too smooth. Real calculated. Milk told me that he changed his pickup and drop-off spots every week, and the rotation was never the same. So tell me, how were the Feds able to run down on him?"

"They knew the pickup and drop spots," Cam said with a shrug.

"But how if the rotation was at random? They knew the exact days, the exact times, and the exact locations."

"Sounds like an inside job to me. Who all knew the rotations of the spots?"

"Jerry, of course, somebody named Amir, Milk, and Drako." At the mention of Drako's name, Cam sat up in his seat. Adrian could see his mind working behind his eyes. He was sure they were on the same page. "Jerry and Amir are locked up. The only ones free are Milk, because he got out of the game years ago, and Drako."

"Hoody said he thought Drako had something to do with Jerry going down." Cam shook his head and then glared at Adrian. "So if this nigga is really rattin' niggas out, you done led him straight to some more cheese. You let his ass walk straight to the door. Fuckin' dumb. And you the motherfucka I'ma have to follow someday?"

Adrian's nose flared at his words. Cam was right about the Drako situation, but his comfort disrespecting Adrian was rubbing him the wrong way. Adrian wanted to put Cam in his place, but then he remembered, he already was in his place.

"You're going to follow me because my family's money is what started this entire operation, and it's our businesses that keep it clean," Adrian said evenly and cut his eyes at him. "Our fathers work well together because they are a team. I made a mistake, and I'm going to fix it. But if while I'm doing so you're just going to keep reminding me of the fuckup, why are you around?"

Cam's chest huffed out but then fell after a few seconds. The glare in his eyes faded, and he ran his hands over his face while groaning loudly. He finally looked back at Adrian and shook his head.

"I hate to say it, but you're right. To our fathers it's one band, one sound. Your fuckup is mine and vice versa. So what's the move, boss?"

Adrian was honestly surprised at Cam's response, so much so that he was only prepared to continue bickering. He processed Cam's question and thought of the only logical answer.

"We need to figure out exactly what Drako is on. We can't just kill him, because if he is working with the law against us, then we all know where the finger will point."

"Then what? You want me to send the whore in after all?"

"Nah. We won't need to. I think we should ask Drako ourselves. That party is tomorrow, right?"

"You really think that man is going to tell us anything?"

"If we show the cards that are in our hands. Not the ones in our lap."

Chapter 20

Kiesha tried her best to cover her puffy eyes with makeup before she arrived at work. She was late due to going to see a doctor with London. Although London said she was fine, Miss Simmons wasn't having it at all. She took one look at her face and bruised ribs and sent them to the ER. Thankfully, everything was okay. London was just given some pain medication and had been advised to get some rest. The swelling in her eye had already gone down, but both girls thought it would be best if London stayed over for a few days, just until the bruising on her face went away.

Kiesha didn't want to, but she left London at home while she went to work for the day. When she walked into Parks Realty, she tried not to let on about all the weight she was carrying, especially since everyone was in such good spirits due to the night before. The fake smile she put on for everyone felt like a grimace, and she was happy when she finally reached Executive Hall so she could hide away in her office for a while. However, that hope came to a crashing halt when she saw Cam and Adrian exiting Adrian's office together. The two men slapped hands, and Cam began walking away. However, he stopped when he noticed Kiesha. He gave her a warm smile, and she tried her best to return it.

"What's up, shawty?"

"Hey," she replied meekly and let him pull her in for an embrace.

Behind him, Adrian was giving her a weird look. He was paying attention to her every move. She even saw his eyes linger on her lower lids. When she pulled back from Cam, she focused her attention solely on him.

"You just now getting here?" he asked, and she nodded.

"Yeah. I had a long night after you dropped me off."

"Oh, yeah. I forgot you and your girl stayed up doin' the best friend thing. I hope you didn't tell her nothin' too bad about me."

"Never," Kiesha said and forced a laugh.

"I'm about to head out and go handle some business. Have a good day, okay, shawty?" Cam told her and kissed her forehead.

He walked away, leaving Kiesha and Adrian standing awkwardly in the hall. When he was gone, Kiesha tried to duck away into her office, but Adrian gently grabbed her elbow to stop her. When she looked at him and saw how hard he was studying her, it was hard to keep the sadness off her face.

"What's wrong?" he asked.

"Nothing. It's nothing." She tried to pull away from him, but his grip on her arm got firmer.

"Did Cam do something to you last night?"

"What? No. He took me right home after the event. I'm just not in the best mood today."

She didn't notice the small look of relief on his face. All she wanted to do was go into her office and use her computer to look up Malcom's address. But Adrian wasn't letting it go.

"Then why were you crying?"

"How do you know I was crying?"

"You never wear this much makeup in the office, but it's still not enough to hide the puffy bags under your eyes. Tell me. Maybe I can help."

He finally let go of her arm, and to her surprise, she didn't will her legs to make a beeline for her office and slam the door. There was something about his presence that made her feet stay planted. He was truly concerned about her. She couldn't just see it. She felt it. She sighed.

"My friend London. Last night she stayed the night to wait for me to get back from the showing. We were going to eat our favorite little snacks and watch movies. Girl stuff. But when I got there, she was all beat up."

"What happened?"

"When she went to the store, an old friend of mine and some other people were there talking shit about me."

"Why?"

"This old friend and I fell out behind a boy, a boy she was always pushing me to talk to, but I found out they were fucking the whole time."

"That's foul."

"What's more foul is I found out she was never my friend. I think she hates me, and I never knew. Anyway, London defended me when they were talking shit, and they jumped her. Even the boys. They beat her up so bad, and it just hurts my heart to see her like that. She's a good friend. So if you don't mind, I need to go look up where this motherfucka lives."

"You can't do that," Adrian said, and Kiesha made a face.

"What do you mean I can't—"

"Your computer has limited access. Mine doesn't. I can pull up any listing: sold, owned, or on the market in the state of Florida. Do you know his first and last name?"

"Malcom Donald."

Adrian led her to his office and motioned for her to sit in the seat she assumed Cam had just gotten up from. He sat down behind his desk and cracked his knuckles before going to town on his computer. After minutes of watching him work, she saw his brow furrow as he was reading something on the screen.

"It might be under his parents' name," Kiesha suggested.

"Nah, it's just . . . how old is this Malcom again?"

"Eighteen, nineteen."

"This is him. How is this motherfucka affording to live in a half-million-dollar home? Hold on. Let me do a background check real quick." His fingers went to town on the keyboard again before he started scrolling. "Well, I'll be damned."

"What is it?"

"It says here that his parents were killed in a car crash a couple years ago, and ever since, he's been living with his older brother. Drako Donaldson."

"Who?"

"He's a dangerous man." Adrian rubbed his chin in wonder. "This is crazy."

"What's the address?" Kiesha asked.

"I'm sorry, I can't give you that." Adrian looked sincerely sorry, but Kiesha wasn't trying to hear that at all.

"So what was the point in all of this?"

"This is bigger than you even know. Malcom's brother is into some dangerous shit. Street shit."

"And how do you know that?"

"I just know. And I can't have you showing up on his doorstep wilding out. I'll handle it."

"If he's so dangerous, what are you going to do? You're a Realtor!"

Adrian held back his chuckle, and Kiesha wanted to reach over and pop him on the side of his head. However, it was he who did the reaching. He took her hand in his and looked her deep in the eyes.

"Kiesha, trust me. I'ma handle it. Malcom won't get away with what he did to your friend."

The annoyance she'd felt toward him subsided. Maybe it was the earnest expression on his face or the way his thumbs caressed her hands. She didn't know how he would do it, but she believed that he would keep his word.

"Okay. I trust you."

There was a sudden tap on his office door, and Adrian could have kicked himself when he saw Megan standing there. Her eyes zeroed in on Kiesha's hand in his before glaring at Kiesha. Adrian pulled his hands back and sat up straight in his seat.

"Can I help you with something, Megan?"

"Yes, um . . ." Megan cleared her throat. "Was I interrupting something?"

"No, no. Kiesha and I were just handling some business."

"Good. Because I thought, after last night, maybe you would want to go grab some lunch together today? I definitely worked up an appetite."

"I'll let you know," Adrian told her quickly.

Kiesha could tell he was trying hard not to look at her. But he looked guiltier than all get-out. She herself didn't understand the pit she felt in her stomach. What had happened last night?

"All right. Well, you know where to find me." Megan winked at him and left.

A silence came across the office, and Kiesha didn't want to ask. But the question was sitting on the tip of her tongue, trying to claw its way out. Adrian was still avoiding eye contact with her.

"That must have been why I couldn't find you last night." She tried to say it like a lighthearted joke. "You were with Megan?"

"I . . . it just happened. I had too much to drink," Adrian exhaled and shook his head.

"I thought you had rules."

"I do. And I'm sure I'm going to pay for breaking them."

He had to have meant with Megan, but when his eyes finally found hers again, there seemed to be a plea in them. She wanted to say something, but the words never found her. Not wanting to think about Adrian and Megan, Kiesha returned her focus to the matter at hand.

"Let me know what happens when you get a hold of Malcom, okay? I don't want what happened to my friend to happen to anyone else." She stood up and made to leave the office.

"Kiesha!" Adrian called, stopping her in her tracks. When she turned around, she saw that he looked just like she felt. There was something he wanted to say, but he was fighting against his tongue to say it. Finally, he just forced a smile. "Good work yesterday. I'm really proud of you."

Disappointed, Kiesha forced her own smile and nodded. Without another word, she went to her own office to get a head start on their next project. She thought the person on her mind would be Cam, or even London for that matter. But the person running laps through her mind was the one across the hall.

Chapter 21

Normally Adrian got a full, good night of rest, but he found himself waking up at 5:00 a.m. Friday morning. That usually happened when his waking thoughts trumped his dreams. He lay in the pitch black of his room, staring upward until his eyes adjusted to the dark. He focused on the ceiling fan while his thoughts formulated in order. They all had a starting point, and it was Steelo. He was there in Florida moving around like there was no problem, when he knew, in fact, there was. Something was making him feel safe, and Adrian had found a lot of dots, but none of them were connecting.

Not only that, but news of his welcome home party had spread like wildfire across social media. There was some outrage due to some people knowing about his snitching history. However, the love he received outshined the hate, and that alone invoked anger in Adrian, mainly because, at that point, Steelo had to know that his being there wasn't a secret anymore. That meant he was sending blatant disrespectful shots to the ones who had banished him.

Adrian was happy that neither his father nor Cam's was active on social media. A war would have broken out if Antonio knew what was going on. He was a "shoot first and later" kind of man. That was where he and Adrian differed. Adrian preferred diplomacy first. Peaceful resolutions in the streets were always best because they kept the wrong kind of eyes off the operation. Bodies dropping left and right was never a good thing, and that was why, for Adrian, a feud was always the last resort. He liked to keep things clean. Still, he wasn't afraid to get things popping if he had to.

He was starting to feel like Steelo was purposely forcing hands. And what bothered Adrian the most was that he'd been so focused on the corporate side of things, he had no clue how long Steelo had really been there in the background, plotting. He didn't like thinking so hard that his head hurt, and that was exactly what he was doing. Adrian forced himself out of bed and to the kitchen to make an early breakfast.

He'd left his phone on the counter the night before, and when he checked it, he groaned. There were three missed calls and several text messages from Megan. He didn't even care to see what they said. He knew it was his own fault that she was on him like that. He'd broken his own rule with her, and that alone probably made her feel special. But the truth was she just wasn't. Beauty and good sex alone weren't enough to hold his attention. Adrian had an old soul, and because of that, he needed depth. The most important things to him were a person's sense of self and their integrity. Megan was too thirsty to have him. And by the way she'd blown up his phone, she was clingy, too. It was something he'd have to officially address the next time he saw her. There was no way in hell he would ever have any kind of sexual interaction with her.

As he cooked, he thought back to Kiesha in the office. It was amazing to him that Cam hadn't picked up that her energy was off. All Adrian had to do was take one look at her to know something was wrong. And he didn't care what he had to do, he just knew he wanted to fix it, whatever it was. However, when he found out what it was, he was almost floored by how close to home it was for him. There was no way he was going to let her confront Malcom on her own. Drako was a cold-blooded killer, and catching a body was nothing to him. Kiesha's body would never be found, but Adrian also knew that it wasn't something she would just drop. After working closely with her even for a short amount of time, he knew how determined she was. That was why he told her he would handle it, which he would—two birds, one stone style.

Adrian poured himself some orange juice and sat down to enjoy his breakfast. By then, the sun was coming up and poking through the blinds in his living room. As he ate his eggs and hashbrowns, he turned on the early morning news.

"Late last night, Miami PD infiltrated a building after receiving an anonymous tip," the black female newscaster was saying.

The cameraman zoomed in on a warehouse that over a dozen officers were outside of. Adrian stopped eating to lean up in his seat and get a better view of the building. The warehouse wasn't just any warehouse. It was one of theirs.

"Our officers here received a tip on possible cartel-level drug trafficking going on at this very location. However, when they arrived at the scene, all they found were a few people inside seeking shelter. Unfortunately, one of the men was injured by officers in the process. More on this story when we come back."

Adrian felt a tension headache coming on and realized he was clenching his jaw out of anger. Someone was sending the police sniffing at their door. Whoever had tipped the police off about the Parks's underground operation couldn't have been too deep in the fold. Otherwise, they would have known that they switched warehouses weeks ago. Still, it was too close to home. Adrian picked up his phone to call Cam, but before he could, Cam was calling him.

"You seein' what I'm seein'?" Cam asked.

"The news?"

"Hell yeah. Somebody's playin' the Feds game with us. I don't like that shit."

"Me either. Tally up everyone who knew the location of the last spot."

"I already did that. And guess whose name came up."

"Drako."

"Yup."

"Damn."

"Yup," Cam said again. "He picked his first order up from the warehouse. He probably thought we moved like dumb niggas and kept all of our spots the same."

"Either way, that was too close a call for me. Have our boys tighten up. I don't want anybody who doesn't need to know shit to know shit. Understand?"

"You already know I'm with the vibes. But about tonight, you thought about how we're goin' about it?"

"Yeah, and I think going through the front doors would be a problem. I want to creep up on that motherfucka."

"And how you gon' do that?"

"Bosses come in through the back. And, Cam? I don't know what to expect tonight, so make sure—"

"The shooters gon' be ready. Don't worry about that. I'm the brawn, and you're the brains. Just make sure you do what you need to do so I don't even have to step in."

"That's the plan."

Chapter 22

"Does my makeup still look okay, Kiesha?" London asked, leaning over the bathroom sink.

Kiesha finished drying her hands and made her way through the small crowd of ladies to get to her friend. The muffled sound of music was making its way into the bathroom from the dance floor of Club Saki, and Kiesha was ready to get back out to it.

All social media had been talking about was the party that was happening that night. Apparently it was the place for anybody to be, and Kiesha thought that getting out of the house would make London feel better. And what was the point of having fake IDs if they never made use of them? So the two of them got dressed real cute, Kiesha in a nude skintight dress and London in a black one. Kiesha had beat London's face and covered the bruises and cuts, but her girl was still feeling a little self-conscious.

"Girl, you look amazing as always," Kiesha reassured her genuinely. "Literally flawless."

"Yeah, flawless," London said sarcastically, looking at her face.

Kiesha took her hands in hers and looked into her face. She really had to give it to herself. She did the dang thing on London's makeup. She was already a beautiful young woman, but the makeup made her look like a goddess.

"Your physical wounds will heal, but right now, nobody can even see those. Let's work on healing this"—Kiesha pointed at London's chest—"because we don't have time for you to be having PTSD!"

"Kiesha!" London exclaimed and burst out laughing. She took one last look at her face and smiled. "You're right. I am a bad bitch. Let's go back out, because I swear I saw too many fine niggas!"

They left the bathroom and made their way over to the bar. Kiesha wasn't really a drinker, but that night they both needed something to take the edge off. She ordered them shots of Patrón, and when they threw those back, they ordered two more. All Kiesha had eaten that day were some tacos earlier at work, so the buzz hit her fast. Soon the girls were lost in a fit of giggles and moving their bodies to the loud music.

"Ooh! This is my song!" London exclaimed when Big Boogie's song "PTPOM" came on. "Let's go shake some ass!"

She grabbed Kiesha's hand and pulled her to the side of the dance floor where they did just that. The men standing around were looking at them like they wanted to eat them for dessert. The girls, on the other hand, weren't too fond of them getting all the attention. They could have joined in on the fun, but the issue with pretty girls was that some of them acted like it was a crime for other pretty girls to exist.

Kiesha saw them and just rolled her eyes. She wasn't about to let a hater ruin her night. She was just happy to see the smile back on London's face. Plus, it had been a long week at the office. She deserved a night out. She and London continued to dance until their feet hurt in their heels, and even after that they danced some more. It wasn't until the DJ started playing slower tunes that they made their way off the dance floor and to a high table. The shots seemed to have gotten to London a little more than Kiesha, so she helped her friend onto one of the chairs.

"Bitch, I got it. I got it!" London said, laughing and trying to swat Kiesha away.

"No, you don't! You're going to fall off the chair!"

Kiesha laughed with her, and when she was sure London wasn't going to topple over, she sat down across from her. She took a moment to survey the club. She was happy that the AC was working because it was packed. There were so many faces that she couldn't focus on just one, so she turned her attention to the stage. At that moment, the handsome DJ cut the music and got on the mic.

"A'ight now, I see a bunch of fine ladies in the building tonight! And, fellas, I see y'all came dressed to impress!" The crowd of people, including London, cheered back at him. "Y'all already know it's your boy DJ Doc on the ones and twos tonight celebrating my boy Steelo. It's his welcome home party, and we're here to have a good time. Make some noise for my big dog one time!"

He pointed at someone sitting over in a VIP section to the side. Kiesha followed his finger as the crowd cheered. A good-looking man rocking a fresh fade and dripping in Gucci stood up, nodding like he was the man. She guessed he was Steelo. Although he was an older gentleman and had one or two people his age with him, his section was filled with younger men and women.

"Ooh, he looks like he has money!" London observed. "Look at his chain!"

"He looks old enough to be your daddy," Kiesha said and made a face.

"Girl, if he's dropping bands, he can be my daddy for the night!"

"Uh-uh! See, that's the liquor talking. No more for you tonight," Kiesha joked.

London was about to say something smart back, but then her face just froze. At first Kiesha thought she was about to throw up, but then she saw that London was looking at something behind her. Kiesha turned around to see what she was so fixated on, and she instantly caught an attitude. It was Stacy, Malcom, and their whole entourage. They had just gotten drinks from the bar and were walking their way. Kiesha glared at the boys with Malcom and wondered if they were the ones who did London dirty.

"Is that them?" Kiesha asked, looking back at London.

"Yeah, that's all of them. Look, let's not make a scene."

London's request was instantly denied when Stacy spotted them in the crowd. A tickled smile came across her face, and she nudged her friends. Soon their entire crew, including the boys, were heading toward their table. Kiesha pursed her lips when Stacy stopped right next to her.

"I didn't know they were lettin' lames up in here," Stacy said loudly, and her friends laughed.

"Yeah, well, I see they let the broke in," Kiesha shot back and looked Stacy up and down, stopping at her shoes. "Actually, aren't those my shoes?"

"Yeah. You can have them back after I stomp your friend's face in again."

Myra and Kennedy laughed loudly behind Stacy. Kiesha couldn't put her disgust into words. She had just been having one of the best nights she'd had in a while, and Stacy was ruining it with her monstrous behavior.

"Bye, Stacy. You can get out of my face now."

"Oh." Stacy faked a gasp and put her hand over her mouth. "Did I upset the virgin? Are you still mad that Malcom is my nigga?"

Kiesha's eyes shifted to Malcom, who blew a kiss at her. She turned her nose up.

"Why would I be mad? He's a loser," she said and directed her next words to him. "You know you're a whole ho for what you did to my friend, right?" she asked him, not holding back.

"Bitch, what did you just say to me?" Malcom stepped forward and leered down at her.

Staring at him in that moment, Kiesha didn't know how she ever found him attractive. Of course he was handsome, but she had been too busy looking at the attributes about him that didn't matter to take notice of what did. Like the hardened look on his face, or the fact that his eyes could turn from hot to cold in a mere second. She then remembered what Adrian had said about his brother being a dangerous man, and Malcom might have been just as dangerous. If he didn't care about hurting London in a public parking lot, he for sure didn't care about harming her right there.

"Go ahead. Repeat that shit, bitch, I dare you, so I can do you just like I did her for talkin' to my girl crazy," Malcom taunted her.

"I—"

"She said you're a ho for what you did to her friend. Excuse me, a whole ho."

Kiesha recognized the voice that interrupted her and found that she was right when Adrian approached them and stood on the other side of the table. His face was expressionless as he stared at Stacy and Malcom's crew, but there was a certain iciness in his eyes. Kiesha was shocked to see him there. Not only that, but he was dressed in regular street clothes. He had a few chains around his neck and was rocking the latest Yeezys. He looked good in suits, but she almost drooled seeing him then.

"A . . . Adrian. I didn't see you walk up."

"You're speaking my name like you know me or something," Adrian said coldly.

"Nah, I . . . you know my brother, Drako. Y'all do business together."

"I guess I'm supposed to be impressed by you name-dropping a runner of mine. I'm not."

Kiesha watched the exchange and was surprised at Malcom's sudden change in posture. He was nervous. Not only did he fix his tone while talking to Adrian, but she swore he was standing up straighter. Not only did his demeanor change, but so did that of the guys he'd brought with him. Stacy was standing beside him, looking mad at the fact that the man on Kiesha's side had that kind of power.

"Why you actin' like that?" she asked Malcom with a stank face.

"That's Adrian Parks," Malcom told her under his breath.

Adrian ignored them to focus on Kiesha and London. He took Kiesha's hand and examined her. It was the same thing he'd done at the office. But that night, the care in his eyes made the butterflies in her stomach swarm. He lifted her chin with one finger and then brushed her hair out of her face with the same finger.

"Are y'all okay?" he asked.

"Yeah, we're fine." Kiesha nodded.

"Good. You and your girl can go to that empty VIP section and tell them that Adrian sent you. They'll take care of you," he said after a few seconds.

"O . . . okay. You coming?"

"I have some business to handle. I'll come check on y'all though."

Everyone, including London, was at a loss for words. She kept looking from Adrian to Malcom, who hadn't said another word or moved. Kiesha rolled her eyes one last time at Stacy before taking London's hand and leading her away to the VIP section.

"Is that Adrian as in the one you work with? That Adrian?" London asked when they were far enough away.

"Yes, girl."

"You told me he was fine, but you didn't tell me he was foine! And who is he again?"

"He's a Realtor."

"No, bitch. You better open your eyes and stop being green. That man back there? He's a boss."

Chapter 23

Adrian waited for Kiesha and her friend to walk away before turning back to Malcom. It wasn't hard to size him up. He was the little brother of someone making money, which meant he was nothing more than a shadow. And that probably made him feel inadequate, which was most likely the reason why he had no problem beating up women.

"Malcom, that's your name, right?"

"Yup."

"I need you to know something about me, Malcom. I'm the last person you want to piss off, understand?"

"Yeah, I understand."

"Good, good. Because see, if you ever again fuck with either of the two girls who were just sitting here, I'm going to kill your whole family and make you watch me do it. Now, do you understand that?"

"I . . . I do."

Adrian gave him one more chilling glance before walking away. His trigger finger itched, and he couldn't lie. He wanted to put a bullet between Malcom's eyes, especially after seeing him threaten Kiesha, but he had other things that required his attention that night.

He walked to the VIP section that Steelo was sitting in. Upon seeing him, the bouncer nodded respectfully and lifted the rope to give Adrian access. He walked up the stairs to the section and instantly saw both Steelo and Drako having a jolly old time. They had alcohol, wings, and big booties twerking in their faces. In fact, their smiles were a little too wide for Adrian's liking.

"Well, well, well. Look what the cat dragged in."

When his voice sounded, everyone looked in his direction. Steelo looked surprised to see him, but not frightened. Drako crossed his arms over his chest and leaned back in his seat. He sucked his teeth and glared. Adrian took that as he wasn't happy to see him.

"Adrian, my boy—"

"We're not boys," Adrian interrupted Steelo's greeting. "We're not anything. In fact, I find it hard to believe I'm really staring at you right now."

"Yeah, why is that?" Steelo asked and smoothly sipped from his glass of dark liquor.

"You know why. You're not supposed to be here. You aren't welcome."

"I beg to differ. All these people came out for me."

"That's because most of them don't know who you really are. Maybe the niggas on this stage rocking with you don't either."

"Whoa, whoa. Calm down," Steelo said, putting his hands up in an amused manner. "No need to be all hostile. Where is your old man? We should talk."

"You and I both know that if it were him instead of me, you and everybody up here with you would already be dead. But me? I'm thinking there must be a logical reason that you were crazy enough to show up back here."

Steelo sipped his drink again and hissed as it went down into his chest. Adrian's eyes might have been on him, but he was scoping out the whole scene. He was paying attention to how far all their hands were from their waists. So far no one had made a move. Steelo set the glass on the table in front of him and stood up. He motioned his head to a bistro table in the section that nobody was sitting at. Adrian followed and sat across from him. He crossed his hands and waited for Steelo to answer his question.

"You want to know why I came back here, huh?" Steel started. "I left too much money on the floor. That's why."

"I think you might have forgotten that it's your fault money was left on the floor. You know what you did. That's something that can never be forgiven. My father was kind enough to banish you instead of killing you."

"Ha. Kind? No, sending a man away from his home and his family is the most inhumane thing a person can do to a hustler. I had no money and no way to eat. Nah, I'm not going for that."

"You say that like you have a choice. We don't have any room for a snitch here."

"You know what's funny is y'all call me a snitch when I call it being a businessman. We all knock our competition off the chessboard in some way. I just went the smarter route about mine."

"What's smart about telling on a motherfucka?"

"It's always a good thing to have the Feds eating out of your pocket. Create a dirty cop and let him get a taste of some real money, he'll be eating out of that same pocket forever." Steelo's lips broke into a slow and sinister smile. "I wish it didn't have to be this way. Your father is a good businessman, but see, there's only room for one king in Miami."

"Were you behind that wannabe drug bust I saw on the news?"

"Nah, that wasn't me. That was my nephew." Steelo nodded toward Drako, who was still sitting on the couch.

"Nephew?" Now that was news to Adrian.

"See, you might not think you're like your old man. But you are just like him in some ways. Arrogant just like him. When Antonio said I couldn't come back, it took me away from my family when they needed me the most. My sister died and left her kids in my care, but how could I care for them with no money? But neph right there, he's just like me. He got that hustle in him."

"He has that snitch in him, too, I see."

"And you led him right into your den not knowing he was a wolf the whole time. And wolves are cunning. It wasn't easy planning all of this. First he had to take Jerry down, and then he had to gain your trust to learn about your operation."

"You almost had us. 'Almost' being the key word."

"Oh, don't worry. Very soon you'll be knocked off the chessboard. You and your father. My nephew is looking forward to expanding our business with more territory. Just you wait."

"Now that I know the type of time you're on, what makes you think I won't kill you right now?"

"Them," Steelo casually said and pointed toward his entourage.

Adrian looked in time to see them all stand up in unison. Their hands were on their waists, signifying that they were ready to shoot once Steelo gave the word. Drako stared at Adrian triumphantly like he had won a competition. To Steelo's surprise, Adrian wasn't moved at all. In fact, he chuckled.

"That's cute. Too bad they'll be dead before they have time to draw their weapons." Adrian lifted a finger up and down by his ear. Almost instantly, red dots appeared on all of Steelo's men. Steelo himself had one on his chest, which Adrian pointed at.

"What is this?" Steelo exclaimed.

"You think I would come alone? I always keep a couple shooters with me. One more signal from me and they're shooting you and everyone you brought with you."

Adrian wanted to give the signal so bad. But as he looked around, there were just too many people. They could get hurt, or worse. They could be witnesses. Killing Steelo and Drako there wouldn't be smart. So instead, he relished the look of fear on Steelo's face and stood up, knowing they couldn't do anything to him. He patted the older man on his shoulder before walking away.

"Remember, Steelo. While you're playing chess, I'm playing *Monopoly*."

With that, Adrian exited the section knowing that a war had been ignited. But that was okay because he was ready.

Chapter 24

When Kiesha and London got to the VIP section, it was once again smooth sailing from there. The girls had an amazing time, and as Adrian promised, they were taken care of. Whatever they wanted, they got it. She and London decided not to drink anymore, but they did indulge in the free chicken wings and fries. Kiesha almost even forgot about the whole Malcom thing. By the end of the night, the girls were full and tired from all the dancing and singing they'd done.

"Let's head out before everyone else," London suggested, and Kiesha nodded.

They grabbed their purses and exited the VIP area. Kiesha tried to look around to find Adrian, but she couldn't spot him. He told her that he would come over to the section, but he never did. Maybe he'd left already. Kiesha felt slightly let down because that meant she wouldn't see him again until Monday.

"You gonna call Cam?" London asked her when they were standing outside the club.

"I don't know." Kiesha shrugged as the hot, humid air hit her stickily. "Probably not."

"I thought you really liked him."

"I mean, he's cool. We vibe. But he's just not—"

"Him?" London asked and pointed at a vehicle approaching them.

Sure enough, a red Cullinan slowed to a stop in front of them. The window was rolled down, so Kiesha could see Adrian in the driver's seat. He leaned out the window toward them with a smile.

"Y'all good?" he asked.

"Yeah, we're fine. I thought you left. You never came to the section," Kiesha said.

"I had to come out here and talk to my people. Do you ladies need a ride or anything?"

"No, she drove us here." Kiesha pointed at London.

He nodded but didn't drive off. They did their usual dance and just stared at each other, both wanting to say something, neither knowing what. Beside Kiesha, London cleared her throat and stepped to the side.

"Kiesh, maybe he can take you home? I'm going to slide on my little boo, and he stays more out this way."

Kiesha was thrown off. London had never mentioned having plans after the club, let alone having a boo. But there she was, put on the spot.

"Umm, I . . . Do you mind?" she finally asked Adrian.

"Not at all. Hop in."

Adrian unlocked his doors, but before Kiesha walked off, she gave London a big hug.

"You sure you're okay to drive?" she asked.

"Girl, that little buzz been done worn off. Make sure you call me in the morning, okay?"

"I will."

Kiesha watched her walk to her car and didn't stop until she saw her friend behind the wheel of the white Dodge Charger. She waved when London pulled off, and then she got into Adrian's car. She closed her eyes and inhaled deeply, because his car's aroma was becoming one of her favorites. When she opened them she found him staring at her.

"What?" she asked shyly.

"Nothing. You just have this ability to look fine as hell every time I see you."

"Thank you, sir. I must say, I like this look on you," she said and tugged at the unbuttoned Cubs jersey. "You look normal."

"Normal? What's that supposed to mean?" Adrian laughed as he started to drive.

"Nothing bad. Just that at work you always seem so much older than what you are. Now you just seem—"

"Normal," Adrian finished for her.

"Yeah. I would say like a regular nigga, but I think you proved tonight that there isn't anything regular about you." She looked over at him in wonder. "What was that tonight?"

"What was what?"

"You know, what happened with Malcom. I've never seen anything like that before. He straightened up at the mere sight of you."

"I don't know. Maybe he just knew I wasn't about to play about you." He shrugged.

"Bull. The way Malcom reacted, that wasn't just fear. That was respect. He knew who you were, but I don't think I do. Not really. Who are you, Adrian?"

"Let's just say I'm a man of a few faces, all of them solid though. But that's all I can tell you, for now."

"For now, huh? Does that mean we'll be spending more time together?"

Kiesha didn't know where that question came from. But she knew she'd asked it because she felt her lips move and heard her voice. She clearly wasn't all the way sober because the liquid courage was still there.

"I thought you and Cam were a thing."

"I mean"—Kiesha shrugged—"he's cool and nice to me. I don't want to hurt him. I just . . . I guess my mind is always on other things."

"Like?"

He took his eyes off the road to glance over at her, and his gaze seemed to burn a hole in her cheek. She was ready to spill everything to him about how he made her feel. However, biology had other plans. Suddenly the overwhelming sensation to pee came over her.

"Oh, my gosh, I need to pee so bad," she said, holding her stomach, and his eyes grew wide.

"Are you serious right now?"

"Yes, Adrian, please! Pull over or something. I need to go bad!"

"Nah, my condo isn't too far from where we are now. We can stop there first before I run you home."

Kiesha didn't have a weak bladder, but right then it felt like she did. She held it until they got to the tall building Adrian stayed in. He led her inside and into an elevator, where she leaned on a wall, crossing her legs. He would, of course, be so dramatic as to live on one of the top floors. Kiesha was so happy when she finally heard the ding and the doors opened.

He took her hand and led her down the hallway to his door. She was too busy trying not to tinkle that she couldn't even pay attention to the beautiful architecture of the building. As soon as he opened the door and flicked the light switch, she burst through and kicked her shoes off.

"There's a bathroom right there in the hall," Adrian said to her, but she was already racing toward it.

She barely cared to shut the door. She hiked her dress up and plopped down on the toilet, happy she'd decided not to wear panties that night. She was also happy that it was just a number one and not a number two. Kiesha didn't think she'd ever be able to look at Adrian the same if she stunk up his bathroom the first time she ever went to his house. When she was done, she washed her hands and left the elegant bathroom. She found him sitting on one of his barstools patiently waiting for her.

"You good?" he asked.

"Much better now, thank you," she said and spun in a circle, taking his place in. "Wow, Adrian. This is really nice."

She walked over to the floor-to-ceiling window in the living room and was blown away by the view of the city. It was beautiful. What she would give to wake up to a view like that every day. He walked up behind her and stood so close she could feel his warm breath on her neck.

"Thank you. This is where I stand sometimes to clear my head. It helps to see everyone down there living their lives. It makes mine seem less important."

"And that helps you?"

"It does. Because it reminds me that everybody has something going on, and that helps me be honest with myself about anything and everything. Maybe it can do the same for you."

"What do you mean?" she breathed.

"In the car, you didn't finish your statement."

"I wasn't going to say anything important," she lied.

"Don't lie to me, Kiesha." His voice got lower and deeper.

Adrian placed his hands on her sides and slowly let them slide to her stomach. She inhaled a sharp breath when he pulled her to him. She felt his warm body on her and almost let her head fall back into his chest, but she tried to keep it together. But when she spoke again, her tone was low and soft.

"I was . . . I was going to say that Cam is nice, but my mind is always on you. I don't understand it, because you don't want me. But this short time with you has felt like a lifetime, and every second I spend with you, I think I fall for you even more."

"Why do you think I don't want you?"

"You fucked Megan the night of our event."

"You showed up with Cam." Adrian sighed behind her. "I don't usually admit shit like this, but I'm a man, and I can admit when I'm wrong. I was jealous when you showed up, looking how you were looking, with him by your side and not me. I didn't get it at the time. I just knew how I felt. Angry. And I kept thinking about the two of you, of him and you having . . . you know. And it made me even more jealous, so I fucked Megan. But the whole time, I was wishing it was you."

"That's stupid as hell. You were mad at me, so you fucked somebody else?"

"You fucked Cam."

"No, I didn't! I've never fucked anybody before. I'm a virgin."

Kiesha didn't mean to blurt it out like that. She swore she felt a pause in Adrian's breathing. His hands loosened on her stomach, and he turned her around to face her. He looked her dead in her eyes, and she gave him the same energy back. There wasn't disbelief in his eyes. More like shock.

"You're a virgin?"

"Yes." Kiesha rolled her eyes. "I'm not a nun or anything. It just hasn't happened yet."

"Wow," he said and took a step away from her.

That hurt her.

"Now what? You don't like me anymore?"

"No, no, that's not it. I just feel like a fucking idiot. I really thought you and Cam—"

"Well, we didn't."

Kiesha crossed her arms and leaned against the window behind her. She felt him staring at her again, but she kept her eyes on the ground. She didn't know why, but she couldn't look at him. She didn't know how she had gotten herself into a love triangle, but she had. And the person who was going to get hurt in it didn't deserve it, but she knew who she yearned for, who she truly wanted, and it was the man standing in front of her.

"Kiesha," Adrian finally said and tried to grab her hands.

"Don't," she said and kept her arms tightly crossed. "You can take me home now."

"All right, if that's what you really want."

"I do." Her lips moved, but her body didn't.

She finally looked at him and felt flutters throughout her whole body, not just her stomach. Her eyes told him the words her lips couldn't, and he just nodded. Adrian reached for her hands again, and that time she didn't resist. He pulled her to him and put her arms on his shoulders.

"I want you," he breathed down at her, holding the small of her back. "So much so that I'll be done with my rules to try this for real. If you'll have me. I don't care about what you have going with Cam. That shit is dead to me. You were mine the moment I laid eyes on you."

"Oh, Adrian," she said right before their lips locked.

Their kiss was so deep and passionate it felt like Kiesha was floating. It took a few moments for her to realize she actually was. Adrian had scooped her up off her feet and carried her to his bedroom. They only broke their kiss when he placed her gently on the edge of his bed. He stood in front of her, and she rubbed his bare chest all the way down to his six-pack. Her lips kissed him there, too. She wanted to feel him inside of her, but she was afraid. Still, her clit throbbed at the sight of his erection. Her hand caressed it through his jean shorts, and he moaned.

"I've never done anything before except kiss," she told him.

"Are you sure you want to do this then?"

"Yes."

"Then I'll show you." He leaned down and placed another kiss on her lips before exiting the room. When he came back, he was holding a warm towel in his hand. "Lay back, baby."

Trusting him, she did as she was told. She watched as he gently lifted her dress, spread her legs, and marveled at the sight of her fat kitty cat. A low moan escaped his lips again, and he shook his head at the beautiful sight. He used the rag to wipe her off, from the rooter to the tooter. She found herself giggling. She forgot she had used the bathroom, but she wasn't embarrassed. She was happy that he was a clean man. When he was done, he set the towel to the side.

"What now?" she asked.

"Now I devour you," he said and positioned his head between her legs.

She didn't have time to have another thought before she felt the first lick on her clit. That first clit lick turned into many, and when she felt his lips wrap around it, her back arched. She'd never felt anything so pleasurable, and many cries slipped through her lips. Her juices began flowing like a river down his chin, but that seemed to turn Adrian on even more.

"I'm going to start with one finger, okay?" he told her, and she nodded.

When he put his middle finger at her tight hole, Kiesha braced herself. She felt the pressure as it slid in and out of her, but quickly the pleasure came with it. As he fingered her, he kept licking her clit. Her hips swirled to match the strokes of his finger thrusts.

"Fuck, Kiesha, you're turning me on," he said in between licks. "This wet-ass pussy. I'm gonna do two fingers now, okay?"

She nodded again, letting him know that she was ready. That time, she felt a small nipping pain, but it went away. He was handling her with care and began making the "come here" motion inside of her love tunnel. Kiesha had to grip the comforter of his bed tightly to keep from running away.

"Adrian! Adrian. I'm . . . I'm . . ."

"Let it come, baby, let it come," he urged and proceeded to beat her clit up with his tongue.

Finally Kiesha exploded. Her orgasm felt like the flood after a river dam broke. Her lips and legs mirrored each other as they quivered. Her brow was crinkled, and she uttered love cries. Adrian came up for air and kissed her again deeply.

"I think that's good for tonight," he whispered, but she shook her head.

"I want more," she told him hungrily. "I want you inside of me."

"Kiesha . . ."

"I want you, Adrian."

He couldn't turn her away. Not when she was lying there looking as sexy as she was. Kiesha pushed him off of her, and he scooted up onto the bed so that his back was against the pillows. She crawled sexily toward him and straddled him. He watched as she pulled her dress over her head and revealed her perfect body. His hands explored every inch of it, squeezing her voluptuous bottom, and he ended up holding on to her perky breasts. Her brown nipples tantalized him so much, and soon his mouth was wrapped around them, sucking ever so gently. And whichever one wasn't in his mouth at the time was pinched and rolled by his fingers.

"Adrian," Kiesha moaned, throwing her head back. "Oh, Adrian."

She ground on his erection, making him grow even more excited. He knocked the pillows from his bad and flipped her back onto her back. Afterward, he took his shorts and briefs off right before reaching into his nightstand for a condom. Her eyes grew wide looking at how big his manhood was, but it didn't make her want to tell him to stop. In fact, she grew hornier. Her vaginal walls were yearning to be separated.

"Kiesha, you're so beautiful," Adrian told her, stroking himself as he stared down at her. "Damn, you're so beautiful. You're going to make me fall in love with you. Is that what you want?"

"Yes," she answered truthfully.

"You want this dick all to yourself?"

"Yes!"

"After tonight it's yours. Only yours."

He rolled the condom down his shaft, and Kiesha opened her legs wide so he wouldn't have to. He looked pleased at her eagerness. He positioned his tip at her opening and lay down on top of her. He kissed her neck and her ear while caressing her hair. The first thrust he made sent the tip through, and Kiesha tensed up. He began whispering sweet nothings in her ear in between his kisses, causing her to relax her body again. That time when he thrust, he did it a little harder, granting him more entrance. The last thrust he gave, he was all the way in. He sucked his teeth at how tight and wet she was. He stroked a few more times slowly, but when he was sliding in and out with ease, he picked up the pace.

Soon her pained cries turned into moans. She wrapped her arms around him and put her mouth by his ear. She wanted him to hear how good he was making her feel. Tears had welled up in her eyes. They were happy tears. Everything about that moment felt right, and if she could stay there forever, she would have. But once again, biology had other plans. She once again felt her orgasm building up, and by the way Adrian was beginning to jerk, his was too.

"Ahhhh!" they moaned loudly in unison as they climaxed together.

She saw fireworks behind her eyelids. When the feeling subsided, Adrian collapsed off of her onto the bed. She wanted to say something, anything, but there were no words to describe the cloud she was riding. Instead, she snuggled closely up to his body, welcomed his arms around her, and fell into a deep sleep.

Chapter 25

The ride home the next morning was a silent one. There, however, were a lot of smiles between Kiesha and Adrian. Not only that, but the only time he let go of her hand the entire ride was when he stopped to grab her some breakfast.

Kiesha was still on a high from the events of the night before. She couldn't believe that she wasn't a virgin anymore, but then again, she didn't feel any different. Except when the flashbacks hit her, and then all she felt were chills. There was a shadow looming over her, though, and that shadow was Cam. She knew she would have to tell him the truth sooner or later, and the sooner, the better.

When Adrian slowed to a stop in front of her house, she looked for her mother's car. Kiesha knew she would be curious as to who was pulling up in such an expensive car. But she had gotten lucky. Her mom didn't seem to be home.

"So," she said when he parked.

"So," he repeated, leaning back into his seat and looking at her.

"Did you mean everything you said last night?"

"I said a lot of things last night. Pinpoint something."

"About giving up your rules for me?"

"Hell yeah! You think I'm going to be one of them 'hit it and quit it' type of men?" Adrian asked, and Kiesha made a knowing face. He couldn't help but laugh. "That was the past. I'm starting fresh with you. I meant everything I said."

"Good, because now I understand why I see girls going crazy behind dick. Hell, I even understand why Megan was so pressed. Speaking of her . . ." She gave him another look.

"I'ma handle that. I'm not going to let anything get in the way of what I want to build with you. But you have to do the same."

"I know," Kiesha told him and sighed. "I'll handle it. I'll see you Monday?"

"If you're my girl now, I'm not waiting until Monday to see you. I'll be back tonight to take you to dinner."

His words were music to her ears. She grinned and leaned forward to give him a kiss goodbye. She loved the way his lips tasted. Once Kiesha had gotten her fix, she got out of the car with her food and went inside her house. As she thought, it was empty, but there was a note on the fridge. It was from her mom, telling her that she had a last-minute meeting with a client. Perfect. That meant she could do what she needed to do. She screamed and spun around in a dreamy circle before falling onto one of the dining room chairs. Kiesha's hands found their way to her chest, and a fit of giggles came from her lips. She was so happy that she couldn't eat.

However, that happiness came to a pause when she finally checked her phone. There were a few missed texts from London, but there was one from Cam that tugged at her chest.

I was at the club last night too. I saw you leave with Adrian. Everything okay?

She stared at the message for a long time. Kiesha knew Cam deserved a face-to-face explanation, or maybe even a phone call. But she opted to take the easy way out. Her thumbs began typing out a message to him, and she hoped it didn't come off too harsh.

I did leave with him, and there is something I need to tell you. I like Adrian. More than like him. I didn't know things would go as far as they did with you, and I was just young and experiencing life. I also didn't know the two of you knew each other, so I'm so sorry about it all. The last thing I want to do is hurt you. You are a great person, and we had some good times. But I choose him. And if you never want to talk to me again, I understand.

Kiesha sent the message before she lost the nerve to. She went to set her phone down, but the loud ding signified that a message had come in. It was from Cam. Kiesha forced herself to read it.

Yup.

That was it. Just "Yup." She didn't know why it made her chest feel so heavy because she didn't regret it. Suddenly it hit her. She realized she'd done to Cam exactly what Stacy had done to her. The only difference was that she'd had the decency to tell him about it. The only thing was that it didn't feel so decent. And she hoped it didn't create a rift in whatever business the two men had together.

The ringing of the doorbell jarred her from her thoughts and back to reality. She smiled big, thinking it was London. She couldn't wait to tell her all about the night before. Kiesha all but skipped to the door and swung it open.

"Girl, I—" She stopped talking midsentence when she saw that it wasn't London standing at her front door.

It was Malcom. And he wasn't alone either. Standing next to him was a man who resembled him greatly, all the way down to the scowls on their faces as they stared at her.

"Damn, Stacy wasn't lyin' when she said your and your mom's crib was nice," he said, looking all in her house.

"What are you doing here, Malcom?" Kiesha asked tersely.

"Oh, my bad. I'm rude as fuck. This is my brother Drako, and we were just dropping by to give you a message."

"I don't need a message from you. I thought Adrian told you to stay away from me." Kiesha told him and tried to shut the door.

Drako put out a hand and stopped it from shutting. In fact, he forced it open farther. She tried to close it again, but he was too strong, and he smiled at her efforts.

"It's funny you bring up Adrian," Drako said and looked around the quiet neighborhood. "Because the message we have is for him. I don't like how he tried to punk my little brother last night at the club."

"Is that the message? Because you can tell him that yourself." Kiesha rolled her eyes.

"Nah. The message we have is louder than that. In fact, it comes wrapped in a nice bag. A body bag."

His eyes twinkled menacingly. Before Kiesha could react, he pulled out a pistol from his waist. Thinking he was about to shoot her, Kiesha turned to run away.

"Grab her!" Drako instructed Malcom.

Malcom grabbed her before she could get too far into the house, and when she tried to fight him off, he punched her hard in the side of the head. Kiesha instantly collapsed, and before she blacked out, she felt them scooping her up and carrying her out of the house.

Chapter 26

Cam wasn't a man who normally let his personal feelings get in the way of business, but the anger he felt in his chest was what caused him to drive all the way to Adrian's condo. After reading Kiesha's message, he couldn't believe that Adrian would do something so low-down and dirty to him. He knew she was the girl he was dealing with. Granted, if she had been any other girl, especially in that short amount of time, he wouldn't have cared. But Cam was really starting to feel her. Kiesha was young, but she moved different from all the other girls her age. Her mind matched her grown-woman body.

When Cam got to Adrian's door, he banged on it. And when it wasn't answered right away, he banged on it again. Adrian finally opened the door wearing only a pair of Nike shorts, and he had a toothbrush dangling from his mouth

"Cam, what the fuck?" he asked, looking at Cam like he was crazy.

"Don't 'what the fuck' me!" Cam exclaimed and pushed Adrian hard in the chest. Adrian stumbled back, and Cam entered the condo, letting the door shut behind him. "Why would you snake me?"

Adrian didn't waste his time looking confused about what he meant. Instead, he took the toothbrush from his mouth and set it on the island.

"She chose up, man. Ain't nothing more to it," he said, giving Cam a bored face. "I was feeling her before you even knew she existed."

"I hollered at her first. You shoulda had enough respect for me to fall back."

"Respect?" Adrian scoffed. "Nigga, you don't respect me. So why would I give a fuck about shit you're talking about? Like I said, she chose up."

"Nah, she'll be back. She knows a real nigga when she sees one."

"I know. And that's why I was her first."

His words stopped Cam in his tracks. He couldn't have said what he thought he'd said. Visions of Adrian with Kiesha flooded his mind and made him clench his fists.

"Nigga, you aren't about to shove me like you just did without me busting your ass. So if you take a swing, just know how I'm coming."

Cam wanted to fight Adrian. He wanted to slam his fist into his face, but if he did, an inevitable fight between two savages would ensue. He didn't know if he was angrier about Adrian being with Kiesha, or about the fact that she had chosen up. He was the one who received the cutoff message, not Adrian. He unclenched his fists and let out a big breath before rubbing his face.

"You good?" Adrian asked.

"Nah. But I will be. Bitches come and go every day."

"It was nothing personal, man. This was just one of them crazy things that happened. We can't let it come between our business."

"Nothing would ever get between me and my money. But you better treat her right, or else a nigga like me will come swooping back in. She's a good girl."

"I know it," Adrian said and began to say something else, but his phone rang. He looked at the phone and made a face before showing Cam that it was Drako. He answered it and put it on speaker. "Hello?"

"You niggas thought you were on to somethin' last night at the club, huh? All you did was piss Steelo off."

"You and Steelo can suck a fat one and get the fuck on. You know what it is with me. If I see you again, it's sparks, nigga." Adrian's lip curled as he spoke.

"Nah. I think we can work something else out. Something everyone can benefit from. And by everyone, I mean Steelo and me."

"Nigga, get off my phone. I said what I sa—"

"Adrian! Adrian, help! Please help me!"

The terrified cries of a woman stopped him midsentence. They weren't the cries of just anybody. It was Kiesha.

"Kiesha!" Adrian shouted, and Cam grew more alert. "If you hurt her, I'll—"

"Too late. I already punched the bitch in the face a few times. But you can save her life by doing one simple thing."

"What?"

"Hand over your crown. He wants your connect and complete list of clientele."

"You sound crazy!" Adrian exclaimed, but he wished he'd bitten his tongue when he heard a loud thud, and Kiesha screamed again. "Stop it!"

"I will once you do what I ask. You have five minutes to decide or she dies. Damn, nigga, didn't your pops ever teach you to hide your heart? You made it too easy to find last night at the club."

On that note Drako hung up the phone, leaving both of them dazed. Adrian paced back and forth while Cam put his hands on his head. He didn't know what they were going to do. There was no way they could give Steelo what he wanted.

"Adrian," Cam said but got ignored. "Adrian!"

"Hold on, I'm thinking. I'm thinking!"

"Thinking about what? We can't give him what he wants!" Cam shouted.

"We can't just let him kill her either."

"I know. Fuck!" Cam wanted to punch a wall. "What we gon' do?"

Adrian didn't say anything. And before they had come up with a solid plan, the phone rang again. It was Drako.

"I'm here," Adrian answered and put it on speaker.

"Did you decide?"

"Yeah. Yeah, man. I'll do it," Adrian said to Cam's surprise.

"Good. Steelo wants to meet you today and get this shit squared away expeditiously. Then you and your bitch can ride off into the sunset."

"Where?"

"Turner."

"The dock?"

"Yup. You know where that's at?"

"I'll be there."

"Five o'clock sharp. And come alone. Don't pull any of the shit you did last night at the club."

He hung up again and left Adrian staring at the phone in his hand. Cam couldn't believe he had made such a decision. He stared at him incredulously.

"Nigga, what did you just do?"

"Bought us some time."

Chapter 27

Five o'clock came both too fast and too slow for Adrian's taste. Cam tried his hardest to talk Adrian out of going to the dock alone, but his mind was already made up. He wasn't going to let Kiesha die due to a part of his life that she didn't even know existed. She was innocent in it all, and she had a long life ahead of her. The decision made itself, really.

There was a small building on the dock that Adrian had been instructed to arrive at. When he parked his vehicle, he tucked one gun in his pants and another on his ankle. He didn't know what to expect, but Steelo was the type to play dirty, so Adrian assumed the worst.

He grabbed a small suitcase from the passenger seat, got out of his car, and walked to the entrance of the old building. As soon as he walked through the door, the strong aroma of fish invaded his nostrils. The building must have been an old packing spot, because there were blood spots all over the ground and a few old tables still set up.

Adrian was immediately greeted with hostility as men armed with assault rifles checked him for weapons. They took the gun that he had on his waistline and a knife that he had in the pocket on the inside of his suit. Once they were done, they let him pass. He didn't have to walk too far being that Steelo was standing in the main area of the building. He, too, was wearing a suit. His was black, and he wore the shades on his face to match. Upon seeing Adrian there on time, he pretended to give him a standing ovation.

As Adrian approached them, he noticed two hallways in either direction that led off to God knew where, but it seemed as though Steelo's whole entourage was right there waiting for him. He stopped walking and rested with his hands in front of him, holding the briefcase. Malcom and Draco were among the people there, and when Drako stepped to the side, he revealed a bound and bloody Kiesha. She was tied to a chair, and the fear in her eyes tugged at Adrian's heart. Her hair was disheveled, and there was a gash under one of her eyes.

"Adrian!" she cried when she saw him standing there.

"I'm going to get you out of this, Kiesha, I promise," he assured her.

"How . . . sentimental," Steelo said, stepping forward. "I'm glad that you decided to take this matter seriously. I'm pleased that you aren't a hothead like that father of yours. Did you bring what I asked of you?"

"It's right here." Adrian patted the briefcase. "The name of our connect and our list of clientele."

"And how can I trust their cooperation with the new management change?"

"Once they find out that I easily folded for a girl, they'll cut ties with me. You shouldn't have anything to worry about. Unless they find out that you're a snitch."

Steelo let Adrian's words settle. Once they did, a chuckle escaped his mouth. He nudged Drako and pointed at the briefcase.

"Go get it," he instructed.

"No," Adrian said and tightened his grip. "You won't be getting anything until she's cut free and standing at my side."

"And why do you think we won't just kill you and take it?"

"Because you need a code to unlock it. The inside is riddled with explosives, so if you try to open it without the code, it will explode."

"Nigga, this ain't Indiana Jones!" Steelo exclaimed, but the look on Adrian's face told him that he was serious. "Fine. Untie the girl. And go get the briefcase."

Drako gave Steelo a funny look at first, but he eventually obliged. He cut Kiesha free and walked her to Adrian with a gun to her head. When they got to him, he snatched the briefcase and glared at Adrian.

"What's the code?" he asked, but Adrian's eyes were too fixated on Kiesha's injuries. "Tell me the code or I blow her brains out!"

"It's three, two, eight, two," Adrian said without taking his gaze off of Kiesha.

Drako tried that number combination, and the briefcase unlocked. He glanced inside and saw the papers. After nodding at Steelo, he shoved Kiesha toward Adrian and took his boss the treasure. When he shoved Kiesha, she lost her footing, but Adrian caught her before she fell to the ground. Her tears hit his neck as she sobbed, and he held tightly. Words couldn't express how sorry he was to her, but that wasn't the place to try. He hurried to put her behind him and watched as Drako handed Steelo the briefcase. Once it was in his hand, he chuckled. Quickly that chuckle turned into a laugh of mania.

"So good doing business with you," he said. "But you know I can't let you walk out of here alive, right?"

"You slimy bastard. We had a deal!" Adrian exclaimed.

"Do you really think I'm going to make the same mistake your father made with me? He should have killed me, because shit like this festers. It turns into rage, and rage turns into get back. And it's time for me to be king again. I don't have time for you to come biting at my ankles in the future. Nah, I'm going to end you now. Kill him, Drako."

"Hold on, let me get the AK for this. I wanna fill their bodies up."

Kiesha whimpered behind Adrian when Drako went to grab the automatic weapon from one of the other men. While he did that, Steelo opened the briefcase to take a look at the files. Curiosity had gotten the best of him. Adrian watched with pleasure as Steelo's victorious smile turned into a scowl as he looked at the papers.

"What is this?" Steelo bellowed.

"What's wrong? Not what you were looking for?" Adrian asked innocently.

"This isn't what I asked for! These papers aren't filled with anything but restaurants and addresses!"

"Shoulda had your mans double-check." Adrian shrugged.

"This was very dumb of you, Adrian. You're going to die. But first I think we'll have some fun with her and make you watch. If you were gonna do something so stupid, you shouldn't have showed up alone. Get the girl!"

Steelo's men made a move at Adrian and Kiesha, but he snatched the .22 from his ankle. Upon seeing the gun, Steelo began to laugh, but Adrian pointed it at the closest man to him in all seriousness.

"What are you gonna do with that? Give him a bruise?" Steelo asked, still laughing.

"Nah. Worse." Adrian aimed at the man's chest and mouthed, "Boom."

Boom!

The gunshot was so loud that it was obvious it didn't come from the .22 in Adrian's hand. However, the man he was aiming at was sent flying back when a bullet opened up his chest. He fell to the ground dead, and Steelo's eyes widened.

"You asked me to come alone. You didn't say I couldn't already have people here." Adrian grinned as his shooter ran out from one of the hallways in the building. Cam was one of them and Milk was another. Milk was the one holding the smoking shotgun, and he stared at Drako with contempt in his eyes.

The moment Drako told Adrian the meeting spot was at the Turner dock, the tables turned to favor him. It was the same dock Milk had a boat at, and the building was one he knew like the back of his hand, including a sliding-door room where fishermen used to store their supplies. With his help, Adrian was able to send his men hours ahead of him to hide out in that room until it was time for the meeting. The only thing was the room was so far back that Adrian had just hoped they would come to his rescue on time. Luck seemed to be on his side.

"Kill them all!" Steelo shouted, and Adrian jumped out of the way with Kiesha as automatic rounds began to spray.

"Adrian, are we going to die?" Kiesha breathed.

"I didn't do all this for us to die. Plus, we just got together last night. I'm trying to at least make this relationship last more than a day. Here." He handed her the .22, and her eyes grew into saucers.

"What am I supposed to do with this?"

"Stay behind this table. If anybody comes up to you, aim and shoot."

Before she could say anything else to him, Adrian took off to where Cam was taking cover behind a pillar. As he ran, bullets ricocheted off the ground, missing him with each step he took. By the time he reached Cam, his adrenaline was pumping, and all he wanted to do was put a bullet between Steelo's eyes.

"I need a gun!" he said to Cam over the gunfire.

"First you take my bitch. Now you take my gun. Here, nigga, damn!"

Cam handed him a Glock 19 and went back to shooting the enemy. He caught one man in his neck and the other in the forehead. While he did that, Adrian scoped out the scene in search of Steelo. He spotted Milk and Drako exchanging fire. Not too far from them, he saw Malcom sprawled out on the ground in a pool of blood with a face full of bullets. Finally, his eyes found Steelo sneaking out the back of the building.

"Cover me!" he shouted, and Cam nodded.

Adrian took a breath and ran after Steelo. As he ran, men aiming at him dropped like flies. Cam's aim was impeccable. When Adrian got to the back door, he burst through it, ready to shoot, but Steelo was nowhere in the distance.

"Ahhh!" The shout came from his side.

He tried to aim his gun, but Steelo tackled him before he could, knocking the weapon out of his hand. The two of them wrestled on the ground, throwing punches when they could. For an older man, Steelo was strong, Adrian had to admit. His nose leaking blood was proof of that, but still he didn't give up. He'd come to Miami and not only caused a ruckus, but he also tried to kill Kiesha. That was unforgivable. Summoning all his strength, Adrian knocked Steelo to the ground and made a quick grab for his gun. When he pointed it at the defeated man, Steelo began to clap again.

"I guess I underestimated you."

"You did. Your first mistake was assuming I was like my father. Your second was being shocked that I wasn't," Adrian spat. "Not knowing your enemy was your demise. I guess that comes with playing nice with the Feds. You start to believe you're really untouchable."

For the next words he had to say, his trigger finger did the talking. By the way Steelo's face nodded with each bullet entering it, he got the message. Adrian spat on his dead body before going back into the building. The gunfire had subsided, and everyone Steelo had come with was laid out dead on the ground. Including Drako.

"He had it coming to him after what he did to Jerry," Milk said when Adrian approached him.

"They all did. Thanks for coming through, man. I'm sorry I had to bring you out of retirement," Adrian said and slapped his hand.

"I don't think you can ever really get away from this life," Milk said and looked around. "You all better get out of here before the police come. The boats are too far away from here for their cameras to have picked up anything, but I'm sure somebody heard the shots."

"What about you?" Adrian asked.

"Me? I was never here."

Milk winked at him and made his way to the door. Adrian would be quick to follow, but there was someone he had to check on first.

"Adrian!" Kiesha ran to him.

Her lip quivered as she looked around at all the dead bodies. Adrian took her gently by the side of her face and forced her to look at him.

"Don't look at them. Look at me. Are you okay?"

"I . . . I'm alive. But they . . . they—"

"They're dead. But we're alive," he said, and they locked eyes. "Now you know about the other side of my business. But you can't tell anyone, okay?"

She didn't say anything at first. She pulled her face out of his hands and looked around at the ground again. Her gaze jumped from one dead body to the next. Finally, she turned back to him and shocked him by hugging him.

"You came to save me. You saved me."

"I'll always be here to save you," he said, tightly hugging her back.

In the distance, Adrian saw Cam looking at them. His eyes were hard to read, but Adrian gave him a nod. Cam sent one back and left the building with the others.

"Come on," Adrian told her, taking her by the hand and leading her outside. "You have to go see a doctor about your bruises."

"The hospital?"

"Nah, you can't go there. Not after something like this has happened. We have a family doctor for shit like this. I'm going to have him come check you out at my house. Afterward, if you make the choice to rock with me, I'll let you know a little bit about the family business."

When they were outside, they walked quickly to his car. He helped her inside and shut the door. He was sure that when she signed up for the internship, her last thought was that she would take part in something like this. But he hoped she would have an open mind. He thought he would be able to ease her into his complete line of work, but the universe had had other plans.

He got into the driver's seat and pulled off from the dock, and when they'd been driving for about five minutes, his phone rang. It was his father.

"Hello?"

"Hey, son. I was just calling to let you know my flight will be in first thing in the morning. How has business been?"

Adrian paused when he felt Kiesha's hand find its way to his. He glanced over at her, and she smiled gratefully at him. He tenderly squeezed her hand before looking back to the long road ahead of him.

"Everything is fine, Pop. Business is business."

Lost and Found

by

Marcus Weber

Chapter 1

After serving ten years in the Marines, Sheba Styles was getting out. She joined when she was 18, and there she found great fulfillment and great personal satisfaction living and fighting as a Marine. But the time had come to put that life behind her and begin a new chapter. Her aunt Millicent had recently died, and it was time for her to come home and take care of her family.

Sheba checked out of the Panzer Kaserne barracks in Böblingen, Germany—the headquarters of the U.S. Marine Corps European and Africa commands—and headed for the States. She planned to visit a friend and fellow Marine, Colin Web, in Albany, New York. He was there on leave spending time with his family. She spent the day with him, getting some much-needed R&R before heading to the Albany bus terminal for the trip to Atlanta.

"Why are you taking the bus?"

"Because I like it. I like to sit back, relax, and look out the window. Despite how fucked up it can be sometimes, this is a beautiful country we live in."

"Greatest country in the world, Marine," Colin laughed.

"True, but that would be ex-Marine."

"Whatever. When you're a Marine, you're a Marine for life." He shook his head. "I still can't believe that you're getting out. I thought we'd be doing what we do until we were old and gray."

"There was a time when I thought that too. I planned to retire after a distinguished thirty-year career. But it's time for me to go home and take care of my family."

Her cousin Chanel had been in her ear for years about the family being in disarray and Sheba needing to come home. Those pleas fell on deaf ears until recently. Her grandfather had always handled all the family's business, and when he passed, that responsibility fell to their oldest daughter, Millicent. Now that her aunt had passed, there was no one to take care of her grandmother's affairs. Miss Pearl was the woman who raised Sheba, and she felt that responsibility now fell to her.

"And I know how close you are to her, so I get it." Colin leaned forward. "I just don't like it, that's all."

She chuckled. "I'm sure you'll be able to push through somehow," Sheba said and got ready to leave for the bus terminal.

The next stop for her was Atlanta, Georgia. Although Sheba was born in New York, she had lived in Georgia for as long as she could remember. And when her mother died when Sheba was 8, her grandmother raised her. This was her first trip stateside in five years. It was a choice that she made to stay away, but now it was something that she regretted. Despite her feelings about her aunt Millicent, Sheba should not have let that separate her from her grandmother and the rest of her family.

Her Greyhound bus was scheduled to depart at ten forty-five p.m. and arrive at New York's Port Authority in Manhattan at one thirty-five a.m. When the bus arrived in New York, Sheba grabbed her backpack and exited the bus. There was layover of an hour and ten minutes before she had to catch the bus departing for Baltimore, Maryland, at two forty-five a.m.

With time to kill, and never having been to New York, Sheba decided that she would leave the terminal and take a walk around the city that she'd heard so much about her entire life. It wasn't like Sheba could see much in the time that she had, but at least she could say that she'd

been to Times Square, the world-famous tourist destination and entertainment center.

There weren't many people on the street as she strolled
casually down Eighth Avenue toward West Thirty-ninth
Street, looking up at the buildings and in the windows
of the stores as she passed thinking that she wasn't
impressed. She had been to cities around the world, and
this was one of the so-called greatest cities on the planet,
so she was expecting better. She had to take into account
that it was damn near two in the morning, and then there
was the fact that bus stations were never located in the
best part of town.

"So cut the Apple some slack," Sheba said aloud as she
heard what sounded like an argument.

Being a trained observer, and curious to the point
of being nosy by nature, Sheba slowed her pace as she
approached the alley where the sound was coming from.

"What do you mean you ain't got it?"

"I mean, I ain't got it with me, but it's close!"

Sheba peeked in the alley and could see four men,
all with guns in hand but they were not pointed at
each other. One of the men was carrying a briefcase
in his other hand. She had accidentally walked up on a
drug deal in progress.

This is what I should have expected, Sheba thought as
she looked on.

After taking a second or two to laugh at the irony,
Sheba was about to move on when one of the men raised
his gun and shot the man with the briefcase in the head.
The sudden sound of the gunshot startled her, and Sheba
watched as the man dropped his gun and then the briefcase before dropping to his knees and falling flat on his
face.

"Oh, shit," she said in a whisper.

That was when the shooting started, and Sheba hit the ground. She lay there with her hand over her head as the shooting continued and then stopped just as suddenly. Sheba got to her feet, brushed herself off, and then looked into the alley. There lay the dead man with the gun and briefcase on either side of him. Sheba looked around the street. There didn't seem to be anybody around, and that included the men who had done the shooting. She looked at the dead body once again and then at the briefcase.

Suppose it's full of money?

Sheba looked around the street once again, then to the dead body and the briefcase, and she started for it. Without doing any serious reconnaissance of the situation, her assessment in the moment was that all the men were dead and that money was there for the taking. Sheba stopped and looked around one more time before she scooped up the briefcase and the gun and made her way back to the bus station as quickly as she could.

Chapter 2

"Where the fuck is the briefcase?" one of the men asked seconds later when they got back to the alley.

"It was right there," the other said, pointing to the spot where the briefcase had been.

"Well, it ain't there now! Come on!" he shouted and ran toward the street.

"You see anybody?"

"No, wait." He pointed down the street. "Blue jacket, heading for the bus station. Come on!"

"That looks like a woman."

"I think you're right," he said as both men ran to the bus station and went inside. "You see her?"

"No, do you?"

"No. It's like looking for a needle in a haystack."

"Fuck that. We gotta find her."

"How?"

"Maybe she's getting on a bus that's leaving soon."

"Good idea. Let's check the departure board."

The men rushed to the board and saw that two buses were departing shortly. One was going to Philadelphia, Pennsylvania, and the other to Baltimore, Maryland.

"I'll take Baltimore, and you head for Philly," one said, and they split up.

As he got closer to the gate, he could see that the bus was boarding. He rushed to the door and was about to grab the handle when a ticket agent stepped in front of him.

"You have a ticket?" he asked, knowing that all the passengers had boarded.

"No, but I gotta get out there."

"Not without a ticket," the agent said firmly as an NYPD officer walked up.

"Any problems?"

He had just killed a man, and the gun was in his pocket. "No, Officer," he said, backing away with his hands up. He went back to the departure board to meet up with his partner.

"Did you see her?"

"If I did, would I be standing here empty-handed waiting for you?"

"What now?"

"I'm thinking she had to get on one of those buses."

"Unless she came in one door and went out another."

"That's possible, but no. She came in here to get on a bus and get out of the city."

"So what do we do now?"

"I take Baltimore, and you head for Philly," he said and began walking quickly toward the exit.

He rushed to catch up before he asked, "You mean drive to Philly?"

"And get there before the bus does, so you better hurry up, because you gotta steal a car first."

"Why I gotta steal the car?"

"Because I got the keys," he said, dangling them in front of him.

"You fuckin' suck."

"I'll call you when I get to Baltimore."

"I knew I should have driven," he said, and the men rushed off in different directions.

Once Sheba was back on the bus, she relaxed in her seat and tried to behave like she hadn't just witnessed a murder and there wasn't a briefcase full of money sitting on the seat next to her. They had crossed the George Washington Bridge into New Jersey, and most of the other passengers had turned off their overhead lights before Sheba picked up the case and placed it gently on her lap. Surprised that it wasn't locked, she cracked open the case slightly and looked inside.

"Dayyymn," she said in a whisper, closing the case and locking it.

Instead of the money that she was expecting, Sheba found four kilos of cocaine.

"I just knew it was money."

She sat looking out the window, wondering what she was going to do with that much cocaine, but she knew the answer.

"Sell it."

It wasn't that she was a stranger to the game. It was sort of the family business. Her parents sold drugs in New York until a warrant was issued for their arrest and they fled to Atlanta. However, her father didn't stay long. He thought it best that they separate, and he went to Detroit, intending to make something happen to get them back in the game. He was killed by undercover police officers during a buy. Her mother stayed involved in the game until she died two years later speedballing heroin and cocaine. Sheba also had a couple of cousins in the game in Atlanta who she would talk to about getting rid of the kilos. With that settled, Sheba looked out the window at the night sky and relaxed in her seat for the ride to Baltimore.

When the bus arrived in Baltimore for a scheduled thirty-five-minute stop, Sheba decided to get off to use the bathroom and get something to eat. But since it wasn't a food stop, she would have to settle for whatever she could find in the vending machine. Not wanting to leave it on the bus, she got the gun that she had taken from the dead man, got her backpack, and took the briefcase with her.

Sheba entered the terminal and looked around for the restroom sign. Once she saw it, she headed in that direction along with a few of her fellow passengers. Therefore, she didn't notice that her pursuer was walking right behind her.

He thought about simply snatching the briefcase from her hand and running, or better yet, he could shoot her in the back of the head and take the case from her dead body. But there were cops in the terminal, and either plan would cause too much attention. He followed her to the restroom and planned to make his approach once she came out. Then he'd walk up behind her, shove his gun in her spine, and walk her out of there quietly.

"Easy peasy."

That plan went out the window when a cop walked by just as Sheba came out of the restroom.

"Shit," he muttered and went after her, thinking that the plan was still viable, but he just needed to catch up with her before she got back on the bus.

As she walked back to the bus, Sheba got a sense that caused her to glance over her shoulder, and she saw the man following. She recalled seeing him in the lobby when she came into the terminal and then again outside the restroom when she came out.

Instead of returning to the bus, Sheba walked a little faster into a crowd of people heading toward the exit. That made it harder for him to see her. He watched her weaving through the crowd but quickly lost sight of her. He rushed outside and looked around, but he didn't see her anywhere. And then he felt the feeling of metal in the small of his back.

"You need to stand real still and don't make a sound." Sheba reached around and took the gun from his waist. "Now we're gonna walk. Nice, slow, and quiet," she said, knowing that she was going to have to kill him.

There was no other choice.

Although Sheba was no stranger to killing in combat, this would be different. This would be murder. But in the back of her mind, Sheba knew that it could come to this as soon as she opened the briefcase and saw that she had stolen four kilos of cocaine. He and his partner had already killed for it, and that brought up another question.

Is he alone?

She needed to end this. It was just a matter of where. Just then, the man turned quickly and lunged for the gun. Sheba stepped back, raised the gun, and fired twice. Both shots hit the man in his chest and the impact took him off his feet.

Sheba stepped up and stood over him. He was still alive, holding his chest and looking up at her. She shot him once more in the chest and once in the head before running away from the scene.

Chapter 3

Once she was a couple of blocks away from the bus station, Sheba stopped running but continued walking quickly. Knowing that she'd just killed a man and there may be more men looking for her, Sheba decided not to get back on the bus. But she still needed to get off the street.

"Taxi!" she shouted and waved her arm in the air until one stopped, and she got in.

"Where to?"

"Take me to a hotel near the airport."

"You got a preference?"

"Is there a Marriott?"

"Courtyard."

"That works," Sheba said, and the driver took Sheba to the Courtyard by Marriott in Linthicum.

Upon her arrival at the Courtyard, Sheba went to check into the king suite and went to the room. Her first order of business was to call Chanel to tell her not to pick her up at the bus terminal.

"I decided to drive instead."

"Why? You hate to distance drive. What's up with that?"

"I need to think and clear my head," Sheba said instead of telling her that she was safer driving than on the bus.

"I thought that was the whole point of catching the bus."

"It was, but the bus wasn't gonna stop where I wanted it to," she said, thinking fast.

"Where did you wanna stop?" Chanel asked, because being naturally curious to the point of being nosy ran in the family.

"I won't know until I see it. It's called being spontaneous. You should try it sometimes."

"I know Miss Rules and Regulations isn't telling me about spontaneity."

"Oh, but I am. It's something that I've discovered lately. Acting on impulse and living in the moment."

"How's that working for you?"

Sheba glanced at the briefcase and the gun on the bed. "I'll let you know."

"So when should we expect you?"

"I don't know. Sometime tonight, early tomorrow maybe."

"Could you be any less specific?"

"Why, what's up?"

"Nothing, I just need to know what to tell Grandma when she asks. You know she's been asking all day."

"Tell her that I'll see her either tonight or tomorrow." She paused. "Chanel?"

"Yes."

"You better not have planned a welcome home party for me."

"Welcome home party, no. Because you already said, 'I don't want no damn welcome home party,'" she said, imitating the way Sheba barked orders that just about everybody in the family followed. If Sheba said it, it was law.

"Better not be."

"What did you tell me? You said you don't want no damn welcome home party, so there isn't gonna be any damn welcome home party."

"All right, then. I will see you when I see you, cuz. I'm going to take a shower and get some sleep before I head out."

"All right, then, Sheba. You drive safe, and I'll see you when you get here."

"You gonna be at Grandma's?"

"I'm not leaving until you get here," Chanel said and ended the call.

After talking to Chanel, as promised, Sheba got undressed and headed to the bathroom. After a long, hot shower, she got into bed and tried to get some sleep. It wasn't easy at first, as Sheba kept replaying the murder over and over again in her mind, trying to think if it could have gone another way, but all the while knowing that it went the only way that it could have.

Not only had Sheba witnessed a drug deal gone terribly wrong and one man murdered, but she had also taken the drugs. She was going to have to kill him no matter how it went. His lunging for the gun just made it easier for her. The question was posed once again.

What now? Sheba asked herself, and the pursuit of an answer was enough to lull her to sleep if only for a little while.

When she woke up a couple of hours later, Sheba had some idea of what she was going to do next. It involved food, so she got dressed and walked across the street to the Chick-fil-A to get something to eat. When she got back to the room, Sheba took out the gun she'd used to kill the man, as well as her service weapon, and placed them both on the table in front of her.

As she ate her food, Sheba took apart the murder weapon and broke it into its four basic parts: the action, the frame, the clip, and the barrel. With those two tasks taken care of, Sheba called to rent a car. Once she was ready, she caught the hotel's airport shuttle to pick up the car for a slow drive to Atlanta.

When she stopped for gas in Richmond, she threw away the action before returning to her vehicle and continuing south on Interstate 95. She threw away the frame during a food stop in Raleigh, the clip in Florence, and the barrel was left in a gas station garbage can in Columbia, South Carolina, before she went and checked into a hotel for the night.

"Hello."

"Where you at?" Chanel asked excitedly, thinking that Sheba should be close to Atlanta by then.

"I'm at the Hampton Inn in Columbia, South Carolina."

"Really, Sheba?"

"Really. I'm tired of driving, so I'm gonna get something to eat, get some sleep, and leave in the morning." She paused. "If that's all right with you, of course."

"It's fine, and please forgive me for being excited about seeing my bestie cousin for the first time in five years."

"It wouldn't have been five years if you had told James no and met me in Abu Dhabi."

"True. But the point is still the same. I miss you, and I'm excited to see you and so is everybody else, especially Grandma."

"See, Chanel, it's when you say stuff like that that makes me think you're planning some big welcome home party."

"And I say again, what did you tell me? You said you don't want no damn welcome home party."

"I'm serious, Chanel."

There was silence on the line. "Let me stop lying. Look, Sheba, it's like this. You're having a welcome home party whether you like it or not because it's Grandma's house, and she wants to have a party for you. So seriously, Sheba, you tell me, what was I gonna say? 'No, Grandma, you know Sheba, and she said she don't want no damn party'?"

"And then you should have ducked before she threw something at you for cussin' in her house."

"Right. Then she would have told me that I sounded like a fool and to do what she said to do."

"You're right. That's exactly what she'd say."

"So face it, you're having a party when you get here." Chanel laughed. "It actually started last night."

"Last night?"

"Yes, Sheba, you were supposed to get here last night. I was supposed to pick you up from the bus and take you to your party. And you know this bunch. Just because you weren't coming . . ."

"Wasn't no reason to cancel the party."

"It's still going on right now, and since you ain't coming until tomorrow, I imagine that it will still be going on when you get here."

"Y'all have fun." Sheba laughed. "I'll see you tomorrow."

Once she ended the call with Chanel, Sheba freshened up and then went to eat at a nearby restaurant called Private Property, where she enjoyed the blackened redfish, before returning to her room. Sheba got a good night's sleep, was on the road a little after noon, and was turning down her grandmother's street just before four that afternoon.

Chapter 4

As Sheba drove down the street she grew up on, a rush of happy memories washed over her as she passed the house looking for a place to park and not finding one. There were cars in the driveway and on the grass in front of the house, so she kept driving. She found a spot to park on the next block and walked back. As she got closer, she could smell the meat burning on the grill. That meant her uncle Willie was back there. So instead of going in the front door, as she was expected to do, Sheba opened the gate and walked around to the back.

She could hear the sound of children playing in the backyard before she saw Chanel's children, the nieces, Jelena, Erica, Sandra, and her nephew Nelson, whom she hadn't seen in so long that she barely recognized them. Sheba walked up behind her uncle.

"You saving one of those bones for me?"

"Sheba," he said, smiling brightly without looking in her direction. "I got these bad boys right here slow grilling on the outside just for you."

"You know I like them just a little burnt on the outside and juicy on the inside."

Uncle Willie turned toward Sheba with his arms out. "Come here, girl," he said and hugged her. "Damn, it's good to see you." He broke their embrace. "You look good," he said and hugged her again.

"How are you doing?"

"Oh, my back's trying to act up more than usual these days, but other than that, I'm doing fine for an old man."

"You ain't old, Uncle Willie—"

"If you say that I'm seasoned or vintage, you can forget about them bones."

"I wasn't going to say either one of those. I was going to say you're not old, you're my favorite uncle," Sheba said and hugged him. "How's Aunt Ella?"

"She's fine, inside with everybody else." He paused. "You haven't been inside?"

"Not yet. I smelled the meat cooking, and I came to say hello to you."

He laughed. "Chanel said you didn't want no party, but you should know that your grandmother was going to insist. Her baby is home."

"Home for good."

"And Miss Pearl is so glad you are. I'm just surprised you got out, that's all."

"Without actually saying it, Chanel made it seem like I needed to do more than just come home for a couple of weeks to see Grandma. So how is she?"

"Hear her tell it, she's fine. But I've been hanging around here the last couple of days, watching her." He shook his head. "Your grandmother is slowing down."

"What do you mean?"

"You know how she is, all over the house, into everything and everybody."

"And?"

"She'll be that way for a while, but . . ."

"But what?"

"Like last night, one minute she was there in the kitchen, and the next she was gone. Chanel went to check on her, and she was in the bed."

"What time was this?"

"Whatever time you called and told Chanel you weren't coming, it was a little while after that."

"That is early for her, and with company in the house."

"See what I'm saying? Chanel's doing the best she can, but them four kids running her ragged. And that sorry-ass James ain't no help."

"You never did like him."

"And he gives me new reasons every day not to like him. That is one sorry-ass man," Uncle Willie said and looked at his grandchildren. "Jelena, Erica! Y'all come here," he said, and all four children came to see what their grandfather wanted. "I want you all to meet your aunt Sheba," he said, and Nelson ran quickly to the house and burst inside.

"Aunt Sheba is here!" he exclaimed and ran back outside.

All the people who were in the house bounced to their feet and rushed outside to greet the returning veteran. There were hugs and kisses and tears of happiness as aunts, uncles, cousins, other family, and old friends welcomed Sheba home. But there was one person in particular she didn't see.

"Where's Grandma?" Sheba asked.

"She was going upstairs to get changed last time I saw her," Chanel advised her.

Sheba headed for the stairs to her grandmother's room and tapped gently on the door. "Grandma," she said, pushing the door gently and walking in.

"There's my baby," Miss Pearl said and hugged her first-born granddaughter. "How are you, Ashebe?" her grandmother asked, calling her by her real name.

Her full name was Ashebe Loretta Styles. However, the name was too many syllables for the toddler, so she began referring to herself as Sheba.

"I'm fine, Grandma."

"I was just on my way down to see you."

"Well, I came to see you first. How are you, Grandma?"

"Doing fine, child. I am just so glad to see you home and home for good this time."

"Yes, ma'am. I am here to stay."

"You thought any about what you're gonna do now that you ain't a slave to Uncle Sam?" Miss Pearl asked and coughed lightly.

"Hadn't even thought about it. Just glad to be here with you. But are you all right? Uncle Willie said that you seemed a little tired."

"Willie needs to mind his business and worry about that young girl he thinks his wife don't know about."

Sheba laughed as they left the room on the way downstairs. "He did say his back was bothering him," she said, and they went to join the family and the welcome home celebration.

As the afternoon wore on and turned into night, Sheba found that it went exactly the way Uncle Willie said it would. At first, Miss Pearl was her usual self, all over the house, into everything, and talking and laughing with everybody, but eventually she slowed down and retreated into her kitchen sanctuary. Sheba was about to go in and check on her when the room erupted.

"Jody!" half of the room shouted enthusiastically when her cousin arrived at the house. He was kind of the family rock star, but that wasn't the reason for their reaction. He and his brother Floyd had been banned from the house, so everybody was surprised to see him there.

"What's up, what's up? Where she at?" he said, high-fiving, fist-bumping, and exchanging hugs with family as he moved through the room. "Where is the guest of honor? There she is!" he shouted when he saw her. "Sheba the queen!"

"How you been doing, Jody?" Sheba asked, walking toward him with her arms out.

Jody picked her up and spun her around. "Doing great. Glad my cousin is home," he said and put her down.

"Glad to be home. Look at you." She felt his muscular arm. "All jacked and shit."

"Not a little boy anymore, Sheba."

She laughed. "You were skinny, but you were never a little boy."

"True, true. Where's Grandma?"

"In the kitchen."

"I'ma get with you in a minute. I need to say hello," he said, hugged her, and walked away toward the kitchen.

As the party continued, everybody was having a good time, laughing, drinking, and telling old stories and new lies. There was plenty to eat, and the music was good. The later it got, Sheba noticed that there were a couple of other people she hadn't seen.

"Where's Floyd?" she asked Jody.

"He said he might stop by, but if not, he'll get with you tomorrow."

"What's up with the whole banned from the house thing?"

"One Sunday after dinner, Grandma said that we couldn't come in the house no more." Jody shrugged his shoulders. "She still calls and checks on us like she always did, and if she doesn't hear from us, she'll call and fuss, and if she needs somebody, she don't mind calling and telling us what to do. We just can't come in the house."

"I'll ask her about it."

"Please do. Maybe then we'll understand it," Jody said and laughed.

"Where's Demi?" Sheba asked of their cousin.

Jody frowned. "Ain't no telling where that girl is."

"Why you say it like that?"

"Chanel ain't tell you? Demi is out of control. That's another reason I'm glad you're home. Maybe you can talk some sense into her. I tried talking to her, but you know how she is. Demi will sit there with that smile on her face, agreeing with everything you say, and she'll promise that she is done with all that and she gonna do better, and then she goes out and does exactly the opposite. I'm done with her, Sheba. All I can do now is to be there for her when she calls."

"I guess she's still doing her thing?"

"Deep into it." He shook and dropped his head. "Like I said, all I can do is be there for her."

"What?"

"What?"

"Tell me."

"Tell you what?"

"Why the look?"

Jody paused. "Like I said, Demi is out of control." He took Sheba by the hand, and they went outside on the back porch. He got both of them a beer from the cooler, and they sat down. "One night, a friend of mine calls me and says that Demi was there and I needed to come get her. So me and Floyd roll over there. When we get there, one nigga lets us in, but there's two or three other niggas in the apartment. My boy is guarding the bedroom door, not letting anybody in. I go in and there's Demi, laying half-naked on the bed, passed out."

"What you mean, half-naked?"

"I mean, her skirt was jacked up around her waist, she wasn't wearing panties, and her titties were hanging out. Half-naked."

Sheba shook her head over what her cousin was doing. "What did you do?"

"What else could I do? I straightened up her clothes, picked her up, and carried her out of there. But no, we didn't confront them niggas about it if that's what you're asking."

"That was what I was asking." She would have expected him to do or at least say something to defend Demi's honor, but she understood why he didn't. "That's fucked up."

"We took her to my apartment, and I had a PA friend of mine look at her."

"Did Demi say what happened to her?"

"She said she didn't remember what happened, but it was pretty obvious to me. To my PA friend too. So like I said, I'm done trying to talk to her. I just come rescue her when she calls."

"What about Floyd?"

"Floyd don't fuck with her at all."

"Why not?"

"I'll let him tell you that," Jody said, and they went back inside.

However, when Sheba got back into the house, she noticed that her grandmother was nowhere to be found. When she went upstairs to look for her, her grandmother said that she was tired and was going to relax for a while before bed. Sheba went straight back downstairs and got everybody's attention.

"I want to thank everybody for coming, but it's late and it's time to go—"

"Aww!" the guests said collectively.

"Grandma's said she's tired and wants to rest, and I'm tired from the drive, so it's time for y'all to go home."

It took a good forty-five minutes after that, but once the house was clear, Sheba looked at the mess in the living room and in the kitchen, decided that she would get on that in the morning, and went up to her old room to sleep.

Chapter 5

It was almost ten by the time Sheba got up and got out of bed. She'd woken up earlier that morning before the sun came up, but with no reason to get up other than getting started on cleaning up the house, Sheba went back to sleep. Once she had showered and dressed, she went downstairs to find that her grandmother had already cleaned the living room and was just about finished in the kitchen. Not only that, but she had also cooked Sheba her favorite childhood breakfast: blueberry waffles and bacon.

"Good morning, Grandma."

"Morning, Sheba," Miss Pearl said as she washed a dish and put it in the dishwasher.

"You didn't have to clean up, Grandma. I was gonna call Chanel, and we would've jumped on it this morning."

"Chanel got enough to do running after them bad kids," she said without looking away from her task. "Besides, I can't stand to walk around in a dirty house, much less cook in a nasty kitchen."

Sheba began clearing the kitchen table and putting items in the trash. "Your kitchen is never nasty, Grandma."

Miss Pearl stopped doing dishes and looked at her granddaughter. "The way you and Chanel left my kitchen last night was nasty."

"That's because we were gonna jump on it this morning."

"Really? And where is Chanel?"

"I—"

"She's at home running after them bad kids," she said before Sheba could answer and went back to doing the dishes. "I needed to get started so I could cook you breakfast."

"Are her kids really bad, Grandma?"

"Not really. Just active, noisy, and mischievous." Miss Pearl stopped. "I guess I'm getting old, because I ain't for all that running around, whooping, and hollering in my house."

"You mean like we used to do?"

"Yes, and I wasn't for it then. I'm glad you grew up and got some sense. Come on and sit down. I made you breakfast."

Miss Pearl went to the refrigerator, got the food, and put it in the microwave before sitting down with Sheba. It was then that she noticed that Miss Pearl was wheezing.

"You all right, Grandma?"

"Just a little tired is all." She coughed.

"And how long have you had that cough?" Sheba asked and got no answer. "When was the last time you checked your blood pressure?"

"It's been a few days."

"And?" Sheba asked as she ate.

"It was a little high."

"What's a little high?" Sheba asked and again got no answer. She started to get up. "I'm gonna check your blood pressure."

"No," Miss Pearl said quickly. "You finish eating, and I'll go get the cuff," she said and got up to get it.

She purposely took her time coming back with it so Sheba could finish eating. Since she hadn't been taking her medication, she had a pretty good idea of what was gonna happen next.

"One ninety-five over one thirty-eight is way too high." Sheba went to the cabinet where her grandmother kept her medication. "The pill box is empty."

"I haven't had time to show Chanel how to set them up."

"Grandma?" Sheba frowned, and Miss Pearl shrugged her shoulders. "I remember how to set them up. Where's your medication list?"

"On the cabinet door."

Sheba looked at the list and matched up the bottles. "You're out of a few medications," she said, picking up her phone to call the pharmacy to get them refilled. "The recording says that you're out of refills and they'll call your doctor for authorization, but we need to get your pressure down." Sheba paused to think. "Come on, get ready. I'm taking you to urgent care."

"I don't think we need to do all that. I just need to rest." Miss Pearl coughed.

"No." Sheba shook her head. "You are going to urgent care. Where are your insurance cards?"

"In the desk drawer in the living room," she said and got up from the table.

Sheba went into the living room and looked through the papers that were on the desk. Not seeing the cards, she began checking the drawers. She did find the insurance cards in the center drawer. What she also found were several past-due notices, including a final notice from the mortgage company. Feeling that the important thing right then was seeing about her grandmother's health, Sheba decided not to mention the bills.

When they got to urgent care, Sheba was informed that her grandmother's insurance was not being accepted and she would have to pay for her to be seen.

"How much would that be?"

"Two hundred and seventy-five dollars."

Sheba reached into her purse and handed the woman her credit card. Once she ran the card, Sheba was given a receipt, and she went to sit down with Miss Pearl.

"What was the problem?"

"For some reason, your insurance wasn't accepted," Sheba said and looked for a number to call on the back of the card.

"That doesn't make any sense."

"I'm calling the insurance company now to see what the problem is."

While Sheba was on hold to speak to customer service, a nurse came and took her grandmother to be seen by the doctor. When a service rep did come on the line, she told Sheba that the policy was canceled for nonpayment, and she was transferred to an agent.

"Unfortunately, your grandmother will need to reapply to be covered."

"I understand. I'm at urgent care with her right now."

"I will call you tomorrow, and we can get your grandmother reinstated. But that coverage won't take effect until the first of next month," the agent stated, and Sheba ended the call. Her next call was to the bank, where she was able to speak with the branch manager, who turned out to be the bearer of more bad news.

"Thank you very much for holding, Miss Styles," the branch manager said when she came back on the line. "And thank you very much for your patience."

"No problem. I just need to know what's going on with her accounts."

There was a second or two of silence.

"I was able to look into the matter and found that the account that the insurance payment was drawn from has been closed, as well as her savings account. The only active account Mrs. Harrison has open is the account that her social security check is deposited into."

"There must be some mistake. Why would my grand-mother close those accounts?"

"Your grandmother didn't close them. The accounts were closed by a Millicent Harrison. She has your grand-mother's power of attorney."

"I see." Sheba paused to exhale past her anger. "Thank you for letting me know."

"There's one more thing."

"What's that?"

"Were you aware that the house is in foreclosure and a final notice has been sent?"

"No, I wasn't aware," she said and thought about the past-due bills and the final notice she'd seen earlier. "How far behind is she?"

"$11,299.68."

"Shit. When was the last time a payment was made?"

"It's been over a year."

"How much would it cost to get the house out of fore-closure?"

"$2,394 will stop the action."

"Do you take credit cards for payment?"

"Yes, we certainly do. What's the card number?"

With that handled for the moment, Sheba's next call was to Chanel. "Did you know that Grandma's house was about to go into foreclosure and that she has no insurance?"

"What? I thought that Aunt Millicent was taking care of all that for her after Granddaddy died."

"I thought so too, but apparently what your aunt was doing was robbing Grandma blind. She closed all her accounts and stole her savings."

"You're kidding."

"I wish I weren't." Sheba saw a nurse come out of the back who appeared to be coming in her direction. "I'm at urgent care with Grandma, Chanel. I'll call you back."

"Why are you at urgent care with Grandma?" Chanel asked, but Sheba had already ended the call and was on her feet waiting for the nurse.

"Miss Styles?"

"Yes. How's my grandmother?"

"She's fine. We were able to get her pressure under control with medication, and she needs to follow up with her primary care physician to get her other medications up to date. However, the doctor is concerned about the persistent cough. Do you know how long she's had that?"

"No. I just got home from the military yesterday."

"I see. First, thank you very much for your service to our country."

"Thank you."

"The doctor would like to transfer your grandmother to Decatur Medical Center for further observation and to run some tests."

After that, Miss Pearl was transported by ambulance to Decatur Medical Center. Sheba sent Chanel a text message to meet her there, and then she headed for the hospital. Upon arrival, she got her grandmother checked in.

"Since your grandmother only has Medicare, she'll be billed for the amount that Medicare doesn't pay."

"I understand," Sheba said, signed as being the party responsible for the bill, and went to sit down in the waiting area. It was forty-five minutes later when Chanel arrived at the hospital and sat down.

"How's Grandma?"

"I haven't heard anything yet."

"What's wrong with her?"

"I checked her blood pressure this morning—"

"She let you check it? I try, but she never lets me. She says she is a grown woman and is more than capable of checking her own pressure."

"Well, it was really high, and when I went to get her meds, she was out of her pressure pills and a couple of others, so I took her to urgent care, and that was when I found out she has no insurance."

"I was sure Aunt Millicent was taking care of all of that for Grandma."

"Apparently not. Apparently, she was robbing her blind before she died."

"That is so foul," Chanel said as Demi came into the waiting room.

"If she weren't already dead, I'd kill her myself," Sheba said.

"If who weren't already dead?" Demi asked.

"Your mother," Sheba said and hugged her. "Hey, Demi." She broke their embrace and looked at her younger cousin. "You lost weight, and your face looks drawn."

"Whatever, Sheba," Demi said and hugged Sheba again. "It's good to see you."

"It's good to see you too."

"Now, what did the Wicked Witch of the West do this time?" Demi asked of her mother, calling her by the name they used to call her as kids.

"She was stealing all of Grandma's money," Chanel said as the doctor approached them.

"Miss Styles? I'm Dr. Kulkarni. I'm a pulmonologist here at Decatur Medical Center, and I conducted the examination of your grandmother."

"How is she?"

"My preliminary diagnosis of her condition is emphysema. It's a disease of the lungs that usually develops after many years of smoking."

"She quit smoking two years ago," Chanel said.

"But she'll be the first one to tell you that she started smoking when she was thirteen," Demi added.

"Emphysema is a condition that involves damage to the walls of the alveoli of the lung. Alveoli are small, thin-walled, very fragile air sacs located in clusters at the end of the bronchial tubes deep inside the lungs," Dr. Kulkarni advised them.

"What's the treatment for emphysema?" Sheba wanted desperately to know.

"Once it develops, emphysema can't be reversed."

Chapter 6

It was late the following afternoon when Sheba got home from the hospital. Dr. Kulkarni recommended that Miss Pearl be kept overnight for observation. However, when Sheba arrived to take her grandmother home the following day, she was informed by the hospital staff that the doctor had ordered the tests she had spoken to Sheba about.

"The diagnosis of emphysema cannot be made based solely on the symptoms," Dr. Kulkarni explained the night before. "There are several tests that are used to make the diagnosis. I'm going to order a CAT scan and spirometry and pulmonary function tests to determine airway blockage. I'd also like to do an ECG to check her heart function and rule out heart disease as a cause of her shortness of breath."

With everything going on with Miss Pearl and her health, Sheba barely had time to think about the fact that her aunt Millicent had stolen from her grandmother and left her uninsured and on the verge of foreclosure. Maybe she had a reason to do it, but for the life of her, Sheba couldn't see one. All she could think was, *how could she do that to her own mother?*

"Did you know what your mother was doing?" Sheba asked Demi the night before at the hospital.

"That she had stolen money from Grandma? No, I didn't know anything about it," Demi said, but it was only partially true. She didn't know that her mother had stolen money from her mother, but she knew the money to pay off the loan sharks came from somewhere. She looked at the rage in Sheba's eyes and knew her cousin well enough to know that she should keep the story to herself at least for the time being.

"You sure?" Chanel asked. "Because this sounds more like some shit you might do."

"Damn, that's fucked up, Chanel."

"What? You trying to act all brand new because Sheba's here. Is that what this is?" She paused. "Because I know you, and I know that you will do whatever, beg for it, borrow it, and if that doesn't work, steal that shit. Ain't that your line?"

"It is, but I swear on Granddaddy's grave that I would never do that to Grandma." She looked at Chanel and pointed. "That hurt. I may be a little on the grimy side, but that's family."

"I'm sorry," Chanel said.

"And it is good to see you, fam," Sheba said and hugged Demi.

"I'm glad you're home, Sheba," she said, and Chanel made it a group hug.

"See, this is more like it."

"What?"

"First you say I'm too skinny, and then you accuse me of robbing Grandma. It's about time y'all show me some love."

"All the love in the world for you."

Sheba looked at Demi. She had lost a lot of weight since the last time she saw her. Demi's once-wide hips were all but gone, as were her once-healthy breasts, and her skin looked dry. It was obvious to anyone who wanted to pay attention that Demi was hooked on cocaine, probably smoking it, and more likely than not, she was running with the wrong crowd.

Just then, Sheba was startled by a loud banging on the door. As the banging continued, she went to the door and looked out. Sheba smiled and opened the door.

"What's up, what's up?" Floyd said and picked Sheba up.

"What's up, Floyd?"

He put her down. "What's up, Sheba the queen?"

"I'm good, I'm good. What's up with you?"

He leaned forward. "Grandma's not here, right?"

"No, she's still in the hospital. You can come in," Sheba said, and Floyd came into the house. "What's up with you and Jody being banned from the house anyway?"

"Grandma said that she knows that we're nice boys, good boys, but she just can't have no drug dealers coming in and out of her house."

Sheba led them into the living room, and they sat down. "You and Jody selling drugs now?"

"It's in the blood. Damn near a family business."

"What you talking about?"

Floyd shook his head. "There's a lot of shit you don't know." He laughed. "Lotta shit about the old days that I didn't know until Pops told me."

"Like what?"

"Any brew left from the party?"

"Cooler on the back porch," she said, and Floyd bounced up to get one.

"You want one?"

"Yeah. But I really need something stronger."

"Not in this house." He handed Sheba a bottle and sat down.

"You were about to tell me what I don't know."

"Did you know that my pops was in business down here and that he used to bring the dope to New York for your mom and pops to sell?"

"I knew my mother kept selling until she died, but I didn't know about your father."

"Did you know that my pops was in Detroit when your pops got shot? My pops kept that shit going for a long time while we were kids before he gave it up."

"No, I didn't know any of that." But it was good to know. "How are Uncle Al and Aunt Tina doing?"

"They're good, still down in Kingsland taking care of Grandpa. He said to tell you hello, and my mother said that she hopes to see you soon."

"Tell your mama I'll get down there to see her. How is Grandpa Pete?"

"Dementia's getting worse. Hard to keep him in the house." Floyd laughed. "Pops hired a nurse to keep up with him, but then he started fucking the woman. So one day while they're fucking, Grandpa leaves, and it took them the rest of the day to find him. Then he had to explain to my moms how two of them were in the house and he still got away."

Floyd laughed, and so did Sheba, because it was a cute story. However, since there were four kilos of cocaine in a briefcase under her bed, Sheba was more interested in the fact that he and Jody were in the drug business.

"So how deep in the game are you two?"

"We doing all right," Floyd answered, and Sheba decided not to push the conversation. One thing that the day before told her was that she needed money to save the house and cover her grandmother's upcoming medical bills.

"What's up with you and Demi?"

"I don't fuck with her. That's what's up with me and Demi."

"Why?"

"Demi called me one night and said that she needed me to come pick her up. When I get there, she says, 'I'm sorry,' and then three masked niggas robbed me. They took my money, the dope I had on me, and my car, and all she got to say is sorry. No, Sheba, I can't fuck with that girl no more. I got nothing but love for her. I just can't fuck with her."

"I hear you."

Floyd looked at his watch. "Look, cuz, it's good to see you. Glad you're home and all that, but I got someplace I need to be."

"Go where you gotta go. I'm home for good, and you know where to find me."

"Cool." He started for the door. "I'ma come scoop you up tonight. We'll hit the clubs, celebrate you being back home where your ass belongs."

"I see this."

"I heard about what Aunt Millicent did." He opened the door. "That's why we need Sheba the queen to straighten shit out. I'm out," Floyd said and closed the door behind him.

It had gotten late in the day, and Sheba was hungry because she hadn't eaten all day, but after looking in the refrigerator, she decided that she didn't want any of the leftovers. She decided to go and get something to eat at Grindhouse Killer Burgers.

It wasn't crowded when Sheba walked in, but there was a line, so she got in it and looked up at the menu. That was when she noticed the man next in line to be served.

"Next in line!"

"I'd like to place an order to go," came a voice so deep that it reverberated in her ear. He was at least six two with a muscular build and deep mahogany skin that seemed to glow.

"Go ahead with your order."

"Grindhouse Style with grilled onions, American cheese, Grindhouse sauce, pickles, and lettuce."

"You wanna make that a combo?"

"Yes, please," he said and turned toward her. Sheba saw full, sexy lips framed by a close-cropped beard that she had seen before.

"Yes, sir, I'll have that for you in just a minute," she said, and he paid for his meal. "Next!" the cashier shouted, and he stepped to the side to wait for his food.

"Dante?" Sheba said softly.

He looked at her. "Sheba."

His name was Dante Manfred, he was once her boyfriend, and he was the reason that she joined the Marines. Ten years ago, she was pregnant with his baby when Sheba caught him coming out of a room with Desinita Shaw, who was once one of her close friends. Both of them were fixing their clothes. Although both swore that nothing happened, Sheba ran out of there feeling hurt and betrayed by two of the people closest to her. She joined the Marines the next day and aborted the baby she was carrying.

"It's me." She waved. "I thought that was you."

"How have you been?" Dante asked and gave her a hug.

"I've been doing fine."

"When did you get home?"

"I got home yesterday."

"You look great."

She looked at the man she once planned to build her world around. "So do you."

"How long has it been?"

"Ten years," she said.

There was a time when Sheba could have told him how many days, hours, and minutes it had been, but she'd moved past that point. It took him a second, but Sheba could tell by the way his expression changed that he remembered the last time he saw her.

Dante remembered the night he kissed Desinita and they broke up over it. Sheba never told him, so he never knew that she was pregnant with his baby. All he knew was that after that night, Sheba avoided him until she joined the Marines, and he never saw her again until that moment.

"How long are you home for?" Dante asked.

"Home for good."

"Next in line!" the cashier shouted impatiently, and Sheba stepped to the counter to order her food.

"I'd like an Apache Style killer burger with grilled onions and Pepper Jack cheese."

"You wanna make that a combo?"

"Nope, just the burger."

"I'll have that for you in just a minute," she said, and Sheba paid for her meal. "Next!" the cashier shouted. Sheba stepped to where Dante was standing waiting for his food.

"Grindhouse Style combo!"

"That's me," he said and excused himself to go and get his food. Once Dante got his food, he walked back over to Sheba, thinking of something clever to say. "What did you get?"

"I got the Apache Style burger."

"Those are good. I get it sometimes."

"You must eat here a lot."

"I do. It's close to the house, and the food is good."

"It's my first time. I was just driving around looking for something. Decatur has changed so much, I just picked a spot and parked," she said and laughed lightly.

"When was the last time you were here?"

"It's been more than five years."

"Oh, yeah, there've been hella changes in the last five years."

"Apache Style burger!"

"That's me," Sheba said and went to the counter. With food in hand, she returned to where Dante was waiting with a smile. "I can't tell you how good it was to see you again, Dante. We should get together sometime soon and catch up."

"I'd like that, but I have a better idea."

"What's that?"

"Let's catch up now." Dante paused. "Looks like you're going to eat alone, and I was going home to eat and binge-watch *The Boys*. Let's get a table and talk."

"I'd like that." Sheba smiled. "But can I get a raincheck? I'm tired, and I have a lot on my mind."

"Hey, I completely understand."

"Do you?"

"Sure, I do."

"But it really was good to see you," Sheba said, inching toward the exit. "I'm sure we'll see each other again."

"Can I get your number?"

"I haven't got a phone yet," Sheba lied. "But stop by the house. I'm sure that my grandmother would love to see you," she said and was out the door before he could offer up his number.

Chapter 7

On the way home from the Grindhouse, Sheba's mind was on Dante. He looked good, really good. He was no longer the tall, lanky kid she dated in high school. Now he was a man, and from what she could tell, he was all muscle. Although the idea of sharing a meal with him to catch up did sound appealing on some level because Sheba was curious about how he was doing, she'd heard from Chanel that he was dating Desinita Shaw, and she wanted no part of that situation.

"Not again."

When Sheba got back to the house with her Apache Style killer burger, she went into the kitchen, heated it up, and got something to drink. She had just sat down and was about to dig in when she heard the front door open, followed by a loud noise. She jumped up from the table and rushed into the living room.

"What the fuck!" Sheba shouted in justifiable horror at the sight of Demi.

She was struggling to get to her feet. Her clothes were torn and stained with blood. One of her eyes was bruised and swelling. Demi's jaw was swollen, and her lip was busted, and blood was trickling down her chin.

"What the hell happened to you?" Sheba asked, rushing to Demi in time for her to collapse into her arms.

"I'm sorry. I won't do it no more," Demi said as Sheba helped her to the couch. "I don't wanna be worthless to you. I can be a good girl for you again."

"What happened to you, Demi?"

"I'm sorry, Ty. I won't do it no more," Demi said, and Sheba called 911.

During the ambulance ride to the hospital, Demi kept repeating those words over and over.

"I'm sorry, Ty. I won't do it no more."

"Who's Ty, Demi? Did he do this to you?" Sheba asked, but she got the same words in response.

"I won't do it no more."

"Do what?"

"I can be a good girl for you again," she said, and figuring that she wasn't going to get an answer, Sheba stopped asking.

At the hospital, the doctor told Sheba that the beating Demi had taken had caused some internal bleeding.

"Internal bleeding?" she questioned.

"Internal bleeding caused by blunt force from the violent beating she apparently took. We're going to keep her overnight for observation. Deeper bleeding, which involves arteries and veins, can result in severe blood loss, which can result in shock."

Sheba talked to the police and told them everything she knew, which wasn't much. Once they had talked to Demi, the police said that there was nothing that they could do because she refused to identify her attacker.

"I'm sorry, but our hands are tied." He handed Sheba his card. "If she changes her mind, please, give me a call, and I'll go get this animal," he said and left the waiting room, passing Jody and Floyd on his way out.

"How's Demi?" Jody asked.

"The doctor said that she had some internal bleeding from the ass kicking she took. They're going to keep her overnight for observation."

"She say who did it?"

"Cops said that she refused to tell them who did it. But she kept saying, 'I'm sorry, Ty.'"

"Ty," Floyd spit out.

"Who is Ty?"

"The nigga she fucks with," Jody said in a combination of disgust and regret.

Floyd pointed in Jody's face. "I told you we should have killed that nigga the last time."

"Last time? What last time?" Sheba asked.

"Tell her!" Floyd said angrily and walked out of the waiting room.

"Tell me what?"

"I told you about me and Floyd having to go get her?"

"Yeah."

"She was with that nigga Ty."

She exhaled angrily and pointed in Jody's face. "Floyd's right, you should have killed him on the spot." Sheba started to leave the waiting room.

"Where are you going?"

"I'm going to see Demi, and then we're gonna go find Ty and kill him."

Jody followed Sheba to Demi's bed in the emergency room. Floyd was there when they got there, sitting on the edge of the bed, holding Demi's hand while she rested her head on his shoulder, crying and softly mumbling, "I don't wanna be worthless. I can be a good girl again."

"Where's Ty, Demi?" Jody demanded to know.

Suddenly, Demi's head shot up, and her eyes burst open. "No! Don't hurt him!" She looked at Sheba. "He didn't mean it. It was my fault. I shouldn't have done it."

"Done what, Demi?" Sheba asked.

"Please, Sheba, don't let them hurt him."

Floyd let go of her hand and stood up. "She doesn't have to tell us. I know where to find the muthafucka."

"No!" Demi shouted, trying to hold on to Floyd. "Please don't hurt him!"

"Let's go," Jody said.

"Please, Sheba, I'm begging you. Don't let them hurt him."

"They won't, because I'm gonna kill him myself."

"No, Sheba!"

Sheba led her cousins out of the emergency room with Demi shouting, "Please don't hurt him. It was my fault! I made him do it!"

As they were leaving the emergency room, Chanel was coming into the waiting room. "Where y'all going?" she needed to know.

"Stay with Demi, Chanel," Sheba said angrily, and she kept walking.

Chanel grabbed Jody by the arm. "Where are y'all going, Jody?"

He stopped and put his hands on Chanel's shoulders. "Stay with Demi, and I'll call you later," he said and caught up with Sheba and Floyd.

"So where do we find him, Floyd?" Sheba asked as they exited the hospital.

"Same place we went to get her last time he did this shit to her," he said angrily. "That's what I think."

"You're probably right."

Jody regretted that they didn't take care of Ty when they had the chance, and he had no problem killing him to make up for his mistake. *But does Sheba really need to be there?* He stopped once they got to his car.

"You serious about killing this nigga, Sheba?"

"I am!" Floyd shouted.

"Yeah, I'm serious. You can't do shit like that to our family and we don't do shit."

"See? Sheba is with me. Now let's stop fuckin' around and go get this nigga," Floyd said. "We should have been killed him."

"He's right," Sheba said. "Now let's go."

"Okay," Jody said, and they got in the car. "Let's go kill a muthafucka."

After they left the hospital, they stopped at Jody's apartment to get more guns. When they were getting ready to leave, Floyd seemed hesitant.

"What's up?" his brother asked, and Floyd looked at Sheba.

"Maybe we should drop you off at Grandma's house and you let me and Jody do this."

"Why?"

"I don't want to see you get hurt."

"Nigga, please," Jody laughed even though he had the same thoughts about the need for Sheba's involvement. "Sheba's a combat Marine. You're more likely to get hurt than she is."

Jody handed Sheba a gun. "He's right, Floyd." She checked the weapon and put one in the chamber. "I'll be fine."

The last time that Jody and Floyd went to rescue Demi, Ty had an apartment in the White Oak Townhomes, so that was where they were going. When they got there, every light in the house seemed to be on, and Ty's car, as well as his partner Rick's, were parked outside. Jody got out to take a look in the window and saw that there were three people inside: Ty, Rick, and another man, whom he had never seen before. He went back to the car to report.

"How you wanna do it?" Floyd asked.

"They ain't ready for us. I say we hit the door and come in blasting," Sheba said and got out of the car.

"You heard her," Jody said, and he and Floyd got out, and they approached the unit.

When Jody kicked in the door, Sheba came in blasting and hit the other man Jody saw in the living room before he could reach for his gun. Ty and Rick began shooting at Jody and Floyd as soon as they came through the door, and they were forced to take cover. Ty fired shots wildly until he emptied the clip. Then he ran up the stairs, ducked into the first room he got to, and closed the door behind him.

As Sheba started up the stairs to go after Ty, Rick kept firing shots at Jody, and he fired back. He ducked behind the wall while Rick fired away. When Rick stopped shooting to reload, Jody came out from behind the wall and hit him with three shots to the chest.

Floyd got to his feet, but when a woman came out of the kitchen and started shooting at him, he dove to the floor and got off a shot. When he got up from the floor, he looked at the woman and saw that he'd hit her with a shot to the head.

Sheba went up the stairs slowly with her gun raised. When she got to the top, she looked around for Ty but didn't see him, so she checked the first room she got to. When she touched the doorknob, Ty fired blindly through the door. The second the shooting stopped, Sheba kicked in the door and saw him going out a window as Jody and Floyd came into the room.

"I'm going after him!" Jody shouted and followed him out the window.

"I'll go out the front and cut him off," Sheba said and ran out of the room.

Floyd put another clip in his gun and went out the window behind Jody. Once he reached the ground, he took out his gun and looked around. He saw Ty run out of the shadows with Jody on his ass and went after them.

When Sheba got downstairs and made it outside, she saw Ty run out into the street with Jody and Floyd running behind him. Sheba raised her weapon and hit Ty with two shots, one to the chest and the other in his head.

Chapter 8

When Sheba arrived at the hospital room that Demi was assigned to, she wasn't at all surprised to see that Chanel was still there, asleep in the chair next to the bed. Demi was asleep as well. During the night, she became agitated and made several attempts to leave the hospital and had to be given a sedative.

Sheba came into the room quietly and shook Chanel enough to wake her. She got up and followed Sheba into the hallway.

"How is she?"

"She's all right now, but she had a bad night."

"What happened?"

"She kept trying to leave so she could get back to Ty so she could apologize, and maybe he'd take her back."

Sheba shook her head in disgust. "What happened to her self-esteem?"

Chanel shrugged her shoulders. "He beat that out of her a long time ago."

"Jody and Floyd told me how out of control she is."

"You're considered legally drunk with a blood-alcohol level of .08."

"What was hers?"

"Demi's blood-alcohol level was .12. And she had cocaine, heroin, marijuana, and opiates in her system."

"Damn, Demi."

"In addition to the ass-kicking she took, she has burn marks on her chest and arms, and there were signs of vaginal and anal tearing. . . ." Her voice trailed off, and Chanel paused before she said, "She told the nurse that the sex was consensual."

"What kind of animal was this muthafucka?"

Sheba had been feeling a little bit of remorse over killing Ty, but after hearing what he had done to Demi, all that was gone. Ty deserved to die, and she was glad that she ended him.

"I think Demi needs to be in rehab."

"I think so too," Sheba agreed. She looked sternly at Chanel and shook her head. "Why didn't you tell me that she was that bad?"

"I did. You're home, aren't you?"

Sheba looked at Chanel and shook her head, only this time her look was affectionate.

"I told you what I needed to tell you to get you to come home."

"You could have just asked."

"I did, repeatedly. For years. All I got out of you was that we would be fine."

"I seriously thought your aunt was taking care of things."

"Be honest, Sheba. You couldn't stand her, and she couldn't stand you."

"Hated me would be more accurate."

"And you let that keep you away."

"I did. Y'all didn't need me."

"Bullshit, Sheba." Chanel pointed in her face. "That was nothing but some bullshit you convinced yourself of so you could feel better about abandoning your family."

"I did not abandon y'all," she said quickly and defensively.

"Whether you did or not doesn't matter," Chanel said because she didn't want to argue. "You're here now when we need you."

"You're right."

"I always am."

"You been up to see Grandma?" Sheba asked.

"After they sedated Demi."

"You tell her she was here?"

"Are you kidding? I didn't even mention Demi's name."

"Okay. I'm going up there to see her."

"You gonna tell her?"

"Yes, Chanel. I'm gonna tell her everything. About Demi, about Aunt Millicent, everything."

"You're right. She needs to know." Chanel laughed. "I just wasn't gonna be the one to tell her."

"Don't you have to go to work today?"

"I already called in. My grandmother and my cousin are both in the hospital. My boss said she understood and told me to take as much time as I need."

"Okay," Sheba said and looked in on Demi. She was still asleep, so she went to see her grandmother.

When she got to the room, Dr. Kulkarni was there making her rounds. She told Sheba that they had run all the tests she'd wanted and that her grandmother would be released from the hospital that day. After Dr. Kulkarni left the room, Sheba sat down on the bed and took her grandmother's hand.

"There are some things that I need to tell you about, Grandma."

Sheba told her about Demi, some of what she'd been doing, what happened to her the night before, and that she was in the same hospital. Miss Pearl listened in horror, and she cried over what her granddaughter had been doing and what she had to endure.

"Chanel and I agree that Demi needs to be in some type of rehabilitation program."

"I think so too. My God, I had no idea all that was going on." She wiped away a tear. "Please tell me that my boys aren't involved in any of this."

"Jody and Floyd? Of course not. They've been protecting her as best they could, Grandma. And what is this I heard about them being banned from the house?"

Miss Pearl folded her arms across her chest and looked away from Sheba. "I can't have them in my house."

"They damn near grew up in that house, Grandma."

"You need to watch your mouth, Ashebe Lorretta Style," she said, smiling. "You ain't that grown that I won't beat your behind."

"There's something else I need to tell you about, Grandma."

"What's that?" Miss Pearl asked, and her smile disappeared.

"Did you know that Aunt Millicent had closed your bank accounts?"

"Why would Millicent do that?"

"I don't know why she did it, Grandma, but that's what she did. She took all your money, and she wasn't paying for your insurance, so it was canceled. She wasn't paying the mortgage on the house either."

Sheba paused as the hurt set in, and tears filled her grandmother's eyes. Miss Pearl was both angry and hurt at the betrayal. She felt overwhelmed by the emotions that were so intense that it just didn't make any sense. How could her own daughter do that to her?

"You don't have to worry. I took care of it."

She squeezed Sheba's hand. "Thank you, Sheba. I always could count on you."

"I'm gonna make this right, Grandma. I promise."

Later that afternoon they were both released from the hospital around the same time, and the four ladies went to Grandma's house. As soon as they got there, Sheba took Demi upstairs, and she got into bed. Once she was comfortable, Demi told Sheba how much she appreciated what she had done for her.

"That's what family is all about. And I'm just sorry that I stayed away so long."

"It's all right. You're back now."

Sheba stood up and started for the door.

"Sheba."

"Yes," she stopped to say.

"I understand that you did what you had to do with Ty. I would have done anything for that man no matter how bad he treated me. I needed to get away from him," Demi said. This was the longest she'd been sober in years, so she was just starting to think clearly and for herself. "I need help."

"I'm glad you see that. I'm gonna look into getting you into some kind of rehab program."

"I think I need that."

"You get some rest, and I'll be back to check on you," Sheba said and left the room.

When she got downstairs, Chanel was on the phone with her husband, James, checking on him and their children.

"I know that you have things to do," an exasperated Chanel said. "And I told you, I will be home as soon as I can."

Sheba didn't see her grandmother and knew where she was. She found her exactly where she expected—cooking in the kitchen.

"What are you doing, Grandma?"

"What does it look like I'm doing, child?"

"You need to be in bed resting, Grandma."

"I've been in bed resting for the last two days. I'm tired of the bed. So I got a little cough. That don't mean I can't cook dinner for my family. Now either you're gonna help me or you can go sit out there with Chanel."

"Just tell me what to do," Sheba said, and her grandma motioned for her to join her at the stove and handed her a spoon.

"Stir this," Miss Pearl said of the gravy for the mashed potatoes.

She set the corn on the cob to boil and went on to fry the chicken. Once the food was ready, Miss Pearl got Chanel off the phone to set the table while Sheba went to get Demi, but she said that she wasn't hungry.

As expected, cooking for everybody wore Miss Pearl out, and after dinner, she allowed Chanel and Sheba to clean her kitchen before she went upstairs to bed. Therefore, the topics of conversation as they did the dishes were their grandmother's health, Demi, and the cost of drug rehabilitation.

"How much does drug rehab cost anyway?" Sheba asked as she washed the plate and handed it to Chanel.

"I don't know," she said, drying the plate and putting it in the dishwasher. Then Chanel dried her hands and took out her phone and searched for the cost of drug rehabilitation. "Rehab services and prices vary," she reported as she read. "Most people go to a drug treatment center for a minimum of thirty days, and the cost is determined by the level of care." She scanned the information. "Various levels of care for residential treatment cost twenty-five thousand dollars or more for thirty days."

"Damn, that's a chunk," Sheba said as she washed the serving dish. "But that really is what she needs."

"Where are we gonna get that kind of money?" Chanel asked as she dried the last dish and put it in the dishwasher.

Sheba knew what she needed to do but was reluctant for some reason. "I'll think of something."

"Let me know what you come up with," Chanel said and picked up her purse to leave. "I'm going home so James can stop sending me 'when are you coming home' texts."

Sheba sat down at the table. "Call me tomorrow when you get free."

"Night, Sheba."

"Good night, Chanel," Sheba said, watching her cousin leave the house.

She sat there for a moment or two thinking about what to do, and then Sheba got up. She went to the refrigerator and made Demi a plate and took the food upstairs to her.

"You need to eat something, Demi," Sheba said when she came into the room.

"I know," Demi said and sat up to eat. "What did Grandma cook?"

"Fried chicken."

"I haven't had Grandma's fried chicken in a while," she said excitedly and bit into a drumstick.

Sheba sat down on the edge of the bed while Demi tore into Grandma's chicken. "You ready to tell me what happened?"

Demi looked at her. "Not really, Sheba," she said with her mouth full.

"Why not?"

Demi took another bite of chicken. "I don't want you to think any less of me than you already do."

"I won't think any less of you. You're my cousin and I love you. I'm not here to judge you. I just wanna help. We all do."

"I know that," Demi said and got started on the mashed potatoes. "And I know you love me," she said with her mouth full.

"Just tell me about the burns then. How'd that happen?"

She exhaled. "Okay, if you really have to know." Demi put the plate down. "I was fucked up, and I accidentally burned Ty with the pipe. This was what he did to me in response," she said and showed Sheba the burn marks on her chest and arms.

"My God, Demi," Sheba said and shed a tear.

Demi started to cry. "He just kept burning me, Sheba," she said as the tears rolled down her cheeks. Sheba hugged her. "I said I was sorry. I said I wouldn't do it again, but he hit me. I tried to run away from him, but he caught me and beat me. Then he forced me to have sex with him and Rick."

"They raped you."

Demi nodded and looked away in shame. "Then he told me that I was useless to him, and he made some woman drop me off here."

"I'm sorry, Demi," Sheba said as her eyes filled with tears. "Sorry you had to go through that. But you're safe now. I won't let anybody hurt you ever again. I promise." Feeling overwhelmed by her emotions, Sheba stood up. "You go on and get some rest, and I'll see you in the morning."

"Good night, Sheba, and thank you," Demi said as Sheba left the room.

After looking in on her grandmother, Sheba went downstairs to the kitchen and got the last bottle of beer from the cooler. She went out on the back porch, sat down, and popped the top. Sheba looked out at the night sky, thinking about what she was going to do. Her grandmother was deep in debt, she needed treatment, and Demi needed to be in rehab. Knowing that all that was gonna cost money, more money than she had, she made a decision to sell the cocaine she had in order to save her family.

She drained the bottle and went into the house and upstairs to her room. Sheba got down on her knees and pulled the briefcase from under her bed. She put the case on the bed, sat down, and opened it. Sheba took one kilo out and closed the case.

Chapter 9

In the morning when Sheba woke up, she felt refreshed. For the first time since she'd taken that briefcase, she slept well. From almost the moment that Sheba arrived, she had watched her family come apart at the seams and felt like everything that was going on in her family was her fault. There was still a lot going on in her world, but after making the decision to sell a kilo, it felt as if some of the weight had been taken from her shoulders. Sheba decided not to beat herself up any longer over not being there and got out of bed.

The house was quiet when she came out of her room. Sheba expected her grandmother to be in the kitchen, so after looking in on Demi, who was still asleep, she came downstairs and was surprised to see that Chanel was in the kitchen with her grandmother drinking coffee.

"Morning!" Chanel said brightly and enthusiastically.

"Good morning, Sheba," Miss Pearl said, taking a sip of her coffee.

"Morning, Grandma," she said and leaned in to hug her. "Morning, Chanel. Ain't you supposed to be at work?" she asked. She got a cup from the cabinet and went to get coffee.

"'Take as long as you need, Chanel,' means take as long as I need. So after I dropped the kids off at school, I came here."

"Do you. You always do." Sheba sat down at the table. "How are you feeling this morning, Grandma?"

"Feeling good this morning."

"How long have you been up?"

"Since about six thirty."

"Did you take your meds this morning?" Sheba asked.

"Yes, Sergeant Styles, I took my medication."

"She did. I was here when she did," Chanel said and exchanged glances with her grandmother, who didn't want to take the new medication that Dr. Kulkarni had prescribed that morning. That was, until Chanel threatened to wake Sheba up. Then Miss Pearl went on and took it.

"Good. And thank you, Chanel."

"No worries." She winked at Miss Pearl. "Demi's not up yet, is she?" Chanel asked.

Sheba shook her head. "She's still asleep. I looked in on her on the way down here."

"How was she last night after I left?" Chanel asked.

"Did she eat anything?" Miss Pearl wanted to know.

"She was okay when I left her, and yes, Grandma, she ate." Sheba laughed and looked at Chanel. "She tore Grandma's fried chicken up."

"Did you bring her a leg?" Miss Pearl asked. "You know she loves legs."

"I brought her two, Grandma, because I know how much she loves them."

"Good," Miss Pearl said and started to get up. "What do you girls want for breakfast?"

Sheba got up. "Sit down, Grandma. I'll make breakfast," she said, and Miss Pearl sat down.

Despite her telling her granddaughters that she was feeling good, the truth was that she was tired and felt a little tightness in her chest. Miss Pearl had been experiencing those symptoms for some time and had attributed them to old age. However, now that she knew it was more than that, it weighed more heavily on her mind, and Miss

Pearl knew that she needed to start taking it easy. Her baby Sheba was home now, so everything would be all right.

Sheba went to the refrigerator. "What y'all want to eat?"

"Just toast for me," Miss Pearl said.

"You sure that's all you want, Grandma?" Sheba asked and took the bread out of the refrigerator.

"That's all, thank you."

"What about you, Chanel?"

She sat up straight. "I want a classic Denver omelet stuffed with smoked ham, melted cheddar cheese, sweet bell peppers, and onions," Chanel said, using her hands to demonstrate her enthusiasm for the meal. "But I'll have whatever you cook."

"I have all of that stuff in the fridge," Miss Pearl said and fought the strong urge to get up and take out the ingredients to cook.

"I'll cook it if you cut up all that stuff," Sheba said, and Chanel got up.

"Deal."

"The two of you need to wash your hands first."

"Yes, Grandma," both Sheba and Chanel said and went to wash their hands before returning to the kitchen to cook breakfast. While they were cooking, Demi came downstairs.

"Morning, everybody," she said.

"Morning, Demi," everybody said almost in unison, and she plopped down in a chair at the table with her grandmother.

"How are you feeling this morning, Grandma?" Demi asked, reaching for her hand.

"Feeling good this morning." She squeezed Demi's hand. "How are you?"

"I'm fine, Grandma," she said, but like her grandmother, the truth was something different. Demi felt anxious and irritable, she was tired, and all she really wanted to do was sleep to avoid thinking. But she was hungry.

"You want some coffee?" Chanel asked.

Demi got up. "I'll get it."

"You hungry?" Sheba asked.

"Starving," Demi said, and once she poured her coffee, she went to sit down. "What you cooking? You know what? It doesn't matter. I'll eat anything."

"She's making classic Denver omelets," Miss Pearl said.

"What's in it?"

"Ham, cheddar cheese, peppers, and onions," Chanel said as she cut up some ham for another omelet.

"It's so good to have all three of you girls here," Miss Pearl said.

"I could call Jody and Floyd so all of your grandchildren would be here," Sheba said, and Chanel and Demi dropped their heads because any discussion of Jody and Floyd in the house was banned too. Sheba looked at her grandmother, and she looked away. "Then we can have family breakfast like we used to." She looked at her timid cousins. "Y'all remember waffle and bacon Sundays with Grandma and how much fun we used to have?"

"I remember you two used to tease me until I cried. That's what I remember," Demi said and sipped her coffee.

"That's because you were a big crybaby," Chanel said and sat down at the table. "And it was Sheba and Jody who used to tease you."

"Stop it, Chanel," Sheba said and placed an omelet in front of Demi. "You know you used to tease her too."

"That was supposed to be mine," Chanel complained as Demi grabbed a fork and shoved some of her omelet in her mouth.

"That's what you get for lying," Demi said with her mouth full.

"Yours is next," Sheba said.

"So you can stop whining," Demi said and kept eating her omelet.

"That was you, Chanel," Miss Pearl. "You were a whiner."

"She's still a whiner, Grandma," Demi said. "'That was supposed to be mine,'" Demi whined to imitate Chanel.

"I am not a whiner," Chanel whined and folded her arms across her chest.

"And then you get all pouty when you don't get your way," Demi said. "This omelet is so good, Sheba."

"Thank you, Demi," Sheba said, and when the omelet was ready, she served Chanel and then made one for herself.

After breakfast, Miss Pearl directed all three of her granddaughters in the proper cleaning of her kitchen. Although she didn't comment on it when Sheba brought it up, she did miss her grandsons coming by the house. She missed cooking for them, but Miss Pearl thought that she was doing the right thing. Drugs and drug dealing had cost her family so much, and she hoped her stance would change their behavior.

However, knowing that grown men were gonna do what they wanted to do, she knew there was nothing she could do to get them to stop. They would come to that conclusion in the same way their father did before he finally let the game go. Maybe she would invite them to dinner on Sunday.

After the kitchen was clean to her satisfaction, Sheba suggested that Miss Pearl go lay down for a while, and to everyone's surprise, she didn't give Sheba any argument and went upstairs.

"Wow," Demi said once she heard the bedroom door close. "She really must not be feeling well."

"She didn't even give Sheba no argument," Chanel commented.

"That tells us all we need to know. We all need to step up and be here for Grandma," Sheba said and looked at Demi. "And we need to be there for you, cuz."

"Because I am so fucked up," Demi said.

"Stop saying shit like that about yourself, Demi. You are a queen. A beautiful African queen," Sheba said, repeating what their grandfather had tried to instill in each of his granddaughters.

"I hear you." Demi remembered those speeches too. "I just don't feel beautiful. What I feel is fucked up."

Chanel felt a chill wash over her as she recalled their grandfather's powerful words. "But it doesn't have to be like that," she said quickly. "Did Sheba talk to you about us getting you into some kind of rehab program?"

"She did, and I'm good with that, because like I keep saying, your girl is fucked up," Demi said and saw the disappointed looks on her cousins' faces. "Okay, okay, I am not fucked up. I'm a beautiful African queen."

"All you gotta do now is start believing it," Sheba said.

"Baby steps, Sheba. I'm not strong like you and Chanel, and I've been fucked up a long time. All I can do is try, because—"

"Don't say it," Sheba said, pointing at Demi.

"Say what?"

"That you've been fucked up a long time," Sheba said, and Demi shrugged her shoulders.

"Well, what can I say? I've been fucked up a long time."

Sheba and Chanel shook their heads.

"So what about rehab?"

Chanel took out her phone. "I searched for drug rehabilitation clinics and found a place called Alliance Recovery Center on East Ponce in Decatur."

"Where it's greater," Demi said.

"What's up with them?" Sheba asked and sat down at the table.

"The Alliance Recovery Center doesn't charge an admission fee, only a per-day rate for treatment. They accept cash and credit cards," Chanel said, reading the site, and then she raised one finger. "But they seem like they're focused more on opioid addiction."

"Opioids really weren't my thing," Demi said.

"You had opioids in your system," Chanel pointed out.

"I did?" Demi asked, looking shocked because opioids truly weren't her thing.

"Yes, you did."

"Damn." Demi dropped and shook her head. "I really did need to get away from that man. Wasn't no telling what all else he was giving me."

"You had heroin in your system, too, Demi," Sheba said, looking sternly at her.

"What else you got, Chanel?" Demi asked, looking away from Sheba.

Chanel kept scrolling and reading the snippets of information. "Most of these seem like they're focused on opioids too."

"No love for us functional crackheads, huh?" Demi chuckled.

"Doesn't seem that way," Chanel said.

"Make a list of the ones nearby, and we'll go check them out. Somebody in this town must still treat cocaine addiction," Sheba said and stood up. "I'll be right back."

She went into the living room, sat down on the couch, and took out her phone.

"Who's this?" Jody questioned because he didn't recognize the number.

"It's Sheba."

"This your number?"

"Yup."

"Saved. What's up, Sheba the queen?"

"I need to talk to you and Floyd."

"This sounds serious."

"It is serious. When can the three of us talk?"

"I'll get with Floyd, and I'll call you back."

"Cool."

"How's Grandma and Demi?"

"Demi is fine, but Grandma went back to bed."

"Wow, really? That says a lot about how she's feeling."

"Don't it?" Sheba paused. "Call me, and let me know what's up," she said, and she went back into the kitchen with Chanel and Demi.

Later that evening, Sheba got Chanel to stay at the house with Demi while she went to see Jody and Floyd at Floyd's apartment. Seeing that being nosy ran in the family, both Chanel and Demi wanted to know what Sheba wanted to talk to them about and wondered why they couldn't go with her. But because Sheba was Sheba, they both accepted, "It's a personal matter," as an answer, and that was that.

"What's up, Sheba?" Floyd asked when he opened the door to let her in.

"Hey, Floyd." Sheba came in carrying the kilo wrapped up in a plastic shopping bag.

"Come on in."

"'Sup, Sheba?" Jody said as she came into the living room. "So you know I'm dying to know what you wanted to talk about."

Sheba sat down. "With all that's going on in the family, I need to make some money," she said, and her cousins looked at one another curiously. "You know Grandma's got back medical bills and future treatment to deal with, and Demi seriously needs to be in rehab."

"For real," Jody said.

"How is she?" Floyd asked. He may have been done with her, but he loved and would do anything for Demi. Being the youngest of the five grandchildren, it was Demi who used to keep Jody, Sheba, and Chanel off him when they were kids.

"Anxious and irritable. If she's not sleeping, she's eating."

"That's to be expected. Where she at?" Jody asked.

"At Grandma's house."

"She's not alone, is she?" Floyd wanted to know.

"Chanel is with her."

"Good. Don't leave her alone. Especially once them cravings hit her ass, she'll be outta there, and she'll be in the streets trying to find a way to get high," Floyd warned.

"I won't. So far, she's been cool, but that might change," Sheba said.

"So what did you have in mind?" Jody asked. "About making money, that is."

Sheba took a deep breath and reached into the bag. "I need to sell this," she said and handed Jody the kilo.

"Whoa. Where did you get this?" he asked.

"Don't worry about that. Can you sell it?"

"Hell yeah!" Floyd said, excited about getting free product. "We can break it down, put a cut on it, and sell it," he said as Jody took a taste.

"No," Sheba said quickly. "I can't wait around for that. I need that money now. Grandma's house is in foreclosure, and now she got medical bills to take care of. So, no, sell it and get what you can for it."

"Damn, Sheba, you sure?" Floyd asked. "We could more than quadruple the money if we break it down, chop it up, and put a cut on it."

"I know that, and I don't care. This is for Grandma to get out of debt and to pay for Demi to be in rehab. So we do this my way or you hand it back," Sheba said with her hand out.

"She's right, Floyd. We need to do this for Grandma and Demi," Jody said to his brother even though he knew it was the wrong move. "Agreed, Sheba. We do this your way."

Chapter 10

The following morning at ten, Sheba was sitting with Miss Pearl in the waiting room of Dr. Anthony Green, her primary care physician, who Miss Pearl hadn't seen since before Millicent died. After examining her and refilling her prescriptions, he advised her on the results of the forced expiratory volume level test he had run, which measures how much air a person can exhale during a forced breath. Her level was 64 percent, which represented a mild obstruction. He spoke with Sheba on the way to check out and told her that he had made the emphysema diagnosis months ago.

"I spoke to your aunt about it, and she was supposed to get back to us so we could schedule the tests Dr. Kulkarni had run. When I didn't hear from her, I thought that she was getting a second opinion. I had no idea that wasn't the case. I am truly sorry."

"She seems all right now, but can it get worse?"

"Yes, Miss Styles, emphysema can get worse over time. You cannot undo the damage to your lungs. Over time, she may find that she gets short of breath even when she does simple things like getting dressed or cooking a meal. She needs to relax and take it easy and avoid stress. People who are stressed often feel anxious, or irritable, and that stress may also cause more frequent flare-ups."

"I understand. Thank you, Doctor."

"See the nurse on your way out, and she'll schedule her next appointment."

After making Miss Pearl's next appointment, they left the office and took the elevator down to the lobby. "Wait here, Grandma. I'm going to get the car."

"I'll be right here," Miss Pearl said and sat down to wait.

"Mrs. Harrison?" a man questioned, and Miss Pearl turned to see who it was.

On her way to the car, Sheba thought that another thing that she needed to do was take back her rental car. Miss Pearl had a 1999 Chrysler 300 that she hadn't driven in years. She would check to see if she could get it running, and if not, she would make other arrangements. Sheba got in the car knowing that, either way, the rental was getting returned today. She was thinking that once she got her grandmother home and settled, Chanel and Demi could follow her to return the car. Sheba was about to pull up in front of the building when she saw her grandmother standing outside, all smiles, chatting up a tall black man in a lab coat.

"Dante?" she questioned as she got closer. "What is he doing here?" she asked herself and put the car in park. "Duh, he works here." She got out.

"Look who I found, Sheba," Miss Pearl said as she and Dante walked toward the car.

"Hey, Sheba," he said and opened the car door for Miss Pearl to get in as Sheba came around the car.

"Hey, Dante. I didn't know you worked here."

"That's because we didn't get a chance to catch up."

"True. So is it Dr. Dante Manfred?" she asked and wondered why Chanel didn't mention that.

"No," he chuckled. "Not a doctor, just a physician's assistant," Dante said as he walked Sheba around to the driver's side and opened her door. She looked him up and down and inhaled his scent.

"We do need to catch up," she said and looked up into his penetrating eyes.

"So you get a phone yet?" he asked, and this time, Sheba gave him her number. "I'll call you tonight."

"Sounds good," Sheba said and got in, and Dante closed the door behind her.

"Dante certainly turned out to be a very handsome man."

"Yes, Grandma," she said and drove off.

"I thought you two were on your way to getting married."

"I thought so too, Grandma," Sheba said, looking in her rearview in more ways than just the obvious as Dante walked back into the building.

"And then you up and joined the Marines." Miss Pearl shook her head. "Never did quite understand that, but I guess you had your reasons."

"I did, Grandma."

"He said that he's not married and he's not dating anybody—"

"You asked him that?" she asked in shock.

"Of course I did. I was gonna give him your number, but I thought that was too much."

"Thank you," Sheba said, relieved, but still embarrassed that she did that.

"It would have made you look desperate. You did give him your number, didn't you?"

"Yes, Grandma. I gave him my number, and he's going to call me tonight."

Later that evening, Dante called, and she invited him to come by the house. He had only seen Chanel in passing, and he hadn't seen Demi in ten years, so the four had a good time catching up and talking about their high school days. It was Chanel who suggested that Sheba and Dante go somewhere, and once Demi promised to be a good girl, Sheba left with Dante. They went to a place called Poor Hendrix and they talked over hibiscus daiquiris.

Sheba was enjoying herself with him. He was older, wiser, and definitely finer than he was all those years ago, but at his core, Sheba found, Dante was still the same kind, considerate person she'd once loved. She listened as he spoke about his journey to becoming a physician's assistant and what made him choose that as a profession. And then there were a few seconds of silence between them. Sheba was starting to feel him, and since it was on her mind, she asked.

"When was the last time you saw Desinita?"

"Shaw?"

"You know any other?"

"No," he chuckled. "I haven't seen Desinita in"—he paused to think—"five . . . no, it's been more like six years since I last saw Desinita."

"I thought you two were dating."

"Who did you hear that from?" He paused. "Chanel." He chuckled. "I was with Desinita the last time I saw Chanel, but that was years ago."

With a new attitude, Sheba sat up and leaned forward. "What happened with you two?"

"Once I found out what a psycho she was, I got away from her."

"Psycho? Desinita? Say it ain't so," Sheba laughed.

"'Slashing tires, keying cars, mad-crazy stalker, threatening to kill herself' kind of psycho," Dante said and signaled for the server. "Two more, please."

"Coming up."

"I didn't know she was all out of control like that," she said and finished her daiquiri, thinking, *Dante must have really put the dick on her.*

"I had to get a restraining order, and even then, she wouldn't stop." Dante dropped and shook his head. "This last time, she called me and said that she was lying under my car and was about to disconnect the fuel line to drink the gas."

"Seriously?"

Dante nodded.

"What did you do?"

"I hung up and called the police. They said she was under the car when they got there. They arrested her and charged her with vandalism."

"Did that stop her?"

"Nope. When she got out of jail, she came to my house and broke in."

"Are you being serious with me right now?"

"Yes, Sheba. She busted out my dining room window and came on in like she was supposed to be there."

"What do you do?"

"I'm telling you, when she got crazy like that, I learned not to fuck with her. I just call the cops and let them deal with her." He laughed. "Because if she called the cops, it would be my black ass going to jail."

"I hear you."

"Wasn't happening. So while I'm waiting for the cops to get there, she searched the house."

"Were you alone?"

"Yes, I was home alone, but she swore that somebody was there with me." He laughed. "What other reason could I have for not taking her calls?"

"Did she feel foolish when there was nobody there?"

"Nope, that just made her madder. But by that time, the cops were there, and they arrested her for breaking and entering. But instead of going quietly, she ran, and when they caught her, she fought with them. They charged her with resisting arrest and assaulting a police officer, and that day in court was the last I saw or heard from her."

"Okay, so she was a little cray-cray," Sheba laughed. "I hope she got some help for herself."

"I'm just sorry that it took all that before she stopped."

Sheba laughed. "Or maybe she stopped because she's still doing time for resisting arrest and assaulting a police officer."

"True. She was a little cray-cray," Dante laughed, and Sheba looked at the time on her phone.

"I had a good time with you tonight, Dante. But it's getting late, and Chanel needs to go home."

"I understand," Dante said and signaled the server to bring the check. Once it was paid, he took Sheba back to her grandmother's house. On the way to the house, Sheba got a call. She looked at the display, and when she saw it was Jody, she answered.

"What's up, Jody?"

"It's done."

"Tell him I said what's up," Dante said as he drove.

"Who that?"

"Dante. He said to tell you what's up."

"Dante." Jody paused. "There's a name I never thought I'd hear again."

It was Jody Sheba ran to the night she caught him with Desinita Shaw. Instead of rushing inside to beat Dante's ass like he wanted to, Jody sat outside holding Sheba while she cried.

"I didn't either, cuz, believe me."

"I need to get with you," Jody said, turning back to business.

"I'm on my way to Grandma's house now."

"I'll call you when I get there, and you can come out."

"No, you come in the house when you get there."

"What's Grandma gonna say about that?"

"You let me worry about Grandma, and come in."

"See you in a few," Jody said and ended the call.

"That's nice that all y'all are still close. I haven't spoken to my sister in over a year, and we were never close to our cousins in Union City. But y'all always had each other's backs."

"We still do," Sheba said as Dante parked in front of the house. "It was good to see you, Dante," she said with her hand on the door handle.

"It was good seeing you again too. I'd like to see more of you."

Sheba opened the door. "You have the number, so call me," she said and got out. "Good night, Dante."

"Good night, Sheba," Dante said, and Sheba shut the door and walked to the house.

"Chanel. Demi! I'm back!" she said loudly and got no answer.

"Sheba." Her grandmother appeared at the top of the stairs. "She's gone."

"Who's gone, Grandma?"

"Demi," she said as Chanel burst through the front door.

"Did she come back, Grandma?" she said, and then she saw Sheba.

"What happened, Chanel?"

"I went to the bathroom, and she was gone when I came out. I've been riding around the neighborhood looking for her, but I didn't find her," Chanel said as Miss Pearl came down the stairs. "I'm sorry, Sheba."

"It's not your fault. I shouldn't have left," Sheba said as the doorbell rang.

"Who is that at this hour?" Miss Pearl asked.

"It's Jody, Grandma. I asked him to come," Sheba said on her way to the door to let him in.

"What's wrong?" he asked as soon as he saw the look on Sheba's face.

"Demi's gone."

"I tried to tell y'all that would happen," Floyd said, following his brother into the house. "She's gone to find a way to get high." Both of them stopped where they stood when each saw their grandmother standing on the stairs.

"Hey, Grandma," Jody dropped his head and said sheepishly.

"You doing all right, Grandma?" Floyd said in the same manner.

"You boys come here," she said with a smile and her arms out. Her grandsons rushed to her, and she hugged them both.

"Love you, Grandma," Floyd said.

"We're sorry we disappoint you, Grandma," Jody said.

"You two hush that fuss and go find your cousin," Miss Pearl said, kissing each one on the forehead before she let them go.

"Yes, Grandma," they both said.

"How long has she been gone?" Jody asked, walking quickly toward the door.

"About fifteen minutes," Chanel said. "I rode around here looking for her, but I didn't see her."

"Ain't no telling where she could be by now," Floyd said, following his brother to the door, and then he looked back at Miss Pearl. "But we'll find her, Grandma. I promise."

"We'll talk about that other thing later, Sheba," Jody said and left the house.

Sheba nodded, and after they were gone, she went upstairs to get her service weapon, and then she came back downstairs.

"Come on, Chanel, let's ride."

Chapter 11

The search for Demi was on. While Jody and Floyd went to check out an abandoned house a couple of blocks from their grandmother's house, where people were known to come to get high, Sheba and Chanel rode up to the convenience store where you could get just about anything you were willing to pay for. They got out of the car and approached some of the men there that night.

"What you ladies need?"

Sheba stepped to him. "I need to know if you've seen her," she said, and Chanel showed him a picture of Demi from her phone.

He looked at the picture and shook his head. "Nah, ain't seen her," he said as two of his boys leaned in to look.

"Let me see," Jamarco said, and Chanel handed him the phone. He and Latravis looked at the image and then handed Chanel back her phone. "I know her. I ain't seen her tonight, but—"

"Sheba Styles?" a voice came from the darkness.

Sheba turned toward the voice. "Jordan?" she questioned when he stepped into the light.

"Couldn't be nobody else," Jordan Mitchell said.

He knew Sheba back in the days when she used to come home when she was on leave. They met in that exact spot, and they got together between her deployments for a couple of years before he got locked up and they lost touch. Those days, he was an arrogant and brash young drug dealer, and Sheba was an angry young Marine who the government was turning into a weapon of war. They were both fearless and thought they could do anything they wanted, and the city belonged to them. Jamarco, Latravis, and Rashard were his boys, and he controlled that spot now.

"Come show your boy some love."

"Hey, Jordan," Sheba said and gave him a hug and thought back to the days when he used to break her back. "How you doing?"

"Living the dream, doing what I do. Trying to keep my money right."

"I see." Sheba looked around at the activity and smiled. "You ain't changed a bit."

"Nope. What about you? You still government property?" he asked, looking hungrily at her.

"Nope."

"What you doing up here?" Jordan questioned because everybody there was either selling drugs, buying drugs, or doing what they had to do to get drugs.

Chanel was quick to shove her phone in his face. "Have you seen her tonight?"

"That's our cousin," Sheba said. "She's missing, and we're trying to find her."

Jordan nodded and smiled, glad that Sheba wasn't up there to buy drugs or sell herself to get them. He briefly wondered what he would do if she were. Jordan took the phone from Chanel and looked at the image. He nodded his head and then handed Chanel back her phone.

"I know Demi." He looked at Sheba. "I didn't know she was your cousin."

"Have you seen her tonight?" Sheba asked and wondered how well he knew her.

"No, sorry, she ain't been up here tonight."

"I tried to tell them she—"

"Shut the fuck up, Jamarco," Jordan said quickly and turned back to Sheba and Chanel.

"You know where she might be?" Sheba said.

"She always be with Ty, Rick, and them. You know him?" Jordan asked, and Sheba shook her head.

"She ain't with them. Anyplace else you can think of around here where she might be?" Sheba asked, and Jordan thought about it.

"There's a crack house around here"—he paused—"not too far from your grandmother's house."

"I know where it is," Chanel said and started for the car.

"It was nice to see you, Jordan," Sheba said, walking away.

"You staying with your grandmother?"

"Yes."

"I might stop by and holla at you," he said as they got to the car. Chanel shook her head as Sheba waved to Jordan and got in the car.

"Good luck with that." Chanel started her car. "Grandma won't even let her own grandsons in the house."

"I know, right."

"He doesn't stand a chance. And who is he anyway?"

"Somebody I used to know a long time ago," she said, smiling.

"Somebody you used to fuck, judging by that smile on your face."

Sheba raised her hand. "We ain't got time for that now, Chanel. Where is this crack house?"

"It's a couple of blocks from Grandma's house."

"Stop by the house on the way and see if she came back," Sheba said, and Chanel drove to the house. When they got there, Jody and Floyd were coming out.

"Did she come back?" Sheba asked when she got out of the car.

"No, she didn't come back," Jody said.

"We were going to see if she's at the crack house." Chanel started to get back in the car.

"We been there already," Floyd said. He knew the men who sold out of there. "She was there, but she left with somebody right after she got there."

"Who?" Sheba demanded to know.

"My boy didn't know," Floyd said.

"What are we gonna do now?" Chanel asked.

"We keep looking," Floyd said like there was no other option and it should be obvious to all of them.

"How's Grandma? She still up?" Sheba asked.

"She's still up. Worried about Demi," Jody said.

"I'm going to check on her. Where were you two going?"

"To another spot where I know she used to hang out," Floyd said, anxious to get back to looking for her.

"I need to talk to Jody, so why don't you and Chanel go check that out?"

"We gone," Floyd said and got into the car with Chanel while Sheba went into the house to check on their grandmother.

Sheba then talked to Jody before they rolled out and continued to look for Demi for the rest of the night, but they didn't find her.

The sun was up the next morning when the four came dragging into their grandmother's house after searching all night. They were tired and feeling frustrated that they couldn't find her, and their grandmother was feeling stressed and anxious about Demi being missing. Nobody really got much sleep before they were back at it, back in the street asking if anybody had seen Demi.

Throughout the day, four of her grandchildren were in and out of her house, leaving her to worry, and her emphysema symptoms began to worsen. She found it hard to breathe at times. Miss Pearl was coughing and wheezing more and producing more phlegm. As she moved around her house, Miss Pearl was having trouble catching her breath and was having headaches. She got some relief from her inhaler. However, by the morning of day three, as her symptoms kept getting worse, Sheba noticed that she was having trouble speaking in full sentences, and she called Dr. Green. He recommended that she go to the hospital right away.

"It's gonna be all right," Sheba said to her grandmother and put the oxygen mask over her nose and mouth. "The ambulance is on the way."

Miss Pearl nodded and motioned for Sheba to come closer. "What about Demi?"

"Don't worry, Grandma. Jody and Floyd are still looking for her."

"It's her fault that Grandma is like this," Chanel said, looking out the window for the ambulance to come. "You heard what the doctor said about it causing flare-ups. Grandma doesn't need all this worry and stress."

"I know," Sheba said, looking at Miss Pearl, who had closed her eyes and dropped her head.

"Ambulance is here," Chanel said and went to let the paramedics into the house.

Once they had Miss Pearl ready to travel, they exited the house and took her to the ambulance. It was at that moment that Demi came staggering down the street in time to see Sheba get into the ambulance with her grandmother to go to the hospital. And when the door was closed, Chanel turned to Demi.

"This is your fault." Chanel started walking toward her car.

"What did I do?"

Chanel stopped and got in Demi's face. "Don't you think Grandma was worried about you? Her stressing about your selfish ass is what brought this on."

"I'm sorry," Demi said, and Chanel started for her car. "Where are you going?"

"To the hospital, and no, you cannot come with me. I don't even want to see your face right now."

"What should I do?"

"I don't give a fuck what you do. I'll worry about what to do with you when Grandma gets better," Chanel said and got in the car.

Chapter 12

With tears streaming down her cheeks, Demi watched the ambulance and then Chanel pull off and head for the hospital. She dropped her head in shame, and in pain, she went inside her grandmother's house.

Sheba and Chanel spent the day at the hospital as they worked to get her flare-up under control before they went back to their grandmother's house.

Demi was still there when they got there, sitting on the couch watching television. She stood up and looked at her cousins.

"I'm sorry. I'm such a fuckup. I didn't mean to make Grandma sick."

"That's because you're selfish and you never think of anybody but yourself and what you want," Chanel spit out and went into the kitchen.

Sheba shook her head. "I need to get you some help. Until then, I can't let you out of my sight."

Demi shook her head and melted into Sheba's arms, crying. "I'm sorry."

The following day, Chanel was still mad, so she decided to stay home while Sheba took Demi with her to the hospital to assure her grandmother that Demi was safe. She was just that disgusted with Demi. For her part, Demi apologized to her grandmother for being so much trouble and for making her sick and causing her flare-up. Then Sheba and Demi visited treatment centers from the list that Chanel had compiled until they settled on the Lakeside Behavioral Clinic. The following day, with Sheba and Floyd there to support her, Demi was admitted into their adult inpatient program.

Demi was taken care of, and her grandmother's flare-up seemed to be under control with antibiotics and oral corticosteroids. Dr. Kulkarni advised that the exacerbations may last for two days or two weeks, depending on the severity of the symptoms. She recommended that Miss Pearl remain hospitalized to see how things went. With those items off her plate, Sheba took the time to get together with Jody.

"You just don't know, and maybe you do, but it just feels good to be here in this house."

"I know what you mean. No matter where I was in the world, this house was always home," Sheba said as they sat down in the living room.

"It was hard not being able to come home." Jody looked around the room and ran his hands up and down the armrests of their grandfather's chair. "But anyway." He pulled an envelope out of his pocket and held it up. "This is what you wanna talk about."

"What's that?" Sheba asked. Jody told her that he had gotten $20,000 for the kilo. She at least thought the envelope would be fatter.

"The money," Jody said and opened the envelope. He pulled out a plastic card. "This is a prepaid debit card. There are four of them actually. Each one has five thousand dollars on it. This way you can use them to pay Grandma's bills and for Demi's rehab without dropping a lot of cash. Cash transactions over ten thousand dollars attract the attention of the IRS."

"They do?"

"Yes, Sheba, they do. The law requires that businesses report cash payments of more than ten thousand dollars to the IRS."

"Why?"

He shrugged his shoulders. "They think it helps to detect money laundering. But there are always ways to work around it. To avoid that shit altogether, keep your transactions under five thousand dollars."

"Which is why you got cards with five thousand dollars on each."

"You always were the smart one in the family."

"Thank you, Jody."

"It's for Grandma and Demi. But Floyd is right. We'd have made a chunk if you had let us work it. But what's done is done."

"Suppose it wasn't?"

"Wasn't what?"

"Done. Suppose it wasn't done and I had more. What then?"

"What do you think we'd do? We'd break it down, chop it up, put a cut on it, and quadruple our money."

"Okay."

"Why, you got more?"

"I do."

"How much more?"

"Three more keys."

"Get the fuck outta here. You know how much money we could make if we handle them right?"

"No, but I'm sure you do."

"So what you gonna do?"

"I'll let you know. I am going to sell them eventually. I just need to think about how and what is best for our family."

"You're talking about Demi."

Sheba nodded.

"I can tell you for a fact that I've never given her anything more than a blunt to smoke to mellow her out, no matter how much she begged me. I told her that I was never gonna be her enabler. Now I can't speak for Floyd."

"The two of them have or had a special relationship," Sheba pointed out.

"They still do. He was really worried about her when she was MIA." Jody chuckled. "I know that he stopped fuckin' with her because of that robbery shit." Jody shook his head. "But that shit hurt him. He won't say it, but I know it did."

"I know neither one of you would do anything to hurt her. I'll let you know what I decide."

"Cool." Jody stood up. "I'm out," he said, and Sheba walked him to the door.

She had thought about using some of the money to buy a car, but in light of her conversation with Jody about the IRS, Sheba decided that the thing to do, at least for the time being, was to try to get her grandmother's old Chrysler 300 running. Once Sheba got home the following day and had changed her clothes, she got the keys and went outside to give it a shot.

She got in and put the key in the ignition. But when she turned the key, nothing happened. She reached for and pulled the latch and got out to have a look under the hood. Sheba lifted the hood and leaned in. *Everything seems to be in place.*

"Everything looks good to me from there," Jordan said, looking at Sheba's ass as he walked up the driveway. It startled her, and he laughed when Sheba jumped.

"You scared me." She took a playful swing at him. "What are you doing here?"

"I told you I was gonna stop by and holla at you." He held his hands out to the side. "Well, here I am."

"How you doing, Jordan?" Sheba asked and leaned under the hood.

"You know what you're looking at?"

"Not really."

"What's wrong with it?"

"It won't start."

He leaned under the hood with her. "The battery is probably dead. When was the last time it was driven?"

"At least ten years ago."

"If you're planning on driving it, you probably need to get a new battery, new belts, filters . . . I'd get a new alternator, but that's just me. And I'd definitely change the oil." Jordan looked at the tires. "They look all right, but they might be dry-rotted, so I'd get new tires, too."

"I didn't know you knew about cars."

"I work on cars." He chuckled. "What'd you think, I just sling dope?"

"Well, yeah. I mean, that's all you used to do."

"I got a shop on Moreland. Them niggas you saw that night, they work for me." Jordan stepped closer to her. "And that is not all I used to do."

Sheba stepped back. "I remember," she said, smiling.

Jordan smiled and pointed out into the street at a 2002 Trans Am. "I damn near built that myself," he said proudly. "Be right back." He went to the trunk of his car and came back with tools.

It didn't take him long to take out the battery and the alternator. After he put them in the trunk, he checked the size of the tires.

"Come ride with me to the store."

"Let me lock up," Sheba said, and as she went to lock the door, Jordan made a call to get her some tires. "Ready."

It took more than half an hour, and they passed by two parts stores, before they got to the store where Jordan got a discount. He got a new battery and alternator, new belts, oil and air filters, seven quarts of oil, spark plugs, and wires for a tune-up. When Sheba insisted on paying, Jordan said that he paid that bill semiannually and promised to let her know what her share was when he got the invoice.

"Whatever, Jordan." Sheba nodded knowingly. "Thank you."

When they got back to the house, the guys Jordan had called for the hookup on the tires had arrived. They already had two Michelin Pilot Sport tires on the front, and they were working on the rear. When they finished, Sheba ignored what Jordan was talking about, and she paid the men for her tires. Once they were gone, Jordan took off his overshirt, got some rubber gloves, and went to work.

Sheba went and got a lawn chair from the garage and sat in the shade, talking to Jordan while he worked on the car. While they talked, she enjoyed the sight of Jordan. His T-shirt was drenched, and sweat was dripping off his honey-kissed skin.

"You look hot," Sheba said. "Do you want something to drink?"

"Got any beer?"

Sheba got up and came to the car. "Let me drive your car and I could go get some."

"Keys are in my left front pocket," he said with his biceps bulging while he tightened the belts. Sheba reached in his pocket. "Little more to the right."

Sheba grabbed the keys. "No need. I already know what's there. You still drink Moosehead?"

"You remembered," Jordan said as Sheba walked to the car.

"I remember more than you think," she said. She got in and drove off.

By the time Sheba got back with the beer, Jordan was finished and was sitting in the lawn chair in the shade. She handed him a beer, and he handed her the keys.

"Start it up."

Sheba got in and turned the key, and it started right up. "Thank you, Jordan."

"No worries. Leave it running for a while," he said, and Sheba came to sit down on the steps next to him.

"You need to tell me what I owe you for this," Sheba said and cracked open a Moosehead.

Jordan picked up the now four-pack between them. "Paid in full," he said, holding it up. "But you could answer a question for me."

"What's that?"

"What did you mean when you said you remember more than I think?"

"Nothing. Just something to say," Sheba said and took a sip.

He pointed his bottle at her. "You say that now, but you remember us."

"Of course I do. We used to have a good time together."

"Lots of fun and lots of sex."

"Sure did," Sheba said, and her mind once again drifted to memories of Jordan being deep inside her, making her scream.

"You remember the first time?"

Sheba pointed to the garage. "In the garage on my grandfather's old workbench."

Jordan drained the bottle and stood up. "Yeah, you remember. I'm out."

Sheba stood up. "You should clean up before you go."

"I'll be all right," he said quickly and then thought about it. "Yeah." He nodded. "I should clean up."

"Right. You don't wanna be going around all funky," Sheba said and led Jordan into the house to the upstairs bathroom, but they didn't make it that far. He kissed her hungrily as they stumbled into the wall in her room. He pinned her against it, and then he kissed and sucked her neck and chest. Her fingers roamed wildly across his body. She pulled the T-shirt over his head, rubbed his chest, and lathered his neck and chest with kisses.

She looked up into his eyes. He reached for her face and pulled her toward him. Their tongues became entangled in passion. He took off his pants and then anxiously helped her get undressed. He kissed her again and gently laid her body down on the bed and lay next to her. Her breasts seemed to glisten, and her nipples grew harder as he ran his tongue across them.

Jordan kissed her lips and kissed his way down her body, lingering at the nipples. He continued working his way down her body. He crawled between her legs, spread her lips, and then he slid his tongue inside her. He tongued her clit, and she grabbed his head to hold it in place while she screamed in ecstasy.

Sheba lay next to him in bed, and she began gliding her hand up and down his dick. He leaned closer to her and lost himself in her chest, licking and gently sucking her nipples.

She gently pushed him on his back, put a condom on Jordan, and straddled his body. Sheba grabbed his dick and eased herself down on it. She rode him slowly while he continued to feast on her nipples. He began to feel her legs trembling on his thighs, and he pushed harder. She bore down on him and increased her pace. She began pounding her hips furiously onto him until she reached a very loud climax.

"Just like old times."

Chapter 13

Over the next couple of days, Sheba went about the business of taking care of her grandmother's affairs. She was determined that when Miss Pearl got out of the hospital, everything would be taken care of. That would allow her to rest easier and not have to worry about her house being foreclosed on. She had been to the bank and used one card to make another $2,394 payment on the mortgage, and then it was off to the DeKalb County courthouse to pay the back taxes on the house.

She'd heard loud and clear what Jody had said about cash transactions over $10,000 attracting the attention of the IRS. Sheba took that advice to the next level and assumed they may flag any large transaction. She was committed to keeping dollar amounts under $2,500 but had to go back on that when she maxed out one card making a payment to Lakeside to cover half of the $25,000 cost of Demi's rehabilitation.

Demi had never worked a day in her life, so she had no insurance. Therefore, she was only admitted when Sheba used a card to pay $5,000. Floyd paid another $5,000 in cash, and Sheba promised to make another $2,500 payment that night. It had only been a couple of days, and she had spent more than half of that money.

It was Lakeside's policy that visitors were not allowed during the detox process, so nobody had seen Demi since she was admitted. When visitation was permitted, Sheba asked Chanel if she wanted to go with her to see her. But

Chanel was still mad at Demi for running out on her and bringing on their grandmother's flare-up, so she refused to go.

"I get it," Sheba said. "I'm mad at her too, but I had to let that go."

"Why, because she's 'sick'?" Chanel made air quotes.

"Yes." Sheba moved closer and put her arm around Chanel. "Demi is family. You know that rock and glass dick were calling her."

Chanel wiggled away. "No, Sheba, I don't know, and I don't wanna know about anything that would make me want to risk my grandmother's life." Sheba moved closer. "And stop doing that."

"Doing what?"

"You know what you're doing." Chanel moved away. "You're trying to make me all sympathetic so I'll change my mind because she's an addict and still family."

She moved closer to Chanel. "Is it working?"

"Yes," Chanel said and got up. "I'm mad at her selfish ass, but I'll go with you next time."

Sheba got up and got ready to go to Lakeside. "Demi has always been selfish. That's just Demi being Demi. You know that."

"I know." Chanel folded her arms across her chest. "And this is me being the whiner Grandma said I am."

"Whatever, Chanel," Sheba said, and they left their grandmother's house. Chanel went home to her husband, who had done his share of whining while she had been away, and Sheba went to take care of some business for their grandmother before going to visit Demi.

When she signed in to visit, Sheba was informed not only that Demi already had a visitor that day, but also that she needed to make another payment on the account.

This money is going fast, Sheba thought on the way to the visitation area, much faster than she thought it would. $20,000 may have sounded like a lot of money, but it went fast in the real world. When she was told that Demi had a visitor, Sheba had assumed that Chanel had a change of mind and came to see her. She was wrong but was surprised to see that Floyd was there. Sheba approached them, thinking that Chanel needed to see this. Last week, Floyd wanted nothing to do with Demi, and now, even though she'd set him up to get robbed, he was doing all he could to be supportive of her.

"Hey, Sheba," Demi said.

"What's up, Sheba?"

The three visited for a while before Floyd got up and said that he had to leave. "Give you two some alone time."

Demi got up and hugged him. "Thank you for coming to see me."

"I'll see you next time. I'll get with you later, Sheba," he said and left the visitation area.

"So how's it going, Demi?"

"I gotta tell you, detox was hard. As much as I wanna say I got the shit outta my system, I really don't know if I did."

"That's all right. You're being honest with yourself."

"I'll be okay," Demi said, and she rested her head on Sheba's shoulder. "I'm a strong African queen. At least, I wanna be."

"You'll get there. And I promise I'll be right here for you. I meant it when I said I won't let anything or anybody hurt you ever again."

Demi enjoyed Sheba's visit until it was time for her to leave. Once a tearful goodbye was shared between Demi and Sheba, she left the building only to find Floyd waiting for her in the parking lot.

"Thought you were gone."

"I wanted to talk to you," Floyd said.

"So you waited?"

"I didn't know how long you'd be, and I didn't have shit else to do, so yeah, I hung out, made a couple of calls." He laughed. "Chatted up a couple cuties who came to visit. Productive time, so it was time well spent."

Sheba leaned against the car next to him. "What you wanna talk to me about?"

He leaned shoulder to shoulder. "Them other keys," he said softly.

"What about them?"

"You need to let me and Jody work them."

Sheba started to object.

"Before you say anything, just hear me out."

"I'm listening."

"How much money you got left from that twenty?"

"Not much."

"That always was my point. That money was only gonna go but so far. You don't have much money left, and Grandma still got bills to pay. And if you think Demi is gonna be ready to leave here and stay clean after only thirty days, you're kidding yourself."

"I know. She's struggling in there."

"You don't know how bad she was. I wouldn't be surprised if she relapses and escapes from here more than once before she gets clean."

"Don't say that," Sheba said, but she knew Floyd was right.

"This ain't about the money. It's about family. It's about us, all of us, doing what we need to do to take care of our family. And right now, this is what this family needs."

"I'll think about it," Sheba said and got off his car. "We'll talk about it tomorrow. Grandma's coming home, so come by," she said, walking to her car.

"I'll see you tomorrow, but you know I'm right."

On her way home from Lakeside, Sheba got a call from Dante. They had been playing phone tag and texting since the night Demi left her grandmother's house.

"Hello," she answered.

"Finally. I was starting to think that we'd never actually speak again and that we were doomed to having our entire relationship via text and messages."

"They tell me that's how relationships go these days."

"I heard that too, but I don't want to be a part of one. I like physical contact too much," Dante flirted, but Sheba didn't bite on the line. He laughed it off. "So how are you doing?"

"Tired. Been ripping and running since the last time I saw you."

"How's Mrs. Harrison?"

"She's doing a lot better. Thank you for asking. She'll be coming home tomorrow."

"That's good to hear. Please give her my best."

"I will."

"How's Demi?"

"I just left her, and she's doing fine." Sheba didn't go into detail about what was going on with Demi. She hadn't told Dante anything about rehab. Unless he absolutely needed to know, she had no plans to tell him.

"That's good." Dante paused. "Listen, the reason I called was to see if you were busy tonight."

"I didn't have any plans. What's up?"

"I got two orchestra seats for *Pretty Woman: The Musical* tonight at the Fox Theatre, and I wanted to know if you wanted to have dinner with me and see the show."

"I loved the movie," Sheba said excitedly. "That sounds like it might be fun. It's a date."

"Great," Dante said, and arrangements were made for him to pick Sheba up at her grandmother's house at five.

They had a four-course dinner for two at The Melting Pot, which included shrimp, teriyaki-marinated steak, chicken potstickers, sesame-crusted ahi tuna, and duck breast as well as cheese fondue, salad, and chocolate fondue.

Since it weighed heavily on her mind, and Dante, being a physician's assistant, was knowledgeable, a good bit of dinner conversation revolved around him answering Sheba's questions about her grandmother's health, and then it was time to leave for the theatre.

"So what did you think?" Sheba asked on the way back to her grandmother's house.

"It was pretty good. They stuck pretty close to the movie. What about you? What did you think?"

"I agree that they stuck pretty close to the original," Sheba said. "But I don't know, it just felt wrong to me. But some of the songs were good, and I had a nice time with you. Thank you for inviting me, Dante. This was a much-needed distraction from everything that I've been dealing with"—she laughed—"and will be dealing with again in the morning."

"Glad to be there for you. I'd like to see more of you," he said as they got close to the house.

"I can tell that you do. But I hope that you understand and can appreciate that my world is crazy right now and what I can really use is a friend. I know it was a long time ago and you say nothing happened, but it hurt. It hurt for a long time. So let's start here and see where it goes."

"I still love you, Sheba. I never stopped loving you."

"And I loved you once. We'll see if we can make it back there from where we are now," Sheba said as Dante parked in front of the house.

"I waited this long for a second chance, so I guess we'll see if we can make it back."

Dante turned off the car and got out. He came around and opened Sheba's door, extending his hand for her to get out. He walked her to the door, and after a hug and a kiss on the cheek, Sheba said, "Good night, Dante. Thank you again for tonight."

"Good night, Sheba," Dante said, and she went inside.

Once she had showered and was about to get in bed, her phone rang. Sheba looked at the display and saw that it was Jordan calling.

"Hello."

"What you doing?" he asked.

"About to get in bed."

"Let me come get in bed with you."

"No."

"Why not?"

"Because you can't come here anymore. That's why."

"Why not?"

"My grandma doesn't allow drug dealers in her house."

"Okay, okay, fair enough. Gotta respect the lady of the house. So let me come get you."

"No." Sheba got out of bed. "Text me your address."

Dante wants a relationship. Jordan just wants some pussy. Some good dick is about all I can stand in my world right now, Sheba thought and went to his house.

Chapter 14

Sheba had just stepped into the hallway at the hospital when she saw Chanel coming. If all went well, Miss Pearl was scheduled to be released that morning, but that all depended on Dr. Kulkarni and the medical staff.

"Morning, Chanel."

"Morning, Sheba. Is the doctor in the room with Grandma?" Chanel asked, and Sheba nodded. "Are they going to release her today?"

"I hope so, but we'll see what the doctor says."

"She was doing fine last night when I left here."

"What time did you leave here?"

"Eight o'clock. Why?"

"You look tired, that's all."

Chanel hissed. "I'm tired of a lot of shit, but I was up late last night, that's all."

"Nope, not buying that." Sheba shook her head. "Give it up. What's really going on?"

"Me and James got into it on the way home last night." Chanel let out a little laugh. "Got into it in the parking lot, really."

"What'd y'all get into it about?"

"He's been drinking a lot lately. You saw how drunk he was at your welcome home party."

"So was just about everybody else. That's what you do at parties."

"Anyway, James was drunk again last night."

"Drunk at the hospital with Grandma?"

"He's got a little flask that he carries with him. So he'll go in the hall, take a swallow, and come back, or he'll take a sip when he thinks nobody's looking."

"I'm sorry, Chanel. I knew James could drink, but damn, it's like that?"

"Yes, it's like that, and he was too drunk to drive. That's what started the argument. He didn't want to let me drive home. Some guy walked up while we were arguing. It was getting pretty ugly by then. I don't know who he was, but he finally convinced James to let me drive. He passed out in the car on the way home. But when we got home, we got right back into it. Sheba, now you know I don't like to argue."

"I know. You keep it all to yourself."

"Not last night. Sheba, I said everything I've always wanted to say because I've had it. I am so tired of his shit."

"You, Chanel, tired of his shit? Say it ain't so."

"I told him I was tired of him drinking so much, and him embarrassing me in public was getting real old. I told him I was tired of carrying all the weight financially. That he needs to get off his ass and start making some money."

"I thought he got a new job and a big raise."

"Big raise, my big ass. Even with the raise, I still make twice what he's making. He makes enough to pay for that Acura he didn't need and his high-ass insurance. He can handle a bill every now and then. But he's always crying broke. But he always got money to buy a bottle or hang out with his drunk-ass friends. But when I bring up his drinking or that car, he gets annoyed."

"What did he say?"

"He tried to make it about me and what I'm not doing."

"Of course he did."

"After a while, I stopped fussing and went to bed. He gets in bed and starts rubbing on me. I say stop because

I really don't feel like being bothered with his drunk ass. But he keeps on, trying to force himself on me. So I got out of bed and went to sleep in the other room, and that futon is not comfortable."

"And that's why you look tired."

"I'm losing respect for him, Sheba. And that's not good."

"I'm sorry, Chanel. I didn't know it had gotten that bad."

"I keep stuff to myself, remember?" Chanel took a sip of her coffee and dropped her head.

"Why do you stay with him?"

"I still kind of love him. And when he's not drunk, he's nice and he promises to do better. He'll stop drinking for a day or two. Maybe even a week. Most of the time I think it's because he's broke. One time, last year, he stopped drinking for a month. I was shocked," Chanel said as the door opened and Dr. Kulkarni came out.

"Good morning, Mrs. Morgan," Dr. Kulkarni said.

"It will be a great morning if my grandmother can come home today," Chanel said.

"As I was telling Miss Styles, her vitals look good. I just wanted to look in on her and do one last breathing test, but I don't see any reason to keep her another day."

"Thank you, Dr. Kulkarni," Sheba said and shook her hand.

"You're welcome. Hopefully, we can get her out before noon," the doctor said as Sheba and Chanel went into the room.

It was more like one in the afternoon when Miss Pearl was finally released from the hospital. But that gave Sheba time to think about her grandmother's future health as well as Demi's. This was her grandmother's second hospital stay in as many weeks. She hadn't even gotten the bill for the first stay yet, and she was sure, with all the tests they ran, that this bill would be higher than the last. Fortunately, Miss Pearl's new insurance coverage would go into effect on the first of next month, but in the meantime, it was Sheba who signed as the party responsible for the bill.

And then there was Demi. Whether she wanted to hear it or not, Floyd was right about her. Even if she made it through these thirty days, it was Demi herself who said that she was fucked up, and she had been fucked up for a long time. It was more than likely that Demi was going to go through the rehabilitation process more than once before she could make a permanent lifestyle change. It was something that would take time.

And now there was Chanel and the kids to worry about. She had always been slow to anger, and she may always have kept things to herself, but she was fed up now. Sheba knew that things could, and most likely would, escalate quickly between Chanel and James. She would need the support of her family if changes needed to be made. There was also the fact that she had put everything on her credit card that first day, so Sheba was in debt, too. She could hear Jody's words: *We do this right, Sheba, and the whole family comes up.*

Sheba knew that she was going to sell the remaining kilos eventually. What she had to consider was if letting Jody and Floyd handle it was best for their family.

Once Miss Pearl was discharged from the hospital, Sheba took her home with Chanel following close behind them. When they got to the house and went inside, Sheba told Miss Pearl that she should go upstairs and get in bed. Miss Pearl was about to tell her that she was tired of bed and was going to cook something when Chanel came into the house. She was on the phone with James, and the argument over money was getting heated.

"I don't know what gave you that idea, but you are out of your freakin' mind if you think that I'm gonna pay for that nonsense," Chanel shouted as she passed through the living room and out onto the back porch. "You sound like a fuckin' fool!" she shouted and slammed the door.

"Chanel," Miss Pearl said to the closed door. "She knows better than to be talking like that in my house."

"I think that's why she went outside, Grandma," Sheba said and sat down in the living room.

"Who is she talking to, cussin' like that?"

"I think she's talking to James."

"I don't know what to say about that boy." Miss Pearl shook her head. "Up in the hospital last night, drunk as Cooter Brown."

"You knew he was drinking?"

"Child, please. Of course I knew. He was making a fool of himself, thinking nobody notices him stumbling and that he can't complete a sentence."

"She said that she's tired of carrying him."

"It's about time. She's been propping him up, trying to make something out of him that just ain't there. He was no good when she met him, you know that, and he ain't got no better. Worse now because he drinks and can't handle his liquor," she said as they heard the back door slam. Chanel came into the living room.

"I'll be back," Chanel said as she passed through the living room.

"Where you going?" Sheba asked.

"To get my kids from school," Chanel said on her way out of the house, slamming the door behind her.

Both Sheba and Miss Pearl looked at their watches. It was just after one in the afternoon. Miss Pearl looked at Sheba.

"She's leaving him, and she's going to get the kids before he does," Sheba said.

"And she's gonna bring those bad children over here." Miss Pearl shook her head. "Don't get me wrong. I love my great-grandbabies."

"I know, Grandma. You just don't need them here right now."

"Running around, whooping and hollering in my house."

"I understand, and I'll take care of it," Sheba said, knowing that circumstances had made her decision clear. "Is it all right if Jody and Floyd come by for a little while this afternoon? There's something I need to give them."

Miss Pearl patted Sheba's thigh, and then she stood. "Yes, Sheba, it's okay if my boys come by," she said. "I'm going upstairs to rest for a minute, and then I'll get dinner ready."

Sheba watched Miss Pearl go up the stairs and waited until her door was closed before she got out her phone and called Jody. He and Floyd came over right away, and Sheba gave them the other three kilos.

"You know, Granddaddy told me that this day would come," Jody said.

"What did Grandpops say?" Floyd asked.

"He said one day it's gonna fall on you and Sheba to make decisions about what's best for our family, and that I should listen to you," Jody said, and Sheba laughed. "What's funny?"

"He told me the same thing, but then he said that I needed to trust you."

"That's because Grandpops knew that both of you think you know everything," Floyd said and laughed.

"I trust you, both of you. Now go on and get that stuff outta here before Grandma comes down or Chanel gets back with the kids."

"We gone," Jody said, and Floyd followed him out of the house just before Miss Pearl came downstairs.

"Was that my boys?" she asked on her way down.

"Yes, Grandma."

"Why didn't they come up and say hello?"

"I told them that you were resting, Grandma, and they didn't want to disturb you."

"I see," she said as the doorbell rang.

Sheba started for the door. "You expecting somebody?"

"I asked Dante to stop by."

Sheba stopped and frowned. "Grandma?"

"Get the door, child," Miss Pearl said and sat down to receive her guest.

"Hey, Sheba."

"How are you doing, Dante?" Sheba asked and let him in, upset with her grandmother for playing matchmaker, but not upset that he was there.

"Doing fine. Mrs. Harrison asked me to stop by this afternoon to check on her." He held up his medical bag. "I hope it's all right."

"It's fine."

"Hello, Dante," Miss Pearl said.

"How are you feeling today, Mrs. Harrison?"

"I'm doing fine," she said and looked at Sheba. "I asked Dante if he wouldn't mind coming by from time to time to check my pressure and my heart rate."

Dante reached in his bag. "And I'll be checking her lung capacity as well. I brought this. It's a spirometer." He showed it to Sheba. "You can check her breathing with this."

"Then I will get out of your way," Sheba said and went to sit down.

Once Dante had finished, he was about to tell Sheba that he was going to leave. He was happy to do this for Miss Pearl, but at the same time, he didn't want Sheba to think he was forcing himself on her. Just then, the door burst open, and Chanel's children came running into the house, whooping and hollering. As for Chanel, she stomped in a few seconds later, still on the phone arguing with James.

"Keep talking and you'll never see these children again!" she shouted.

"Oh, but no," Sheba said. "Okay, everybody stop!" And everybody did. "We are not gonna have all this noise in this house." She looked at Chanel and then at Dante. "We need to find you someplace to stay." She turned to Dante. "And I need a big favor from you."

"What's that?"

"Could you take the children someplace for a while?"

"No problem. You go ahead and get Chanel situated and call me when you're done."

Dante thought that this was what being a friend meant. Although this wasn't how he had seen his evening going, he agreed to take them to get something to eat and to a movie while Sheba and Chanel got someplace for her and the children to stay until other arrangements could be made.

Chapter 15

As weeks passed, things began to settle for the once-chaotic family. Sheba's decision had the desired effect. Jody and Floyd believed in the concept of making money on volume. Therefore, they didn't put a lot of cut on it. Once the word got around that they were rolling with quantity and very high quality, the money rolled in.

In those few short weeks, all of Miss Pearl's outstanding bills had been paid. The mortgage was current, the back taxes had been paid, and she once again had insurance. Although you couldn't tell by looking at her, her emphysema was very severe. Therefore, there were days when Miss Pearl didn't feel well and it slowed her down, but she was determined not to let it hold her down. Some days were better than others, and each day came with its own challenges. But if Miss Pearl was nothing else, she was a fighter, and she was up to the challenge.

"You need to stay healthy, eat a well-balanced diet, and get moderate exercise. With the aid of medications and therapies, you can live a long, healthy life with emphysema," Dr. Kulkarni explained.

"I'm just lucky to have the support of an amazing family," Miss Pearl replied during their last visit.

The influx of capital also allowed Sheba to pay Lakeside the balance of Demi's rehabilitation costs. Part of the treatment and recovery process was structured around developing new, healthy habits intended to become routine in post-discharge life. Demi was engaged and participating in the program, getting up early in the morning to enjoy a healthy breakfast. That was followed by morning classes in yoga and meditation to help her begin each day in a relaxed state of mind. It was working for her until the night Sheba got a call from Lakeside that Demi had broken curfew and left the center.

Everybody feared the worst.

Demi had escaped as Floyd said she would and would surely find a way to get high. As it turned out, their fears were unwarranted. She was immediately tested upon her return to the center at five in the morning, and there was no trace of drugs in her system. Later that morning, when Sheba arrived at Lakeside and was allowed to visit with Demi, she told her what happened that night.

"I was horny."

"What?"

"I needed some dick, Sheba, and I am not interested in anybody here, male or female."

"So you escaped?"

"With Floyd's help."

"What?"

"I called Floyd, and I told him what I was thinking about doing."

"What did he say?"

"Once I promised to be a good girl and keep my nose clean," Demi chuckled, "he came and got me and took me to the dick."

"I guess that's not so bad," Sheba said and was about to move on when she noticed the look on Demi's face. She'd seen that look before and knew that there was more to the story. "Tell me the rest."

Demi was silent, and then she looked away from Sheba. "After we did it, the guy fell asleep."

Sheba smiled. "You must have put it on him."

"I was really horny. But while he was asleep, I took his car and left, and the only reason I didn't get high was that I didn't have any money and the person I knew who would let me smoke free wasn't home."

Sheba shook her head. "Oh, Demi."

"But then I felt guilty. I got Floyd to trust me. After the foul shit I did to him, he still trusted me. Then I thought about all that everybody was doing for me. So I brought the car back and called Floyd to come get me, and he brought me back here. But I wanted to, Sheba. I just wasn't going to sell myself to get it."

From that, Sheba knew that Demi getting and staying sober was going to be a long process if she could do it at all. The way that she sounded was as if Demi was in rehabilitation trying to get clean for everybody but herself. Other than agreeing with Sheba that she needed to get help, Demi never said that she wanted to stop getting high. She drove away from Lakeside knowing it was something that Demi had to want, and her thoughts turned to Chanel.

After staying a couple of nights at a motel, Chanel moved her family into a three-bedroom long-term vacation rental for a week until they found a house to rent. What she didn't tell Sheba at the time was that James had been cheating on her.

While they were talking after Chanel left the hospital, James put Chanel on hold to take a call. When he came back on the line, he received another call and once again put Chanel on hold, or so he thought.

"Look, Shay, let me get my wife off the phone, and I'll call you back."

"Who is Shay?" Chanel asked, and James said nothing. "Hello."

"I'm here," James said, wondering how he could have made such a stupid mistake.

"Who is Shay?" Chanel calmly asked again, and James paused for a few seconds before he answered.

"She's a friend of mine."

"You need to tell me something more than that," Chanel demanded. "Who is Shay?"

"I was out with Vic one night, and he introduced me to her," James admitted, and they went round and round about that and the definition of a friend. Chanel was relentless, asking question after question until James broke. "Okay, Chanel. I've been having an affair with her."

It took a second or two before his words settled in, and they were first met by anger and rage. The usual screaming questions followed.

"How long has this been going on?"

"How could you do this to us?"

"Why aren't I enough for you?"

"Do you love her?"

All were good questions that James could but didn't really answer. By then, the anger and rage had subsided and were replaced by the hurt and pain of his betrayal.

"That's probably why we don't make love anymore. You've been having sex with her."

"I'm sorry, Chanel," was all that James could manage. "How can I make this right between us?"

"You can't." Tears cascaded down her cheeks. "If you want her that bad, you need to go on and be with her," Chanel said and ended the call. She went to see a lawyer the next day, and she began divorce proceedings.

"You sure you're doing the right thing?" Miss Pearl asked, not knowing the whole story. "I mean, I never thought that he was good enough for you—"

"Nobody did, Grandma, and you all were right," Chanel added.

"But he is the father of your children."

"And I have every intention of him having a relationship with his children, but that's up to him."

Sheba sat quietly and listened as Chanel explained her rationale to their grandmother. Chanel was listing all the reasons that friends and family had told her about James not being right for her and saying them with a conviction that she'd never displayed before.

There's more to this story than she's telling, Sheba thought. But knowing Chanel the way she did, Sheba knew that it would be pointless to ask. Chanel would keep her reasoning to herself and would only share it if she had to.

"Maybe if he were to quit drinking and you two got some counseling—" Miss Pearl began.

"No, Grandma," Chanel said, speaking more sternly to her grandmother than she ever had. It raised an eyebrow or two. "There's not gonna be any counseling for the two of us. He can quit drinking and get some help for himself." Chanel paused, thinking that she could make James quitting drinking and getting into a program a condition of visitation. "But it is over between us, Grandma, and that's that."

"You need to watch your tone, young lady."

"Sorry, Grandma," she dropped her head to say. "I didn't mean you no disrespect, but I mean what I say."

"I know you do," Miss Pearl said.

"There is nothing left between me and James. Right now, I'm not even sure that there ever was anything between us," she said, and a tear rolled down her cheek. Then she smiled. "You never liked him anyway, Grandma." Chanel wiped away her tear.

"I know. I'm just an old lady who still believes in the sanctity of marriage. You and James made vows before God, for better, for worse, until death do you part. It may be a quaint and outdated idea, but I believe in it."

"I believed in my vows," Chanel said, dropping her head and thinking that one of those vows was to forsake all others. "But I was the only one."

Miss Pearl and Sheba looked at one another, and then they looked at Chanel. Her eyes were closed, and her chin was resting on her chest. Knowing that she needed to change the mood in the room, Sheba bounced up.

"Who's hungry?" She raised her hand. "I know I am."

Chanel looked up. "I haven't eaten since breakfast, and that was just a cold sausage biscuit." She giggled. "I ate half of it."

"You gonna cook, Sheba?" Miss Pearl asked because she was feeling a little tired and didn't feel like cooking.

"No, it's too hot to cook, and besides, I'm hungry. Let's go to Golden Corral on Lawrenceville Highway."

Chanel got up. "I'm for that," she said, glad not to be talking about James. "Come on, Grandma."

"All right, all right. Let me get my purse," Miss Pearl said, and they left the house and the discussion of Chanel's divorce behind.

Chapter 16

And then there was Dante.

As the weeks passed and things began to settle for the once-chaotic family, Sheba began spending more time with Dante. It started simply, as things often do. Dante had been coming to the house in the evening after he got off from work to check Miss Pearl's vitals and to walk her through her breathing exercises every few days. Once he was done, he'd leave, until the night Miss Pearl asked, "Are you hungry?"

"Starving. I was going to grab something on my way home."

"Sheba cooked meatloaf and mashed potatoes. Would you like some?"

"No, thank you," Dante said but didn't mean it. He was hungry and more than ready to eat.

"You sure?" Sheba asked. "There's plenty."

"Okay," Dante said, smiling. "I didn't know you could cook," he said as Sheba got up and went into the kitchen.

"She couldn't grow up in this house and not know how to cook."

"Apologies." He bowed toward Miss Pearl and got up. "So I am dying to taste your cooking," Dante said, following Sheba into the kitchen.

That night, the three talked while he ate, and then Sheba walked him to the door. The next time, he stayed longer, and on his next visit, after he ate and Miss Pearl said she was going up to bed, which was usually his cue to leave, something different happened.

"Good night, Mrs. Harrison," Dante said, and he stood up as she left the kitchen. "I'm gonna head out too."

"What's your rush?" Sheba asked.

"No rush at all."

Sheba stood up. "Let's talk outside," she said and led him outside.

That was how it began.

Now that her life wasn't as chaotic as it once was, Sheba relaxed. She appreciated that Dante had been there for her during that time as she had asked him to be. But more importantly, Dante had been there for her family. As the weeks passed, they began to spend more time together, and the hurt that she'd held on to for so many years faded. That allowed her to remember that they were friends, best friends, before they became lovers, and that gave them the space to become friends again.

On that particular evening, Dante had invited Sheba to the Atlanta Jazz Festival in Piedmont Park. Sheba thought that she would make it romantic and planned a candlelight picnic for their evening.

"Sorry I'm late," Dante said when he arrived to pick her up.

"What happened?"

"I was supposed to be meeting with my Realtor at three. But she called and rescheduled the meeting at the last minute to five."

"No worries. How's house hunting going?"

"We've looked at a few places, but I haven't seen anything that's stood out and spoken to me."

"I like a man who knows what he wants." Sheba picked up the picnic basket and walked toward the door. "I'm ready," Sheba said on her way out. "Piedmont Park awaits."

When they got to the park, Sheba and Dante decided to leave the basket in the car and walk around for a while first. As they walked around the park listening to the music, it was hard, but Dante fought the urge to hold Sheba's hand.

"So tell me, are you hungry?" Sheba asked on the way back to the car.

"I haven't eaten a thing all day," Dante answered.

"Good. I brought some food."

"I know, and I've been wondering what was in the cute picnic basket."

He opened the trunk, he got the basket, Sheba got the blanket, and they headed off in search of as secluded a spot as they could find. Once the blanket was laid out, Sheba began taking out the food she'd made.

"Chicken Caesar pitas and homemade potato salad from Grandma's recipe," she began, looking into his penetrating eyes with a smile. "I made strawberry, cucumber, and honeydew salad and strawberry-watermelon lemonade to drink. And these," she said, holding up a plastic container.

"What's in there?"

Sheba opened it. "Wray and Nephew gelatin cubes."

Dante took one and ate it. "Just the thing for an evening of jazz in the park," he said of the 126-proof rum gelatin cubes. While they ate, Sheba decided to ask the question she'd been wondering about since they met again.

"Why aren't you seeing anybody, Dante?"

"I was."

"What happened between you two?"

"We agreed to disagree."

"How come?"

"Control more than anything else. Control of my agenda."

"She wanted to monopolize your time, huh?"

"It was always about what she wanted to do. All about her needs."

"Aww. Did Dante feel that his needs weren't being met?" Sheba said mockingly.

"Very funny. But maybe you're right."

"See, another sensitive man dying to come out." Sheba laughed.

"Or maybe I just felt smothered."

"Or maybe she was in love and wanted to spend all her time with you?"

"Maybe."

"People's feelings evolve at different rates," she said, thinking that Dante wanted this type of relationship with her since he saw her that night at Grindhouse Killer Burgers, and her feelings for him had evolved over time to get to this point.

"I know that." Dante popped a gelatin cube. "Just once I'd like them to evolve at the same rate."

"Would be nice, wouldn't it? But I know what you're saying."

They ate, sipped strawberry-watermelon lemonade, and had gelatin cubes, but mostly they talked. Anytime there was a conversational lull, suddenly one or the other would say something, and the conversation would take off in another direction until Sheba said, "It's getting late. We should probably go."

On the way home from the park, Dante stopped to get gas, and Sheba went inside to get a Goody's Powder just in case those 126-proof rum gelatin cubes got the best of her later that evening. She was on her way back to the car when she saw Jordan coming toward her with his arms out.

Fuck. He is the last person I want to see.

It had been weeks since she'd seen or talked to him. Sheba spent enough time with him to know that he had gone from an arrogant and brash young drug dealer, which she found sexy, to an obnoxious and egotistical asshole, and that made Jordan intolerable to be around, good dick or not.

"What's up, Sheba?" Jordan said loud enough that it got Dante's attention.

"Hey, Jordan," she said and kept walking to avoid hugging him.

"Where you been? I've been calling you."

"I've been busy, you know, with my grandmother and Demi and all that," she said instead of telling him that he was an obnoxious asshole and she'd been ignoring his calls.

"Well, we need to get together then," Jordan said, walking alongside her.

Sheba stopped. "I don't think that's a good idea."

"Why not?" Jordan asked, and that was when he noticed that Dante was staring him down. "Oh." Jordan put his hands together and bowed at the waist. "No problem. I'll call you," he said and walked to his car.

"Who was that?" Dante asked.

"Somebody I used to know years ago," Sheba said and got in the car.

Knowing that he had no choice but to accept that as an answer, Dante got in the car and said nothing else about it.

Chapter 17

With the influx of free product, Jody and Floyd's business was expanding, and with that, so were their enemies. They were still operating out of the same spot, but as they continued to grow, it cut into somebody else's business, and issues with those enemies grew as well.

One morning around two a.m., they were coming out of a convenience store and heading for the car. As they got closer to his car, Floyd saw an Acura coming at them fast. When he saw the gun come out the window, he pushed Jody to the ground and yelled, "Get down!"

Jody and Floyd lay motionless as bullets rained over their heads. Once the car drove on, both men got up and fired, but the car was too far away.

"You all right?" Jody asked.

"Yeah, you?"

"Yeah. I'm all right."

"You have any idea who that was?" Floyd asked as they continued toward their car, but he had his suspicions.

"No idea." But he had his suspicions too. "One thing is certain," Jody said and got in the car.

"What's that?"

"We need to go on offense and start taking this shit to them."

"But who? We don't even know who tried to kill us."

"Does it matter?" Jody asked. "Right now, everybody is our enemy until they prove not to be."

Floyd laughed. "Ain't no allies in this game. Business arrangements, maybe. But as soon as the arrangement no longer serves their interest, it's back to being enemies."

"I know that, so like I said, does it matter who we go at?"

"I see your point, I do. But I would like to go at the niggas who are going at us, instead of making more enemies. You feel me?"

"I do. And trust me, brother, I agree with you. But we gotta do something. You feel me?"

"Yeah, I feel you. So who?"

"If I were a gambling man, my money would be on Jordan and them," Jody said as they arrived at the apartment complex where their business was set up.

"I agree. We've been set up in here for years, and the muthafucka ain't never had no problems with it before."

"It's a new day, and we coming hard and strong. You know they gotta be feeling it."

"So what are we gonna do?"

Jody sat on the hood of a car and thought for a while. "Two things."

"I'm listening."

"We start looking for new spots to do business from."

"Smart. What's number two?"

He pointed. "We send Brooks and Taylor to pay them a visit," Jody said and called his men over. Once he told them what he wanted, they headed out to one of the corners that Jordan's people controlled.

"There they are," Taylor said from the car that he and Brooks were waiting in.

"Showtime," Brooks said and started the car.

"Let's do this!" Taylor shouted.

Brooks dropped the car in gear and slowly rolled toward their unsuspecting targets. He picked up speed, and Taylor took aim and opened fire at the men. At the sound of gunfire, some dropped to the ground as bullets flew, and others tried to run. The shooting didn't last long, and nobody was killed, but a couple of the men had minor injuries. But a message was sent, one that was heard loud and clear.

"DeKalb County Police are seeking information about a drive-by shooting. The shooting happened around three forty-five a.m. Police say somebody opened fire from a car that took off after the shooting. According to witnesses, several men were wounded in the attack, but all fled the scene. Anyone having information about the shooting is encouraged to call the number on the screen."

"My God."

"Probably drug-related," Sheba said as she and Miss Pearl sipped coffee and had toast.

"I don't know what it's gonna take before these boys realize that they're killing each other and the community. It's more than just the people who abuse the drugs. It's their families and friends and the children of those people who are often abused or neglected." Miss Pearl got up to get another cup of coffee. "Never did make sense to me to do that to your own people." She held up the pot. "You want another cup?"

"No, thank you, Grandma. I was about to go shower and get dressed."

It wasn't that she was in any hurry, but Miss Pearl had her feeling bad. Everything that her grandmother had just said now applied to her. She was feeling bad because she didn't have to look any further than Demi to see the effects that drugs had on their family. Drugs had killed her parents, and no matter how Sheba rationalized that she was doing it for the family, she was now responsible for whatever effect what she had done would have on the community.

"Before you rush off," Miss Pearl began as she refilled Sheba's cup, "now that you did what you felt you needed to do for your family, I want to ask you what your plan is."

"What do you mean?" Sheba asked, surprised and wondering how she could possibly know what she had done.

Miss Pearl sat down. "It's been two months since you've been home," she began, and Sheba breathed a sigh of relief. "And since you been here, you've been taking care of me, and seeing about Demi and running behind Chanel helping to get her and her family situated. What I wanna know is what you have planned for yourself."

"I haven't given it much thought, Grandma."

"Well, you need to. You've been spending money like it's going out of style paying my bills, and I know getting Demi in that clinic cost you some money for sure."

"I had some money saved, so I'll be all right, Grandma."

"All the same, you didn't save that money to go in that direction. You need to start thinking about yourself."

"I know."

"Now as much as I've enjoyed having you here and being able to spend this time with you, you need to be thinking about what you plan to do in the future."

"I know that, Grandma. But like you said, I've been so busy that I haven't given it much thought."

Sheba hadn't had to think about money because money wasn't an issue. In the short time that she had been in the drug business, Sheba had already recouped all the money that she had spent taking care of Demi and Miss Pearl. That, and she had what amounted to a year's pay for an E5 Marine upstairs in her room.

"But I will, Grandma. I promise. But right now, I'm just enjoying being home. So unless you're saying that you're tired of me hanging around with you all day and I need to get a job, I'm fine doing just what I'm doing."

"That is not what I'm saying. I am so glad for the company."

"I didn't think so. So I'm about to go shower and get dressed so we can get to the farmers market before it gets crowded." Sheba got up and took their cups and plates to the sink. "And I suggest you do the same."

Miss Pearl stood up. "And you know the later in the day it is, the ruder people get," she said, and they both left the kitchen to get ready to go shopping.

Sheba and Miss Pearl enjoyed their morning at the farmer's market. Although she only came there to get a few things, while they were there, Sheba mentioned that she hadn't had any conch salad or conch chowder in years, so Miss Pearl also picked up some conch, fresh vegetables, tomatoes, green and red bell peppers, pepper, sweet onions, oranges, and limes to make conch salad and potatoes for the chowder. And since she didn't plan on cooking it until the next day because she was always a little tired after walking the market, Sheba picked up some jumbo pasta shells stuffed with mild Italian sausage. She didn't feel like cooking either.

"Too hot to cook," Miss Pearl said, putting away the food.

"That's what I'm saying," Sheba said while putting the pasta shells in the microwave.

Once Miss Pearl had finished putting away the food, she sat at the kitchen table, and they were enjoying their shells when her phone rang.

"Ain't you gonna get that, Grandma?" Sheba asked.

"I'm eating. If it's important, they'll leave a message or call back," she said and kept eating. When the phone rang again a minute later, Sheba got up and went to get the phone from Miss Pearl's purse.

"It might be one of your doctors calling."

"And I say again, if it's important, they'll leave a message or call back when I'm not eating," she said and kept eating.

Sheba looked at the display. "It's Dante calling."

"Go ahead and answer. He's probably calling for you anyway."

"Hello."

"Hey, Sheba," he said, surprised but happy that she answered. "How are you doing today?"

"I'm awesome."

"Is your grandmother available?"

"She's eating," Sheba said, and Miss Pearl nodded. "Can I take a message?" she giggled.

"Ask her if it's all right if I come by early today. The Realtor moved up our appointment to see a house that she thinks I'll love."

"I'm sure that it'll be fine, but hold up. Let me ask her," Sheba said and glanced toward Miss Pearl. "Grandma, Dante wants to know if he can come by early today."

"Of course he can," she said and kept eating.

"She said of course you can."

"Great. I'll see you around three," Dante said and rushed off the phone.

"See, Grandma?" Sheba said as she sat down to finish eating. "It was important."

"And you took a message," Miss Pearl said and kept eating.

It was almost three thirty when Dante arrived at the house to check Miss Pearl's vitals and to walk her through her breathing exercises. He hadn't quite finished up when his phone rang.

"Excuse me, Miss Pearl. It's my Realtor," Dante said and took the call. "Hey, Bebel." He listened for a while. "I'm so sorry to hear that." He looked at Miss Pearl. "I completely understand." Dante glanced at Sheba and smiled. "Go ahead and text me the code, and we'll talk tomorrow," he said and ended the call. "She said that she had a family emergency, so she has to cancel. But she is texting me the lockbox code so I can still look at it."

"She must want you to see it badly," Sheba said as Dante got back to Miss Pearl and her breathing exercises.

"She does. The house just came on the market, and we've been looking for so long. She really thinks I'll like this one."

"Or she hopes you'll stop being so picky so she can sell you a house," Sheba said and chuckled.

"Maybe. Like I said, we've been looking for so long." Dante finished the breathing exercise. "You did great, Miss Pearl. A little stronger than yesterday."

"Thanks, good to know. Thank you again for doing this," Miss Pearl said as he packed up to leave.

"My pleasure, Miss Pearl. I'm glad to do it," Dante said. It gave him the second chance with Sheba, and it was truly all he had wanted for years.

"So you're off to see this house now?" Sheba asked as she walked him to the door.

"Sure am. Wanna come with?" He paused. "You can tell me if I'm being too picky."

"You serious?"

"Sure am."

"Grandma! I'm gonna ride with Dante to see this house. I won't be gone long," Sheba said and left the house with Dante.

The two walked through the beautiful five-bedroom, three-full-bath home with laminated wood flooring throughout and all-new granite countertops in the kitchen and bathrooms.

"I like this, Dante," Sheba said, coming out of the beautiful, bright sunroom.

"I do too. I think Bebel was right. This may be the one," he said, walking into the kitchen.

"New over-the-stove microwave oven. New dishwasher."

Dante opened the back door and stepped out on the deck. "New rear deck and front steps, and the front yard has security lighting." He went back inside and stepped close to Sheba. He put his arms around her. "What do you think?"

Sheba put her arms around his neck. "I told you that I like it. But if you like it, I love it," she said, looking up into his eyes.

Dante cradled her face in his big hands, and he kissed her. Their first kiss in ten years was slow and tender, but that next kiss was hard and passionate as they each were hungry for the other. Sheba kissed him, afraid to even breathe and lose this groove between them.

As his lips moved across her cheek and down to her throat, her head fell back, and her eyes drifted closed. Sheba leaned against the counter as he kissed her neck. His hands caressed her body, making her wet for him. The heat was rushing through her body, and her swelling clit was making her grind against his dick.

His lips trailed a path down her chest to her breasts, and he pressed them together, drawing both nipples into his warm, wet mouth. He used his tongue, lips, and teeth to tease the tips of her nipples, causing her spine to arch and her hands to grip the back of his head, holding him tightly against her.

"I want you inside me," Sheba whispered, aching for more as desire pounded through her body. In one fluid motion, Dante pulled down her shorts and panties, grabbed her full, round, ample hips, picked her up, and sat her down on the counter, all the while trying to come out of his pants and underwear.

"Yes," she cried out.

He felt so good as he moved in and out of her, hard and deep, and she felt overwhelmed by each penetrating stroke. His thrusts were hard and intense, which caused her body to spasm uncontrollably. She was rolling her hips as his hands gripped her ass, encouraging her to work harder against him. She quickly wrapped her legs around his waist, and he dicked her down with long, hard, slow, and constant strokes, sliding in and out of her just like she needed him to.

"Yes!" Dante grunted, and he pumped harder to bring her to climax again. Sheba came over and over in waves, shuddering and screaming.

"Now that we've christened the house, does that mean you have to buy it?" Sheba asked as they left the house.

Chapter 18

It took some time, a lot more time than it should have, but Chanel finally went to visit Demi at the Lakeside Behavioral Clinic. She used the excuses that she had left James and she'd been busy with the move and getting the children situated in their new school.

Chanel had been mad at Demi for running out on her to get high, which caused their grandmother to have the emphysema episode, so she hadn't visited. Sheba had been sharing information about what was going on with her and her recovery, and it hadn't all been positive.

"And I've just been dealing with a lot of other stuff," Chanel said but didn't tell Demi how the knowledge of the affair that James was having had affected her.

Demi nodded. "Tell the truth, Chanel. You were mad at me, and that's why you haven't come to see me until now."

"You're right. I was mad at you. Hell, I'm still mad at you."

"I know. And I'm sorry that I ran out on you. I hope you can forgive me."

Chanel looked strangely at Demi because this was different. "Okay."

"Don't look at me like that. They told me that I need to start taking responsibility for my fuckups, so this is me taking responsibility," she said without any real commitment to what she was saying.

"Wow, I'm impressed. And yes, Demi, I forgive you."

"Thank you. I need to make better choices and be accountable to them."

What she was saying was all positive, but it was delivered in such a lackadaisical manner that, after seeing her, Chanel wished that she had come to visit sooner. After seeing Demi for herself, Chanel drove away from Lakeside believing that Demi was depressed.

She had spoken briefly with a member of Demi's treatment team who suggested that Demi's symptoms of depression may be associated with withdrawal. The team member explained that feelings of hopelessness, pessimism, and overwhelming sadness can and sometimes do persist well after the withdrawal period ends.

"Or her depression may have existed before her addiction, and she may have turned to the use of alcohol and drugs to help mask the negative effects of whatever she was dealing with."

Chanel was so shaken that, once she got home, she called Sheba to share her thoughts.

"Hey, Chanel," Sheba answered.

"Hey, Sheba. When was the last time you visited Demi?" she wasted no time in asking.

"Day before yesterday. Why?"

"I just left her and—"

"About time," Sheba interrupted to say. "But I'm glad you finally made it out there."

"I am too." Chanel chuckled. "She didn't buy my excuse about James and the kids."

"Did you really think she would?"

"I was hoping, but anyway, did she seem depressed to you?"

"No, not really. She seemed real positive about the way the counseling was going. Did you seem that way to you?"

"Yes, so I talked to a member of her treatment team, and they said that in her sobriety she might be realizing the consequences of how she was living."

"I know she told me that she feels guilty, and she is ashamed of some of the things that she was doing to get high and make that man happy, so you may be right. I'll go see her, try to cheer her up."

"Where are you?"

"At Grandma's, watching *Jerry Springer* with her and Floyd."

"Tell them I said hey."

"Chanel says hey, y'all," Sheba said, and since they were into *Jerry*, their response was weak.

"Wow. *Jerry* must be good today."

"This woman got mad at her friend, so she decided to get even by sleeping with the friend's boyfriend, but they just found out that the boyfriend is married, and his wife just came out."

"Drama!"

"You coming by?"

"No, I'm going to pick up the kids and go home. I'll call you tomorrow."

"Talk to you then," Sheba said and ended the call with Chanel.

"What is Chanel talking about?" Floyd asked.

"She said she just left Demi at Lakeside, and she thinks Demi is depressed about the things she used to do."

"Demi was out there." Floyd nodded. "So we have no idea what she was doing."

"Or how it might be affecting her, my poor baby," Miss Pearl said.

"I told her that I might roll out there, spend time with her," Sheba said and started to get up.

"As soon as this is over, I'll ride with you," Floyd said.

"What you all need to do is get together and come up with a schedule so somebody is going to see her every day," Miss Pearl suggested. "I know the poor thing must get lonely out there by herself."

"Plenty of time to think of all the foul shi . . ." Floyd looked at Miss Pearl. "All the foul things she used to do."

"I don't even want to hear about any of that," Miss Pearl said as the commercial ended and *Jerry*'s brand of daily drama resumed.

After the show went off, as promised, Floyd rode with Sheba to Lakeside to see Demi. Although she was genuinely happy about the surprise visit from her cousins, after a while, her mood changed. By the end of their visit, Sheba and Floyd agreed with Chanel. It was almost eight that evening when Sheba and Floyd said good night to Demi and left Lakeside. Sheba left knowing that she would be back at Lakeside the following day to speak with Demi's treatment team about her family's observations.

"I've never seen Demi like that," Floyd said as Sheba drove away.

"You would know better than I do," Sheba said, once again feeling guilty for not being there all those years.

Floyd looked at Sheba. "Don't do that."

"Do what?"

"Make yourself responsible for Demi and her shit." He reached out and took her hand. "I know you, Sheba, and I know it's probably too late, but don't put her addiction on your shoulders."

"You're right. It's way too late for that. I shouldn't have stayed away so long."

Floyd laughed. "You probably think it's your fault that Chanel married James."

"I do," Sheba admitted. "If I had been here—"

"You would have told her that James was a worthless waste of flesh." Floyd laughed. "Everybody did. What makes you think she would have listened to you?"

Sheba laughed as she remembered coming home for the wedding and everybody telling her about James and what Chanel said when Sheba shared those concerns with her. "He just needs a good woman, that's all," was what Chanel had told Sheba.

"You're right about that, too," she conceded.

Floyd squeezed Sheba's hand. "You were gone a long time, living your life. You are not responsible for the choices grown-ass women make."

"Thanks, Floyd."

"No worries." He paused before he said, "Why don't you roll me by the spot? I'll pick up my car from Grandma's later."

"Okay. Where to?"

"Jody never took you by there?"

"Nope."

"Boy be slippin' sometimes. You're the reason we stepped up, and he didn't show you the operation." Floyd shook his head. "Unacceptable. Make a left here," he said and directed her to the apartments where they did the bulk of their business.

Jody was surprised when he saw Sheba's car pull into the apartment complex until he saw Floyd in the passenger seat. When they parked, he approached the car and then bowed at the waist.

"What's up, Sheba the queen?"

"What's up, Jody?"

"'Sup?" Floyd said and shook his brother's hand. "I brought Sheba by to show her how we do it."

Jody chuckled as a car drove past them and parked. "Sit back and watch," Jody said as the driver of the car got out and approached one of the buildings. "You say what you want and drop your money on the ground." Sheba watched as the man dropped his money. "And go up the steps," Jody said as another car drove up, only this time it was the passenger who got out.

After looking long and hard at Sheba, Jody, and Floyd, she dropped her head and headed for the building, and the cycle began again.

"On the ground at the top of the steps, you find what you paid for."

"Smooth," Sheba said as she watched the man come down the back stairs and head back to his car. Having absolutely no experience in the game, Sheba didn't really know if it was smooth. All that she knew was that it seemed to be working for them.

For the next half hour, Sheba hung out with Jody and Floyd and watched as car after car rolled in. She was about to leave when she saw a familiar car pull into the apartment complex.

"What's he doing here?" Sheba asked.

"That's Jordan," Floyd said when he saw Jordan's 2002 Trans Am. He discreetly checked his weapon.

"Y'all know Jordan?" Sheba asked as he parked and got out of the car.

"Yeah, we know him," Jody said and put his hand on his gun. "I didn't know you knew him."

"Sheba!" Jordan said as soon as he got out of his car. "We keep running into each other, and with a different man every time."

Jody and Floyd looked at one another and then at Sheba.

"They're my cousins."

"Cousins." Jordan nodded his head. "I didn't know they were your cousins," he said and paused. "Don't matter. You muthafuckas need to find somewhere else to do business."

"Fuck that!" Floyd said. "We ain't going nowhere."

"You been warned." Jordan started to walk away but stopped and looked at Sheba. "Sheba."

"Yes."

"It was fun while it lasted," he said and walked back to his car, got in, and drove away.

"Fuck that shit," Floyd said.

"Let him come," Jody said.

"We can handle them," Floyd concurred. "And what the fuck is going on with you and this nigga?"

"That ain't none of your fuckin' business. But I know these niggas, and they are coming, so you need to recruit some more soldiers."

"You don't need to worry about that, Sheba. We can handle Jordan and whatever he got."

They were caught totally off guard when seconds later two cars came roaring into the complex with bright lights on. As soon as the cars were close enough to the building, the cars came to a screeching halt, four men exited, and they opened fire. Both of Jody and Floyd's men in front of the building were hit with multiple shots. Jordan's men, Jamarco, Latravis, and Rashard, jumped out of the other car and fired at Sheba, Jody, and Floyd. Both men drew their weapons and opened fire blindly as they ran for better cover.

Jody and Floyd's men Brooks and Taylor came out of the building firing and forced their adversaries to take cover. While their men kept firing, Jody fired and hit one man with three shots to the chest. Then he laid down cover fire while Floyd fired and killed the other man. The two other men fired blindly as they tried to run, but Brooks and Taylor killed them as they ran.

"Give me a gun!" Sheba yelled over the gunfire.

Jody handed Sheba his 9 mm and got the AK-47 from the back seat of his car. Latravis and Rashard opened fire with AR-15s and forced Jody, Floyd, and Sheba to take cover behind the car. Sheba rose up and tried to get off a shot, but she was outgunned. She dropped back behind the car and looked over at Floyd as bullets bounced off the car and the wall behind them.

Jody took a deep breath before he came up shooting with the AK. He fired until the AK was empty. Latravis and Rashard went down. As Jody fired away, Sheba rose up and fired, hitting one with shots to the head and chest. When she took cover to reload, Floyd fired and hit the other one with three shots. Jamarco and the remaining shooter ran for their cars. Jody fired and shot one in the back as they ran. But Jamarco made it to his car and drove away firing the AR out the window.

"Everybody all right?" Sheba asked.

"I'm good," Jody replied. "You good?"

"Yeah, I'm all right," Floyd said. "But we gotta get outta here."

"Pack up!" Jody yelled to his remaining men. "Meet me at the house," he said, and as quickly as possible, they shut down their operation and the three left the apartment complex.

Chapter 19

After leaving the apartment complex, Sheba drove Floyd back to their grandmother's house to pick up his car. As he was about to leave, he stopped and took Sheba's hand.

"Don't worry. Jordan ain't nothing we can't handle. He just caught us today, but that won't happen again." He shook his head. "Next time he comes at us, we'll be ready."

Sheba squeezed Floyd's hand. "You shouldn't wait. This is war, and war is something I know about. Y'all need to take it to him. I'm talking about gearing up right now while they're sitting back thinking about what just happened, and it's hitting them hard. Give the ones who live something to think about. That would be my advice."

Floyd hugged Sheba. "I like the way you think."

"I think like a soldier." Sheba turned toward the house, and then she stopped. "I can take care of myself, but you need to send some men here to make sure Grandma is protected at all times. Chanel and Demi, too."

"I'm on that, Sheba," Floyd said and turned toward his car. She watched him drive away from the porch before she went inside.

After checking on her grandmother, Sheba got her gun and a beer from the cooler she now kept stocked and went out on the back porch. It was a clear night, so she could see the stars shining brightly in the night sky, and she thought about what she had done. Even though Sheba cautioned herself against it, carefully laying out for herself all the consequences, she still felt that where her family found itself was her responsibility.

If she hadn't run off and joined the Marines, or at least if she'd come home more often, she'd have been watching her aunt Millicent like a hawk. Demi was 15 years old when Sheba signed up, but even then, she could see that Demi was already running with a rough crowd. Had she been there, looking out for Demi as she had all her life, she could have ridden shotgun over her and kept her straight. Sheba chuckled. "Straighter than she is now."

She took a swallow. And yes, despite what Floyd said, Sheba was confident that had she any more to do with it, James's worthless lech ass would have never gotten close to Chanel.

As far as Jody and Floyd were concerned, she had no idea that their fathers were in business together and he had been grooming them to take over what apparently had always been the family business. That may have been out of her control, but she was the one who supplied the drugs that brought them to this point. Sheba drained the bottle and went up to bed thinking that this was all her fault and she needed to do something to turn it around.

Early the next morning, Sheba was awakened when her phone rang. She groggily picked up the phone and looked at the display. Seeing the word Lakeside on the screen brought her to complete alertness.

"Hello."

"May I speak with Miss Styles?"

"Yes, this is she speaking."

"Miss Styles, this is Aillen Senedra. I'm a member of Demitra Harrison's treatment team."

"Yes. What can I do for you?"

"I need to inform you that Miss Harrison left the facility last night after bed check."

"What?"

"Miss Harrison left the facility and has not returned."

"She escaped."

"Yes, ma'am."

"Thanks for letting me know," Sheba said and ended the call. Her first call was to Floyd. She had told him to put somebody on Demi for protection. Maybe he felt that she wasn't safe there at all.

He was out cold when his phone rang. "What?"

"It's Sheba. Is Demi with you?" Sheba asked.

"No, she's not with me." And then it hit him. "She escaped from rehab. I'm not surprised."

"Neither am I. But we need to find her."

"Damn, Demi," Floyd said as he rolled out of bed. "I'm on that."

"Thank you, Floyd."

"And I just wanted you to know that I took the advice you gave me."

"We'll talk about that when I see you, so I'll call you later."

Sheba ended the call and got ready to go out to Lakeside. While she was in the shower, she made the decision not to tell her grandmother about Demi just yet. If she could avoid upsetting her, that was what was going to happen.

Sheba spent the rest of the morning at Lakeside speaking with the treatment team, and she made the decision that perhaps Lakeside wasn't the right place for Demi.

"What's up, Sheba?" Floyd answered when she called.

"Where are you?"

"At Jody's."

"I'll be through there. I need to pick up some hardware."

After meeting with Jody and Floyd to pick up a couple of 9mm pistols, Sheba spent the rest of the day and night riding around to the places they'd checked the first time Demi went missing, without success. It seemed that nobody had seen her, and none of the people they sent Sheba to had seen her either.

She was mad at herself for not asking more questions the last time that Demi escaped from Lakeside. She had gone to see a man about some dick and then used his car to try to get high once he passed out. She could have found out who this man was and where he lived, because it was a good bet that Demi was with him.

It was early the next morning when Sheba was awakened once again by her phone ringing. She groggily picked up the phone and looked at the display. Although she didn't recognize the number, she answered.

"Hello."

"It's Demi."

She was feeling down after Sheba and Floyd left her that night, and then the cravings hit her hard, and she had to get outta there. So Demi called Ervan Garland. He was the man she'd had sex with the night Floyd came and got her from Lakeside. All Demi had to do was offer him some pussy, and he was outside the facility within twenty-five minutes. Once she had fucked him real good, instead of him taking her back to the facility, Demi convinced him to take her somewhere else.

"Are you all right?"

"No, I need you to come get me. He won't let me leave."

"Where are you?"

"Somebody's coming. I gotta go. I'll text you my location."

"Demi, wait," Sheba said, but she had already ended the call.

Sheba checked her messages and saw the text with the location from Demi. She quickly called Jody and Floyd, but they didn't answer their phones.

"It's Sheba. I'm sending you both the address where Demi is. I'm on my way there now. Meet me there when you get this message."

Sheba got the gun she just got and went to get Demi from whoever was holding her. It wasn't until Sheba was

halfway to her destination that she realized she had been to that address before. It was Jordan's house where Demi was being held.

"What's she doing there?" was Sheba's first question. But the closer she got, the madder she got, and the more it made sense to her. Sheba was sure that Jordan was the one Demi went to that night to get high for free. Jordan said that he knew her that first night Demi went missing, and there was something about the way he looked when Sheba said Demi was her cousin. And Jordan knowing she was her cousin made Sheba madder.

When she got there, Sheba didn't see any cars, so she walked right up to the front door and kicked it open.

"Demi!"

"I'm back here!" Demi yelled.

When Sheba started toward the rear of the house, a man appeared in front of her with a gun in his hand.

"What you doing in here?"

Sheba raised her gun and kept walking toward him.

"I'm here to get my cousin," she said and shot him once in the chest. "Demi!" she yelled as the man dropped his gun and slumped to the floor.

"I'm back here!"

The sound of Demi's voice was coming from a room in the rear of the house. The door had a padlock on it. "Stand back, Demi," Sheba said, shooting the padlock off.

Sheba opened the door. "You all right?"

Demi rushed out of the room. "I'm okay," she said and hugged Sheba.

"Come on. I need to get you outta here."

The two were on their way out of the house and had reached the kitchen when Jordan came in with a gun in his hand. He lowered it a little when he saw Sheba.

"What the fuck?" was all he could get out before Sheba shot him.

As Jordan went down from the shot to the stomach, Sheba picked up his gun and left the house with Demi. Once they reached the car and Demi was in, Sheba shut her door.

"I'll be right back."

When she got back inside, Jordan was on the floor, trying to pull himself up in a chair. Sheba saw that his cell phone was on the floor next to the chair, so she had to assume that he called his boys for help and that they would be there soon.

Sheba kicked the chair out of the way, and Jordan fell to the floor.

She stood over him and pointed her gun at his head. "You knew she was my cousin."

Sheba shot Jordan once in the head and then twice in the chest with his own gun. She dropped the gun on his chest and left the house. As Sheba was driving away from Jordan's house with Demi, she passed Jamarco on his way to the house.

She started to take Demi back to rehab, but then she thought better of that idea and took her to Miss Pearl's house. What Demi needed more than counseling at that time was the love of her family, and there was no better place for her to be than with her grandmother.

Once she had Demi situated at the house and she promised to stay put and not run out on her grandmother, Sheba told Demi that she would be back. She went to tell Jody and Floyd that it was Jordan who had had Demi and that she had killed him and one of his boys.

"Then it ain't over," Jody said because Jordan's crew would certainly retaliate.

"This shit is just getting started," Floyd said.